BUY JUPITER
AND OTHER STORIES

SHORT STORY COLLECTIONS
by ISAAC ASIMOV

I, ROBOT
THE MARTIAN WAY AND OTHER STORIES
EARTH IS ROOM ENOUGH
NINE TOMORROWS
THE REST OF THE ROBOTS
THROUGH A GLASS, CLEARLY (BRITISH PUBLICATION ONLY)
ASIMOV'S MYSTERIES
NIGHTFALL AND OTHER STORIES
THE EARLY ASIMOV
THE BEST OF ISAAC ASIMOV
HAVE YOU SEEN THESE? (LIMITED EDITION)
TALES OF THE BLACK WIDOWERS
BUY JUPITER AND OTHER STORIES

BUY JUPITER AND OTHER STORIES

ISAAC ASIMOV

DOUBLEDAY & COMPANY, INC.
GARDEN CITY, NEW YORK 1975

ACKNOWLEDGMENTS

"DARWINIAN POOL ROOM," copyright 1950 by World Editions.
"DAY OF THE HUNTERS," copyright 1950 by Columbia Publications, Inc.
"SHAH GUIDO G.," copyright 1951 by Stadium Publishing Corporation.
"BUTTON, BUTTON," copyright 1952 by Better Publications, Inc.
"THE MONKEY'S FINGER," copyright 1952 by Better Publications, Inc.
"EVEREST," copyright 1953 by Palmer Publications, Inc.
"THE PAUSE," copyright 1954 by Farrar, Straus & Young.
"LET'S NOT," copyright 1954 by the Trustees of Boston University.
"EACH AN EXPLORER," copyright 1956 by Columbia Publications, Inc.
"BLANK!" copyright 1957 by Royal Publications, Inc.
"DOES A BEE CARE?" copyright 1957 by Quinn Publishing Company, Inc.
"SILLY ASSES," copyright 1957 by Columbia Publications, Inc.
"BUY JUPITER," copyright © 1958 by Mercury Press, Inc.
"A STATUE FOR FATHER," copyright © 1958 by Renown Publications, Inc.
"RAIN, RAIN, GO AWAY," copyright 1959 by King-Size Publications, Inc.
"FOUNDING FATHER," copyright 1965 by Galaxy Publishing Corporation.
"EXILE TO HELL," copyright © 1968 by the Condé Nast Publications, Inc.
"KEY ITEM," copyright © 1968 by Mercury Press, Inc.
"THE PROPER STUDY," copyright 1968 by the Boy Scouts of America.
"2430 A.D.," copyright © 1970 by International Business Machines Corporation.
"THE GREATEST ASSET," copyright © 1971 by the Condé Nast Publications, Inc.
"TAKE A MATCH," copyright © 1972 by Robert Silverberg.
"THIOTIMOLINE TO THE STARS," copyright © 1973 by Random House, Inc.
"LIGHT VERSE," copyright 1973 by The Saturday Evening Post Company.

Library of Congress Cataloging in Publication Data
Asimov, Isaac, 1920–
    Buy Jupiter and other stories.

    CONTENTS: Darwinian pool room.—Day of the hunt-
ers.—Shah Guido G. [etc.]
    1. Science fiction, American. I. Title.
PZ3.A8316Bu [PS3551.S5]   813'.5'4
ISBN 0-385-05077-1
Library of Congress Catalog Card Number 74–33738
Copyright © 1975 by Isaac Asimov
All Rights Reserved
Printed in the United States of America
First Edition

To all the editors, whose careers,
at one time or another,
have intersected my own—
good fellows, every one.

STORIES INCLUDED

BUY JUPITER
AND OTHER STORIES

It has always been my custom, Gentle Readers, to take you into my confidence, since I have nothing to hide.* Let me tell you, then, how I came to put this book together.

I was tapped to be Guest of Honor at Boskone XI (the name given a science fiction convention held in Boston from March 1 to 3, 1974) and it turned out that it had become traditional for the committee in charge of the convention to publish a small collection of the works of the Guest of Honor. So they grinned toothily and asked me to put together a few stories for the purpose.

This placed me in a quandary. My science fiction stories are published by that esteemed publishing house of excellent repute, Doubleday & Company, and I was afraid that a hurt look might come into their corporate soft, brown eyes if I were to do fiction for anyone else. The Boskone committee, apprised of my suspicion that I would be torn limb from limb by maddened editors, assured me that the book they intended to do would be a limited edition of no more than five hundred copies.

So I approached Lawrence P. Ashmead, my chief editor at Doubleday, in a diffident manner and asked if it would be all right to accede to the request. I pointed out that I would just use a few stories that had never appeared in any of my Doubleday collections. Larry, that gentlest of all souls, said, "Sure, Isaac. Go ahead." So I went ahead.

The result was a little book entitled HAVE YOU SEEN THESE? (The Nesfa Press, 1974) containing eight stories. It was designed to be ready just before Boskone XI, where it was hoped that hundreds (even dozens) of copies might be sold. Alas, need I tell you that the vagaries of the publishing game made it inevitable that the book was not ready for sale until immediately *after* the convention, so that in actual sales it proved to be an even more limited edition than had been planned.

But Larry was biding his time. His gentleness covers an editorial acumen without flaw.

* Literarily, that is.

Eventually he said, "Has that little book come out, Isaac?"

"Oh, yes," I said with a smile (for it always gives me a kind of artless pleasure to talk about my books), and the next time I saw him I gave him a copy.

He looked it over and said, "What a shame these stories don't have a wider circulation. Couldn't Doubleday do an edition?"

I pointed out an insuperable objection. "It's only twenty thousand words long, Larry," I said.

And Larry said at once, "So add more stories." (Now why didn't *I* think of that?)

It turned out, as a matter of fact, that Doubleday has as its ambition the inclusion, eventually, of all my stories into one collection or another. I'm not sure that that's a good idea, really, since surely some of my stories are not as good as others and perhaps a few do not really deserve immortalization.

Larry (who is more of an Asimov partisan than I am) laughed that aside. He pointed out that 1) no story appears bad to all readers, 2) that no Asimov story can be really bad, and 3) that, good or bad, they all are of historical interest.

(That third point makes me uneasy. I have the definite feeling that in the world of science fiction I am a national monument and that young readers are always amazed—and perhaps even indignant —to find that I am still alive.)

So I gave in (for who can withstand Larry's glittering eye?) and added enough stories to bring the total to two dozen. They are for the most part not long stories (averaging twenty-five hundred words in length), they have not appeared in any of my earlier collections, and I have arranged them in chronological order of appearance.

Those of you who have read my books BEFORE THE GOLDEN AGE (Doubleday, 1974) and THE EARLY ASIMOV (Doubleday, 1972) know that they form, together, a sort of literary autobiography up to 1949, the year in which I sold my first book to Doubleday and then moved to Boston to join the faculty of Boston University School of Medicine.

In this book I will continue my practice of adding biographical commentary to the stories. Partly this is because of the number of letters I get from readers who tell me that the commentary is "even more enjoyable" than the stories. (Is that a tribute to the charm of my writing or a slur at my fictional talent? I wonder.) Partly also it is intended to blunt the pressures from certain editors (hi there,

Larry) to the effect that I write an autobiography—full-length and discussing every aspect.

I keep telling them that there is no aspect except my typewriter, and that nothing ever happened to me, but that seems to fall on deaf ears. But if I tell enough of my autobiography in these books, you see—

During most of the 1940s I had written exclusively for John Campbell and his magazine, *Astounding Science Fiction*. I had done so to such an extent, in fact, that I had grown nervous over the fact that if anything happened either to editor or to magazine, my writing career might be over.

To be sure, I had sold my first science fiction novel, PEBBLE IN THE SKY, to Doubleday, and it was published on January 19, 1950, less than three weeks after my thirtieth birthday, but it seemed to me I could scarcely count that. I had no assurance that I could repeat, and I felt comfortable only with the magazine sales that I had grown accustomed to over the first eleven years of my literary career.

The decade of the 1950s, however, opened with a rapid expansion of the science fiction magazine market and I quickly became the beneficiary of the fact.

One new magazine being planned for 1950, for instance, was to be entitled *Galaxy Science Fiction*. It was to be edited by Horace L. Gold, whose stories I had read and admired, and I was very flattered when he asked me for a story for the first issue of the magazine, which he naturally wanted to start off in top form.

The trouble was that the time allotted me was short. He needed it in a week, he said, and I was very nervous indeed about writing for anyone but John Campbell. After all, I hadn't the slightest idea of what Horace liked, whereas John and I had come to fit each other like yin and yang.

I tried, however, and produced DARWINIAN POOL ROOM. Horace accepted it, but without noticeable enthusiasm, and I had the rotten feeling that he took it only because he needed something immediately for that all-important first issue, October 1950.

Let me tell you, out of personal experience, that the feeling you get at having sold a story undeservedly for the sake of your name, or out of an editor's desperation, is far worse than the feeling you get at a rejection (unless you're desperate for money, I suppose).

I at once offered to write another story for Horace, therefore, and I did.† Horace took that one, too, and used it in his second issue, November 1950. This time he was not in a bind and could afford to be selective, so I was greatly relieved when he took the story—but I could not help but notice that he took that one without noticeable enthusiasm, too.

Gradually, as the months and years passed, I finally realized that Horace *never* accepted a story with noticeable enthusiasm— and often did so with very noticeable lack of enthusiasm. (And his rejections were savage ones, indeed, so savage that he eventually lost a great many writers who would not subject themselves to the kind of vituperation with which he accompanied his rejections.)

In any case, I came to realize that my agony over DARWINIAN POOL ROOM was unnecessary. It might not have been my best story, but Horace was as satisfied with it as he was ever satisfied with any story, which wasn't much, perhaps.

The importance of DARWINIAN POOL ROOM to me is that, together with PEBBLE IN THE SKY, it marked the beginning of my diversification into a variety of outlets, and an end to my sole dependence on John Campbell (though never an end to my intense gratitude to him).

† This was *Misbegotten Missionary,* which you will find in my book NIGHTFALL AND OTHER STORIES (Doubleday, 1969) under my own original title, *Green Patches.*

DARWINIAN
POOL ROOM

"Of course the ordinary conception of Genesis 1 is all wrong," I said. "Take a pool room, for instance."

The other three mentally took a pool room. We were sitting in broken down swivel chairs in Dr. Trotter's laboratory, but it was no trick at all to convert the lab benches into pool tables, the tall ring stands into cues, the reagent bottles into billiard balls, and then set the whole thing neatly before us.

Thetier even raised one finger, closed his eyes, and muttered softly, "Pool room!" Trotter, as usual, said nothing at all, but nursed his second cup of coffee. The coffee, also as usual, was horrible, but then, I was the newcomer to the group and had not callused my gastric lining sufficiently yet.

"Now consider the end of a game of pocket pool," I said. "You've got each ball, except the cue ball, of course, in a given pocket—"

"Wait awhile," said Thetier, always the purist, "it doesn't matter which pocket as long as you put them in in a certain order or—"

"Beside the point. When the game is all over, the balls are in various pockets. Right? Now suppose you walk into the pool room when the game is all over, and observe only that final position and try to reconstruct the course of previous events. Obviously, you have a number of alternatives."

"Not if you know the rules of the game," said Madend.

"Assume complete ignorance," I said. "You *can* decide that the balls were pocketed by being struck with the cue ball, which in turn was struck by the cue. This would be the truth, but not an explanation that is very likely to occur to you spontaneously. It is much more likely that you would decide that the balls were individually placed in their corresponding pockets by hand, or else that the balls always existed in the pockets as you found them."

"All right," said Thetier, "if you're going to skip back to Genesis, you will claim that by analogy we can account for the universe as either having always existed, having been created arbitrarily, as it is now, or having developed through evolution. So what?"

"That's not the alternative I'm proposing at all," I said. "Let us accept the fact of a purposeful creation, and consider only the methods by which such a creation could have been accomplished. It's easy to suppose that God said, 'Let there be light,' and there was light, but it's not esthetic."

"It's simple," said Madend, "and Occam's Razor demands that of alternate possibilities, the simpler be chosen."

"Then why don't you end a pool game by putting the balls in the pockets by hand? That's simpler, too, but it isn't esthetic. On the other hand, if you started with the primordial atom—"

"What is that?" asked Trotter, softly.

"Well, call it all the mass energy of the universe compressed into a single sphere, in a state of minimum entropy. If you were to explode that in such a way that all the constituent particles of matter and quanta of energy were to act, react, and interact in a precalculated way so that just our present universe is created, wouldn't that be much more satisfactory than simply waving your hand and saying, 'Let there be light!' "

"You mean," said Madend, "like stroking the cue ball against one of the billiard balls and sending all fifteen into their predestined pockets."

"In a pretty pattern," I said. "Yes."

"There's more poetry in the thought of a huge act of direct will," said Madend.

"That depends on whether you look at the matter as a mathematician or a theologian," I said. "As a matter of fact, Genesis 1 could be made to fit the billiard-ball scheme. The Creator could have spent his time calculating all the necessary variables and relationships into six gigantic equations. Count one 'day' for each equation. After having applied the initial explosive impetus, he would then 'rest' on the seventh 'day,' said seventh 'day' being the entire interval of time from that beginning to 4004 B.C. That interval, in which the infinitely complex pattern of billiard balls is sorting itself out, is obviously of no interest to the writers of the Bible. All the billions of years of it could be considered merely the developing single act of creation."

"You're postulating a teleological universe," said Trotter, "one in which purpose is implied."

"Sure," I said, "why not? A conscious act of creation without a purpose is ridiculous. Besides which, if you try to consider the course of evolution as the blind outcome of nonpurposive forces, you end up with some very puzzling problems."

"As for instance?" asked Madend.

"As for instance," I said, "the passing away of the dinosaurs."

"What's so hard to understand about that?"

"There's no logical reason for it. Try to name some."

"Law of diminishing returns," said Madend. "The brontosaurus got so massive, it took legs like tree trunks to support him, and at that he had to stand in water and let buoyancy do most of the work. And he had to eat all the time to keep himself supplied with calories. I mean, *all the time.* As for the carnivores, they afflicted such armor upon themselves in their race against one another, offensive and defensive, that they were just crawling tanks, puffing under half a ton of bone and scale. It just got to the point where it didn't pay off."

"Okay," I said, "so the big babies die off. But most of the dinosaurs were little running creatures where neither mass nor armor had become excessive. What happened to them?"

"As far as the small ones are concerned," put in Thetier, "there's the question of competition. If some of the reptiles developed hair and warm blood, those could adapt themselves to variations in climate more efficiently. They wouldn't have to stay out of direct sunlight. They wouldn't get sluggish as soon as the temperature dropped below eighty Fahrenheit. They wouldn't have to hibernate in the winter. Therefore, they would get out front in the race for food."

"That doesn't satisfy me," I said. "In the first place, I don't think the various saurians are quite such pushovers. They held out for some three hundred million years, you know, which is 298 million more than genus *Homo* has to its credit. Secondly, cold-blooded animals still survive, notably insects and amphibia—"

"Powers of reproduction," said Thetier.

"*And* some reptiles. The snakes, lizards, and turtles are doing very well, thank you. For that matter, what about the ocean. The saurians adapted to that in the shape of ichthyosaurs and plesiosaurs. They vanished, too, and there were no newly developed forms of life based on radical evolutionary advances to compete with them. As near as I can make out, the highest form of ocean life are the fish, and they antedate the ichthyosaurs. How do you account for that? The fish are just as cold-blooded and even more primitive.

And in the ocean there's no question of mass and diminishing returns, since the water does all the work of support. The sulfurbottom whale is larger than any dinosaur that ever lived. —Another thing. What's the use of talking about the inefficiency of cold blood and saying that at temperatures below eighty, cold-blooded animals become sluggish. Fish are very happy at continuous temperatures of about thirty-five, and there is nothing sluggish about a shark."

"Then why did the dinosaurs quietly steal off the Earth, leaving their bones behind?" asked Madend.

"They were part of the plan. Once they had served their purpose, they were unnecessary and therefore gotten rid of."

"How? In a properly arranged Velikovskian catastrophe? A striking comet? The finger of God?"

"No, of course not. They died out naturally and of necessity according to the original precalculation."

"Then we ought to be able to find out what that natural, necessary cause of extinction was."

"Not necessarily. It might have been some obscure failure of the saurian biochemistry, some developing vitamin deficiency—"

"It's all too complicated," said Thetier.

"It just seems complicated," I maintained. "Supposing it were necessary to pocket a given billiard ball by making a four-cushion shot. Would you quibble at the relatively complicated course of the cue ball? A direct hit would be less complicated, but would accomplish nothing. And despite the apparent complication, the stroke would be no more difficult to the master. It would still be a single motion of the cue, merely in a different direction. The ordinary properties of elastic materials and the laws of conservation of momentum would then take over."

"I take it, then," said Trotter, "that you suggest that the course of evolution represents the simplest way in which one could have progressed from original chaos to man."

"That's right. Not a sparrow falls without a purpose, and not a pterodactyl, either."

"And where do we go from here?"

"Nowhere. Evolution is finished with the development of man. The old rules don't apply anymore."

"Oh, don't they?" said Madend. "You rule out the continuing occurrence of environmental variation and of mutations."

"In a sense, I do," I insisted. "More and more, man is controlling his environment, and more and more he is understanding the mechanism of mutations. Before man appeared on the scene, creatures could neither foresee and guard themselves against shifts in climatic conditions. Nor could they understand the increasing danger from newly developing species before the danger had become overwhelming. But now ask yourself this question: What species of organism can possibly replace us and how is it going to accomplish the task?"

"We can start off," said Madend, "by considering the insects. I think they're doing the job already."

"They haven't prevented us from increasing in population about ten-fold in the last two hundred and fifty years. If man were ever to concentrate on the struggle with the insects instead of spending most of his spare effort on other types of fighting, said insects would not last long. No way of proving it, but that's my opinion."

"What about bacteria, or, better still, viruses," said Madend. "The influenza virus of 1918 did a respectable job of getting rid of a sizable percentage of us."

"Sure," I said, "just about one percent of us. Even the Black Death of the fourteenth century only managed to kill one third of the population of Europe, and that at a time when medical science was nonexistent. It was allowed to run its course at will, under the most appalling conditions of medieval poverty, filth and squalor, and still two thirds of our very tough species managed to survive. Disease can't do it, I'm sure."

"What about man himself developing into a sort of superman and displacing the old-timers," suggested Thetier.

"Not bloody likely," I said. "The only part of the human being which is worth anything, as far as being boss of the world is concerned, is his nervous system; the cerebral hemispheres of the brain, in particular. They are the most specialized part of his organism and therefore a dead end. If there is anything the course of evolution demonstrates, it is that once a certain degree of specialization sets in, flexibility is lost and further development can proceed only in the direction of greater specialization."

"Isn't that exactly what's wanted?" said Thetier.

"Maybe it is, but, as Madend pointed out, specializations have a way of reaching a point of diminishing returns. It's the size of the human head at birth that makes the process difficult and painful. It's the complexity of the human mentality that makes mental and emotional maturity lag so far behind sexual maturity in man, with *its* consequent harvest of troubles. It's the delicacy of mental equipment that makes most of all of the race neurotic. How much further can we go without complete disaster?"

"The development," said Madend, "might be in the direction of greater stability or quicker maturity rather than in that of higher intensity of brain power."

"Maybe, but there are no signs of it. The Cro-Magnon man existed ten thousand years ago and there are some interesting indications that modern man is his inferior, if anything, in brain power, and in physique, too, for that matter."

"Ten thousand years," said Trotter, "isn't much, evolutionarily speaking. Besides, there is always the possibility of other species of animals developing intelligence, or something better, if there is anything better."

"We'd never let them. That's the point. It would take hundreds of thousands of years for, let us say, bears or rats to become intelligent, and we'd wipe them out as soon as we saw what was happening—or else use them as slaves."

"All right," said Thetier. "What about obscure biochemical deficiencies, such as you insisted on in the case of the dinosaurs. Take vitamin C, for instance. The only organisms that can't make their own are guinea pigs, and primates, including man. Suppose this trend continues and we become impossibly dependent on too many essential food factors. Or what if the apparent increase in the susceptibility of man to cancer continues. Then what?"

"That's no problem," I said. "It's the essence of the new situation, that we are producing all known food-factors artificially and may eventually have a completely synthetic diet. And there's no reason to think we won't learn how to prevent or cure cancer someday."

Trotter got up. He had finished his coffee but was still nursing his cup. "All right, then, you say we've hit a dead end. But what if all this has been taken into the original account. The Creator was prepared to spend three hundred million years letting the dinosaurs develop something or other that would hasten the development of man, or so you say; why can't he have figured out a way in which man could use his intelligence and his control of the environment to prepare the next stage of the game? That might be a very amusing part of the billiard-ball pattern."

That stopped me. "How do you mean?" I asked.

Trotter smiled at me. "Oh, I was just thinking that it might not be entirely coincidence, and that a new race may be coming and an old one going entirely through the efforts of this cerebral mechanism." He tapped his temple.

"In what way?"

"Stop me if I'm wrong, but aren't the sciences of nucleonics and cybernetics reaching simultaneous peaks? Aren't we inventing hydrogen bombs and thinking machines at the same time? Is that coincidence or part of the divine purpose?"

That was about all for that lunch hour. It had begun as logic chopping on my part, but since then—I've been wondering!

———————— ◆ ————————

DARWINIAN POOL ROOM is essentially a conversation among a number of people. I have always had a hankering to tell stories of this sort, perhaps because I had read so many stories I enjoyed that began with people about a roaring fire on a stormy night, swapping tales, and then one of them would start with, "It was on just such a night as this that I . . ."

This particular story was strongly influenced by my situation at the medical school. Lunchtime there was frequently one long bull-session with other faculty members—particularly with Burnham S. Walker, who was head of the biochemistry department, William C. Boyd of immunochemistry, and Matthew A. Derow of microbiology. (They are all retired now, but, as far as I know, all alive.)

All three, particularly Boyd, were science fiction fans, and it was Boyd who had first suggested my name for the modest post of instructor (at what to me, at that time, seemed the gorgeously extravagant stipend of five thousand dollars each and every single year).

Eventually, I wrote a biochemistry textbook with Walker and Boyd, entitled BIOCHEMISTRY AND HUMAN METABOLISM (Williams & Wilkins, 1952). It went through a second edition in 1954 and a third edition in 1957, and was a failure in each edition. Another textbook, with Walker and with a nurse from outside the school, was intended for student nurses and was called CHEMISTRY AND HUMAN HEALTH (McGraw-Hill, 1956). It was an even worse fail-ure.*

Although a failure, BIOCHEMISTRY AND HUMAN METABOLISM in-troduced me to the delights of writing nonfiction, and neither I nor my writing career was ever the same again.

It had been my intention to write a whole series of talk-stories like DARWINIAN POOL ROOM. I was dissuaded from this (perhaps fortunately so) by my misinterpretation of Horace's dour accept-ance of the story and by Dr. Walker's remark when he read the story once it was in print. He said in his usual laconic fashion, "*Our* talks are better."

But nothing is lost. The time was to come when I was to be in-spired again, this time by the dinner conversations at the Trap Door Spiders, a peculiar club to which I belong. With a distinct memory of DARWINIAN POOL ROOM, I have written an entire series of mystery stories in terms of conversations over a dinner table. Most of these have appeared in various issues of *Ellery Queen's Mystery Maga-zine,* beginning with that of January 1972. Twelve of them have been collected in my book TALES OF THE BLACK WIDOWERS (Dou-bleday, 1974). At the present moment, I have completed twelve more for MORE TALES OF THE BLACK WIDOWERS.

In THE EARLY ASIMOV I mentioned the fact that there were eleven stories that I had never succeeded in selling. What's more, said I in that book, all eleven stories no longer existed and must remain forever in limbo.

However, Boston University collects all my papers with an as-siduity and determination worthy of a far better cause, and when they first began to do so back in 1966, I handed them piles and piles of manuscript material I didn't look through.

Some eager young fan did, though. Boston University apparently allows the inspection of its literary collections for research pur-poses, and this young fan, representing himself as a literary his-torian, I suppose, got access to my files. He came across the faded manuscript of *Big Game,* a thousand-word short-short which I had

* I eventually wrote about some of my textbook experiences in my article *The Sound of Panting,* which appeared in the June 1955 *Astounding* and was in-cluded in my book ONLY A TRILLION (Abelard-Schuman, 1957).

listed in THE EARLY ASIMOV as the eleventh and last of my lost rejections.

Having read THE EARLY ASIMOV, the fan recognized the value of the find. He promptly had it reproduced and sent me a copy. And I promptly saw to it that it got into print. It appeared in BEFORE THE GOLDEN AGE.

When I read the manuscript of *Big Game,* however, I discovered that, in a way, it had never been lost. I had salvaged it. Back in early 1950, Robert W. Lowndes, then publishing several science fiction magazines for Columbia Publications, and reveling in the science fiction boom of the period, asked me for a story. I must have remembered *Big Game,* written eight years earlier, for I produced DAY OF THE HUNTERS, which was an expanded version of the earlier story, and Bob published it in the November 1950 issue of *Future Combined with Science Fiction Stories.*

DAY OF THE HUNTERS

It began the same night it ended. It wasn't much. It just bothered me; it still bothers me.

You see, Joe Bloch, Ray Manning, and I were squatting around our favorite table in the corner bar with an evening on our hands and a mess of chatter to throw it away with. That's the beginning.

Joe Bloch started it by talking about the atomic bomb, and what he thought ought to be done with it, and how who would have thought it five years ago. And I said lots of guys thought it five years ago and wrote stories about it and it was going to be tough on them trying to keep ahead of the newspapers now. Which led to a general palaver on how lots of screwy things might come true and a lot of for-instances were thrown about.

Ray said he heard from somebody that some big-shot scientist had sent a block of lead back in time for about two seconds or two minutes or two thousandths of a second—he didn't know which. He said the scientist wasn't saying anything to anybody because he didn't think anyone would believe him.

So I asked, pretty sarcastic, how *he* came to know about it. —Ray may have lots of friends but I have the same lot and none of them know any big-shot scientists. But he said never mind how he heard, take it or leave it.

And then there wasn't anything to do but talk about time machines, and how supposing you went back and killed your own grandfather or why didn't somebody from the future come back and tell us who was going to win the next war, or if there was going to be a next war, or if there'd be anywhere on Earth you could live after it, regardless of who wins.

Ray thought just knowing the winner in the seventh race while the sixth was being run would be something.

But Joe decided different. He said, "The trouble with you guys is you got wars and races on the mind. Me, I got curiosity. Know what I'd do if I had a time machine?"

So right away we wanted to know, all ready to give him the old snicker whatever it was.

He said, "If I had one, I'd go back in time about a couple or five or fifty million years and find out what happened to the dinosaurs."

Which was too bad for Joe, because Ray and I both thought there was just about no sense to that at all. Ray said who cared about a lot of dinosaurs and I said the only thing they were good for was to make a mess of skeletons for guys who were dopy enough to wear out the floors in museums; and it was a good thing they did get out of the way to make room for human beings. Of course Joe said that with *some* human beings he knew, and he gives us a hard look, we should've stuck to dinosaurs, but we pay no attention to that.

"You dumb squirts can laugh and make like you know something, but that's because you don't ever have any imagination," he says. "Those dinosaurs were big stuff. Millions of all kinds—big as houses, and dumb as houses, too—all over the place. And then, all of a sudden, like that," and he snaps his fingers, "there aren't any anymore."

How come, we wanted to know.

But he was just finishing a beer and waving at Charlie for another with a coin to prove he wanted to pay for it and he just shrugged his shoulders. "I don't know. That's what I'd find out, though."

That's all. That would have finished it. I would've said something and Ray would've made a crack, and we all would've had another beer and maybe swapped some talk about the weather and the Brooklyn Dodgers and then said so long, and never think of dinosaurs again.

Only we didn't, and now I never have anything on my mind but dinosaurs, and I feel sick.

Because the rummy at the next table looks up and hollers, "Hey!"

We hadn't seen him. As a general rule, we don't go around looking at rummies we don't know in bars. I got plenty to do keeping track of the rummies I do know. This fellow had a bottle before him that was half empty, and a glass in his hand that was half full.

He said, "Hey," and we all looked at him, and Ray said, "Ask him what he wants, Joe."

Joe was nearest. He tipped his chair backward and said, "What do you want?"

The rummy said, "Did I hear you gentlemen mention dinosaurs?"

He was just a little weavy, and his eyes looked like they were bleeding, and you could only tell his shirt was once white by guessing, but it must've been the way he talked. It didn't *sound* rummy, if you know what I mean.

Anyway, Joe sort of eased up and said, "Sure. Something you want to know?"

He sort of smiled at us. It was a funny smile; it started at the mouth and ended just before it touched the eyes. He said, "Did you want to build a time machine and go back to find out what happened to the dinosaurs?"

I could see Joe was figuring that some kind of confidence game was coming up. I was figuring the same thing. Joe said, "Why? You aiming to offer to build one for me?"

The rummy showed a mess of teeth and said. "No, sir. I could but I won't. You know why? Because I built a time machine for myself a couple of years ago and went back to the Mesozoic Era and found out what happened to the dinosaurs."

Later on, I looked up how to spell "Mesozoic," which is why I got it right, in case you're wondering, and I found out that the Mesozoic Era is when all the dinosaurs were doing whatever dinosaurs do. But of course at the time this is just so much double-talk to me, and mostly I was thinking we had a lunatic talking to us. Joe claimed afterward that he knew about this Mesozoic thing, but he'll have to talk lots longer and louder before Ray and I believe him.

But that did it just the same. We said to the rummy to come over to our table. I guess I figured we could listen to him for a while and maybe get some of the bottle, and the others must have figured the same. But he held his bottle tight in his right hand when he sat down and that's where he kept it.

Ray said, "Where'd you build a time machine?"

"At Midwestern University. My daughter and I worked on it together."

He sounded like a college guy at that.

I said, "Where is it now? In your pocket?"

He didn't blink; he never jumped at us no matter how wise we cracked. Just kept talking to himself out loud, as if the whiskey had limbered up his tongue and he didn't care if we stayed or not.

He said, "I broke it up. Didn't want it. Had enough of it."

We didn't believe him. We didn't believe him worth a darn. You better get that straight. It stands to reason, because if a guy invented a time machine, he could clean up millions—he could clean up all the money in the world, just knowing what would happen to the stock market and the races and elections. He wouldn't throw all that away, I don't care what reasons he had. —Besides, none of us were going to believe in time travel anyway, because what if you *did* kill your own grandfather.

Well, never mind.

Joe said, "Yeah, you broke it up. Sure you did. What's your name?"

But he didn't answer that one, ever. We asked him a few more times, and then we ended up calling him "Professor."

He finished off his glass and filled it again very slow. He didn't offer us any, and we all sucked at our beers.

So I said, "Well, go ahead. What happened to the dinosaurs?"

But he didn't tell us right away. He stared right at the middle of the table and talked to it.

"I don't know how many times Carol sent me back—just a few minutes or hours—before I made the big jump. I didn't care about the dinosaurs; I just wanted to see how far the machine would take me on the supply of power I had available. I suppose it was dangerous, but is life so wonderful? The war was on then— One more life?"

He sort of coddled his glass as if he was thinking about things in general, then he seemed to skip a part in his mind and keep right on going.

"It was sunny," he said, "sunny and bright; dry and hard. There were no swamps, no ferns. None of the accoutrements of the Cretaceous we associate with dinosaurs,"—anyway, I think that's what he said. I didn't always catch the big words, so later on I'll just stick in what I can remember. I checked all the spellings, and I must say that for all the liquor he put away, he pronounced them without stutters.

That's maybe what bothered us. He sounded so familiar with everything, and it all just rolled off his tongue like nothing.

He went on, "It was a late age, certainly the Cretaceous. The dinosaurs were already on the way out—all except those little ones, with their metal belts and their guns."

I guess Joe practically dropped his nose into the beer altogether. He skidded halfway around the glass, when the professor let loose that statement sort of sadlike.

Joe sounded mad. "*What* little ones, with whose metal belts and which guns?"

The professor looked at him for just a second and then let his eyes slide back to nowhere. "They were little reptiles, standing four feet high. They stood on their hind legs with a thick tail behind, and they had little forearms with fingers. Around their waists were strapped wide metal belts, and from these hung guns. —And they weren't guns that shot pellets either; they were energy projectors."

"They were what?" I asked. "Say, when was this? Millions of years ago?"

"That's right," he said. "They were reptiles. They had scales and no eyelids and they probably laid eggs. But they used energy guns. There were five of them. They were on me as soon as I got out of the machine. There must have been millions of them all over Earth— millions. Scattered all over. They must have been the Lords of Creation then."

I guess it was then that Ray thought he had him, because he developed that wise look in his eyes that makes you feel like conking him with an empty beer mug, because a full one would waste beer. He said, "Look P'fessor, millions of them, huh? Aren't there guys who don't do anything but find old bones and mess around with them till they figure out what some dinosaur looked like. The museums are full of these here skeletons, aren't they? Well, where's there one with a metal belt on him. If there were millions, what's become of them? Where are the bones?"

The professor sighed. It was a real, sad sigh. Maybe he realized for the first time he was just speaking to three guys in overalls in a barroom. Or maybe he didn't care.

He said, "You don't find many fossils. Think how many animals lived on Earth altogether. Think how many billions and trillions. And then think how few fossils we find. —And these lizards were intelligent. Remember that. They're not going to get caught in snow drifts or mud, or fall into lava, except by big accident. Think how few fossil men there are—even of these subintelligent apemen of a million years ago."

He looked at his half-full glass and turned it round and round.

He said, "What would fossils show anyway? Metal belts rust away and leave nothing. Those little lizards were warm-blooded. I *know* that, but you couldn't prove it from petrified bones. What the devil? A million years from now could you tell what New York looks like from a human skeleton? Could you tell a human from a gorilla by

the bones and figure out which one built an atomic bomb and which
one ate bananas in a zoo?"

"Hey," said Joe, plenty objecting, "any simple bum can tell a
gorilla skeleton from a man's. A man's got a larger brain. Any fool
can tell which one was intelligent."

"Really?" The professor laughed to himself, as if all this was so
simple and obvious, it was just a crying shame to waste time on it.
"You judge everything from the type of brain human beings have
managed to develop. Evolution has different ways of doing things.
Birds fly one way; bats fly another way. Life has plenty of tricks
for everything. —How much of your brain do you think you use.
About a fifth. That's what the psychologists say. As far as they
know, as far as anybody knows, eighty per cent of your brain has no
use at all. Everybody just works on way-low gear, except maybe a
few in history. Leonardo da Vinci, for instance. Archimedes, Aris-
totle, Gauss, Galois, Einstein—"

I never heard of any of them except Einstein, but I didn't let on.
He mentioned a few more, but I've put in all I can remember. Then
he said, "Those little reptiles had tiny brains, maybe quarter-size,
maybe even less, but they used it all—every bit of it. Their bones
might not show it, but they were intelligent; intelligent as humans.
And they were boss of all Earth."

And then Joe came up with something that was really good. For a
while I was sure that he had the professor and I was awfully glad he
came out with it. He said, "Look, P'fessor, if those lizards were so
damned hot, why didn't they leave something behind? Where are
their cities and their buildings and all the sort of stuff we keep finding of the cavemen, stone knives and things. Hell, if human beings
got the heck off of Earth, think of the stuff we'd leave behind us.
You couldn't walk a mile without falling over a city. And roads and
things."

But the professor just couldn't be stopped. He wasn't even
shaken up. He just came right back with, "You're still judging
other forms of life by human standards. We build cities and roads
and airports and the rest that goes with us—but they didn't. They
were built on a different plan. Their whole way of life was different
from the ground up. They didn't live in cities. They didn't have our
kind of art. I'm not sure what they did have because it was so alien

I couldn't grasp it—except for their guns. Those *would* be the same. Funny, isn't it. —For all I know, maybe we stumble over their relics every day and don't even know that's what they are."

I was pretty sick of it by that time. You just *couldn't* get him. The cuter you'd be, the cuter he'd be.

I said, "Look here. How do you know so much about those things? What did you do; live with them? Or did they speak English? Or maybe you speak lizard talk. Give us a few words of lizard talk."

I guess I was getting mad, too. You know how it is. A guy tells you something you don't believe because it's all cockeyed, and you can't get him to admit he's lying.

But the professor wasn't mad. He was just filling the glass again, very slowly. "No," he said, "I didn't talk and they didn't talk. They just looked at me with their cold, hard, staring eyes—snake's eyes —and I knew what they were thinking, and I could see that they knew what I was thinking. Don't ask me how it happened. It just did. Everything. I knew that they were out on a hunting expedition and I knew they weren't going to let me go."

And we stopped asking questions. We just looked at him, then Ray said, "What happened? How did you get away?"

"That was easy. An animal scurried past on the hilltop. It was long—maybe ten feet—and narrow and ran close to the ground. The lizards got excited. I could feel the excitement in waves. It was as if they forgot about me in a single hot flash of blood lust—and off they went. I got back in the machine, returned, and broke it up."

It was the flattest sort of ending you ever heard. Joe made a noise in his throat. "Well, what happened to the dinosaurs?"

"Oh, you don't see? I thought it was plain enough. —It was those little intelligent lizards that did it. They were hunters—by instinct and by choice. It was their hobby in life. It wasn't for food; it was for fun."

"And they just wiped out all the dinosaurs on the Earth?"

"All that lived at the time, anyway; all the contemporary species. Don't you think it's possible? How long did it take us to wipe out bison herds by the hundred million? What happened to the dodo in a few years? Supposing we really put our minds to it, how long would the lions and the tigers and the giraffes last? Why, by the time I saw those lizards there wasn't any big game left—no reptile more than fifteen feet maybe. All gone. Those little demons were chasing the little, scurrying ones, and probably crying their hearts out for the good old days."

And we all kept quiet and looked at our empty beer bottles and thought about it. All those dinosaurs—big as houses—killed by little lizards with guns. Killed for fun.

Then Joe leaned over and put his hand on the professor's shoulder, easylike, and shook it. He said, "Hey, P'fessor, but if that's so, what happened to the little lizards with the guns? Huh? —Did you ever go back to find out?"

The professor looked up with the kind of look in his eyes that he'd have if he were lost.

"You still don't see! It was already beginning to happen to them. I saw it in their eyes. They were running out of big game—the fun was going out of it. So what did you expect them to do? They turned to other game—the biggest and most dangerous of all—and really had fun. They hunted that game to the end."

"What game?" asked Ray. He didn't get it, but Joe and I did.

"Themselves," said the professor in a loud voice. "They finished off all the others and began on themselves—till not one was left."

And again we stopped and thought about those dinosaurs—big as houses—all finished off by little lizards with guns. Then we thought about the little lizards and how they had to keep the guns going even when there was nothing to use them on but themselves.

Joe said, "Poor dumb lizards."

"Yeah," said Ray, "poor crackpot lizards."

And then what happened really scared us. Because the professor jumped up with eyes that looked as if they were trying to climb right out of their sockets and leap at us. He shouted, "You damned fools. Why do you sit there slobbering over reptiles dead a hundred million years. That was the first intelligence on Earth and that's how it ended. That's *done*. But we're the second intelligence—and how the devil do you think *we're* going to end?"

He pushed the chair over and headed for the door. But then he stood there just before leaving altogether and said: *"Poor dumb humanity!* Go ahead and cry about that."

------◆------

The story, alas, seems to have a moral, and, in fact, ends by pounding that moral over the reader's head. That is bad. Straightforward preaching spoils the effectiveness of a story. If you can't resist the impulse to improve your fellow human beings, do it subtly.

Occasionally I overflow and forget this good maxim. DAY OF THE HUNTERS was written not long after the Soviet Union had exploded its first fission bomb. It had been bad enough till then, knowing that the United States might be tempted to use fission bombs if sufficiently irritated (as in 1945). Now, for the first time, the possibility of a real nuclear war, one in which both sides used fission bombs, had arisen.

We've grown used to that situation now and scarcely think of it, but in 1950 there were many who thought a nuclear war was inevitable, and in short order, too. I was pretty bitter about that— and the bitterness shows in the story.*

DAY OF THE HUNTERS is also told in the framework of a conversation, by the way. This one takes place in a bar. Wodehouse's stories about Mulliner, the stories set in Gavagan's Bar by L. Sprague de Camp and Fletcher Pratt, and Clarke's stories about the White Hart were all set in bars, and I'd read them all and loved them.

It was inevitable, therefore, that someday I would tell a story in the form of a bar conversation. The only trouble is that I don't drink and have hardly ever sat in a bar, so I probably have it all wrong.

My stay in Boston quickly proved to be no barrier to my literary career. (In fact, nothing since my concentration on my doctoral research in 1947 has proved to be a barrier.)

After two months in a small sublet apartment (of slum quality) very close to the school, we moved to the suburbs—if you want to call it that. Neither my wife nor I could drive a car when we came to Boston so we had to find a place on the bus lines. We got one in the rather impoverished town of Somerville—an attic apartment of primitive sort that was unbelievably hot in the summer.

There I wrote my second novel, THE STARS, LIKE DUST (Doubleday, 1951), and while there a small, one-man publishing firm, Gnome Press, put out a collection of my positronic robot stories, I, ROBOT, in 1950, and the first portion of my Foundation stories as FOUNDATION in 1951.†

---

* Mankind's suicide seems now, a quarter century after DAY OF THE HUNTERS was written, to be more likely than ever, but for different reasons.
† Gnome Press did not do well with these books, or with FOUNDATION AND EMPIRE and SECOND FOUNDATION, which they published in 1951 and 1952. To my great relief, therefore, Doubleday, playing the role of White Knight on my behalf, pressured Gnome Press into relinquishing these books in 1962. Doubleday handled them thereafter and succeeded in earning (and is still continuing to earn) very substantial sums out of all of them for myself and for themselves.

In 1950 I learned to drive an automobile, and in 1951 we even had a son, rather to our surprise. After nine years of marriage we had rather come to the opinion that we were doomed to be childless. Late in 1950, however, it turned out that the explanation to some rather puzzling physiological manifestations was that my wife was pregnant. The first person to tell me that that must be so, I remember, was Evelyn Gold (she was then Mrs. Horace Gold). I laughed and said, "No, no," but it was yes, yes, and David was born on August 20, 1951.

Having thus become prolific in books and having made a start in the direction of automobiles and offspring, I was ready for anything and began to accept all kinds of assignments.

Among the many science fiction magazines of the early 1950s, for instance, there was one called *Marvel Science Fiction*. It was the reincarnation of an earlier *Marvel* that had published nine issues between 1938 and 1941. The earlier magazine had specialized in stories that accented sex in a rather heavy-handed and foolish manner.‡

After *Marvel* was revived in 1950 (it lasted only for another half-dozen issues) I was asked for a story. I might have recalled the unsavory history of the magazine and refused to supply one, but I thought of a story I couldn't resist writing because, as all who know me are aware, I am an incorrigible punster.**

The story was SHAH GUIDO G. and it appeared in the November 1951 issue of *Marvel*.

‡ In a very indirect way this eventually led to my writing a story called *Playboy and the Slime God* which appeared in the March 1961 *Amazing Stories* and was then included in my collection NIGHTFALL AND OTHER STORIES under the much better title *What Is This Thing Called Love?*

** I once asked a girl named Dawn if she had ever used one of those penny weighing machines on a trip to Florida she was telling me about. She said, "No. Why?" and I said because there was a song written about it. She said, "What are you talking about?" and I said, "Haven't you heard 'Weigh Dawn Upon the Swanee River'?" and she chased me for five blocks before I got away.

SHAH GUIDO G.

Once every year Philo Plat returned to the scene of his crime. It was a form of penance. On each anniversary he climbed the barren crest and gazed along the miles of smashed metal, concrete, and bones.

The area was desolate. The metal crumplings were still stainless and unrusted, their jagged teeth raised in futile anger. Somewhere among it all were the skeletons of the thousands who had died, of all ages and both sexes. Their skully sightlessness, for all he knew, was turning empty, curse-torn eye holes at him.

The stench had long since gone from the desert, and the lizards held their lairs untroubled. No man approached the fenced-off burial ground where what remained of bodies lay in the gashed crater carved out in that final fall.

Only Plat came. He returned year after year and always, as though to ward off so many Evil Eyes, he took his gold medal with him. It hung suspended bravely from his neck as he stood on the crest. On it was inscribed simply, "To the Liberator!"

This time, Fulton was with him. Fulton had been a Lower One once in the days before the crash; the days when there had been Higher Ones and Lower Ones.

Fulton said, "I am amazed you insist on coming here, Philo."

Plat said, "I must. You know the sound of the crash was heard for hundreds of miles; seismographs registered it around the world. My ship was almost directly above it; the shock vibrations caught me and flung me miles. Yet all I can remember of sound is that one composite scream as Atlantis began its fall."

"It had to be done."

"Words," sighed Plat. "There were babies and guiltless ones."

"No one is guiltless."

"Nor am I. Ought I to have been the executioner?"

"Someone had to be." Fulton was firm. "Consider the world now, twenty-five years later. Democracy re-established, education once more universal, culture available for the masses, and science once more advancing. Two expeditions have already landed on Mars."

"I know. I know. But that, too, was a culture. They called it Atlantis because it was an island that ruled the world. It was an island in the sky, not the sea. It was a city and a world all at once, Fulton. You never saw its crystal covering and its gorgeous buildings. It was a single jewel carved of stone and metal. It was a dream."

"It was concentrated happiness distilled out of the little supply distributed to billions of ordinary folk who lived on the Surface."

"Yes, you are right. Yes, it had to be. But it might have been so different, Fulton. You know," he seated himself on the hard rock, crossed his arms upon his knees and cradled his chin in them, "I think, sometimes, of how it must have been in the old days, when there were nations and wars upon the Earth. I think of how much a miracle it must have seemed to the peoples when the United Nations first became a real world government, and what Atlantis must have meant to them.

"It was a capital city that governed Earth but was not of it. It was a black disc in the air, capable of appearing anywhere on Earth at any height; belonging to no one nation, but to all the planet; the product of no one nation's ingenuity but the first great achievement of all the race—and then, what it became!"

Fulton said, "Shall we go? We'll want to get back to the ship before dark."

Plat went on, "In a way, I suppose it was inevitable. The human race never did invent an institution that didn't end as a cancer. Probably in prehistoric times, the medicine man who began as the repository of tribal wisdom ended as the last bar to tribal advance. In ancient Rome, the citizen army—"

Fulton was letting him speak—patiently. It was a queer echo of the past. And there had been other eyes upon him in those days, patiently waiting, while he talked.

"—the citizen army that defended the Romans against all comers from Veii to Carthage, became the professional Praetorian Guard that sold the Imperium and levied tribute on all the Empire. The Turks developed the Janissaries as their invincible advance guard against Europe and the Sultan ended as a slave of his Janissary slaves. The barons of medieval Europe protected the serfs against the Northmen and the Magyars, then remained six hundred years longer as a parasite aristocracy that contributed nothing."

Plat became aware of the patient eyes and said, "Don't you understand me?"

One of the bolder technicians said, "With your kind permission, Higher One, we must needs be at work."

"Yes, I suppose you must."

The technician felt sorry. This Higher One was queer, but he meant well. Though he spoke a deal of nonsense, he inquired after their families, told them they were fine fellows, and that their work made them better than the Higher Ones.

So he explained, "You see, there is another shipment of granite and steel for the new theater and we will have to shift the energy distribution. It is becoming very hard to do that. The Higher Ones will not listen."

"Now that's what I mean. You should *make* them listen."

But they just stared at him, and at that moment an idea crawled gently into Plat's unconscious mind.

Leo Spinney waited for him on the crystal level. He was Plat's age but taller and much more handsome. Plat's face was thin, his eyes were china-blue, and he never smiled. Spinney was straight-nosed with brown eyes that seemed to laugh continuously.

Spinney called, "We'll miss the game."

"I don't want to go, Leo. Please."

Spinney said, "With the technicians again? Why do you waste your time?"

Plat said, "They work. I respect them. What right have we to idle?"

"Ought I to ask questions of the world as it is when it suits me so well?"

"If you do not, someone will ask questions for you someday."

"That will be someday, not this day. And, frankly, you had better come. The Sekjen has noticed that you are never present at the games and he doesn't like it. Personally, I think people have been telling him of your talks to the technicians and your visits to the Surface. He might even think you consort with Lower Ones."

Spinney laughed heartily, but Plat said nothing. It would not hurt them if they consorted with Lower Ones a bit more, learned something of their thinking. Atlantis had its guns and its battalions of Waves. It might learn someday that that was not enough. Not enough to save the Sekjen.

The Sekjen! Plat wanted to spit. The full title was "Secretary-General of the United Nations." Two centuries before it had been an elective office; an honorable one. Now a man like Guido Gar-shthavastra could fill it because he could prove he was the son of his equally worthless father.

"Guido G." was what the Lower Ones on the Surface called him. And usually, with bitterness, "Shah Guido G.," because "Shah" had been the title of a line of despotic oriental kings. The Lower Ones knew him for what he was. Plat wanted to tell Spinney that, but it wasn't time yet.

The real games were held in the upper stratosphere, a hundred miles above Atlantis, though the Sky-Island was itself twenty miles above sea-level. The huge amphitheater was filled and the radiant globe in its center held all eyes. Each tiny one-man cruiser high above was represented by its own particular glowing symbol in the color that belonged to the fleet of which it was part. The little sparks reproduced in exact miniature the motions of the ships.

The game was starting as Plat and Spinney took their seats. The little dots were already flashing toward one another, skimming and missing, veering.

A large scoreboard blazoned the progress of the battle in conventional symbology that Plat did not understand. There was confused cheering for either fleet and for particular ships.

High up under a canopy was the Sekjen, the Shah Guido G. of the Lower Ones. Plat could barely see him but he could make out clearly the smaller replica of the game globe that was there for his private use.

Plat was watching the game for the first time. He understood none of the finer points and wondered at the reason for the particular shouts. Yet he understood that the dots were ships and that the streaks of light that licked out from them on frequent occasions represented energy beams which, one hundred miles above, were as real as flaring atoms could make them. Each time a dot streaked, there was a clamor in the audience that died in a great moan as a target dot veered and escaped.

And then there was a general yell and the audience, men and women up to the Sekjen himself, clambered to its feet. One of the shining dots had been hit and was going down—spiraling, spiraling. A hundred miles above, a real ship was doing the same; plunging down into the thickening air that would heat and con-

sume its specially designed magnesium alloy shell to harmless pow-
dery ash before it could reach the surface of the Earth.

Plat turned away. "I'm leaving, Spinney."

Spinney was marking his scorecard and saying, "That's five ships
the Greens have lost this week. We've got to have more." He was
on his feet, calling wildly, "Another one!"

The audience was taking up the shout, chanting it.

Plat said, "A man died in that ship."

"You bet. One of the Green's best too. Damn good thing."

"Do you realize that a man *died*."

"They're only Lower Ones. What's bothering you?"

Plat made his slow way out among the rows of people. A few
looked at him and whispered. Most had eyes for nothing but the
game globe. There was perfume all about him and in the distance,
occasionally heard amid the shouts, there was a faint wash of gentle
music. As he passed through a main exit, a yell trembled the air
behind him.

Plat fought the nausea grimly.

He walked two miles, then stopped.

Steel girders were swinging at the end of diamagnetic beams and
the coarse sound of orders yelled in Lower accents filled the air.

There was always building going on upon Atlantis. Two hundred
years ago, when Atlantis had been the genuine seat of government,
its lines had been straight, its spaces broad. But now it was much
more than that. It was the Xanadu pleasure dome that Coleridge
spoke of.

The crystal roof had been lifted upward and outward many times
in the last two centuries. Each time it had been thickened so that
Atlantis might more safely climb higher; more safely withstand the
possible blows of meteoric pebbles not yet entirely burnt by the thin
wisps of air.

And as Atlantis became more useless and more attractive, more
and more of the Higher Ones left their estates and factories in
the hands of managers and foremen and took up permanent resi-
dence on the Sky-Island. All built larger, higher, more elaborately.

And here was still another structure.

Waves were standing by in stolid, duty-ridden obedience. The
name applied to the females—if, Plat thought sourly, they could be
called that—was taken from the Early English of the days when

Earth was divided into nations. There, too, conversion and degeneration had obtained. The old Waves had done paper work behind the lines. These creatures, still called Waves, were front-line soldiers.

It made sense, Plat knew. Properly trained, women were more single-minded, more fanatic, less given to doubts and remorse than ever men could be.

They always had Waves present at the scene of any building, because the building was done by Lower Ones, and Lower Ones on Atlantis had to be guarded. Just as those on the Surface had to be cowed. In the last fifty years alone, the long-range atomic artillery that studded the underside of Atlantis had been doubled and tripled.

He watched the girder come softly down, two men yelling directions to each other as it settled in place. Soon there would be no further room for new buildings on Atlantis.

The idea that had nudged his unconscious mind earlier in the day gently touched his conscious mind.

Plat's nostrils flared.

Plat's nose twitched at the smell of oil and machinery. More than most of the perfume-spoiled Higher Ones, he was used to odors of all sorts. He had been on the Surface and smelled the pungence of its growing fields and the fumes of its cities.

He said to the technician, "I am seriously thinking of building a new house and would like your advice as to the best possible location."

The technician was amazed and gratified. "Thank you, Higher One. It has become so difficult to arrange the available power."

"It is why I come to you."

They talked at length. Plat asked a great many questions and when he returned to crystal level his mind was a maze of speculation. Two days passed in an agony of doubt. Then he remembered the shining dot, spiraling and spiraling, and the young, wondering eyes upon his own as Spinney said, "They're only Lower Ones."

He made up his mind and applied for audience with the Sekjen.

The Sekjen's drawling voice accentuated the boredom he did not care to hide. He said, "The Plats are of good family, yet you amuse yourself with technicians. I am told you speak to them as equals. I *hope* that it will not become necessary to remind you that your estates on the Surface require your care."

That would have meant exile from Atlantis, of course.

Plat said, "It is necessary to watch the technicians, Sire. They are of Lower extraction."

The Sekjen frowned. "Our Wave Commander has her job. She takes care of such matters."

"She does her best, I have no doubt, Sire, but I have made friends with the technicians. They are not safe. Would I have any other reason to soil my hands with them, but the safety of Atlantis."

The Sekjen listened. First, doubtfully; then, with fear on his soft face. He said, "I shall have them in custody—"

"Softly, Sire," said Plat. "We cannot do without them meanwhile, since none of us can man the guns and the antigravs. It would be better to give them no opportunity for rebellion. In two weeks the new theater will be dedicated with games and feasting."

"And what do they intend then?"

"I am not yet certain, Sire. But I know enough to recommend that a division of Waves be brought to Atlantis. Secretly, of course, and at the last minute so that it will be too late for the rebels to change any plans they have made. They will have to drop them altogether, and the proper moment, once lost, may never be regained. Thereafter, I will learn more. If necessary, we will train new men. It would be a pity, Sire, to tell anyone of this in advance. If the technicians learn our countermeasures prematurely, matters may go badly."

The Sekjen, with his jeweled hand to his chin, mused—and believed.

Shah Guido G., thought Philo Plat. In history, you'll go down as Shah Guido G.

Philo Plat watched the gaiety from a distance. Atlantis's central squares were crawling black with people. That was good. He himself had managed to get away only with difficulty. And none too soon, since the Wave Division had already cross-hatched the sky with their ships.

They were maneuvering edgily now, adjusting themselves into final position over Atlantis's huge, raised air field, which was well able to take their ships all at once.

The cruisers were descending now vertically, in parade formation. Plat looked quickly toward the city proper. The populace had grown quieter as they watched the unscheduled demonstration, and it seemed to him that he had never seen so many Higher Ones upon the Sky-Island at one time. For a moment, a last misgiving arose. There was still time for a warning.

And even as he thought that he knew that there wasn't. The cruisers were dropping speedily. He would have to hurry if he were himself to escape in his own little craft. He wondered sickly, even as he grasped the controls, whether his friends on the Surface had received his yesterday's warning, or would believe it if they had received it. If they could not act quickly the Higher Ones would yet recover from the first blow, devastating though it was.

He was in the air when the Waves landed, seven thousand five hundred tear-drop ships covering the airfield like a descending net. Plat drove his ship upward, watching—

And Atlantis went dark! It was like a candle over which a mighty hand was suddenly cupped. One moment it blazed the night into brilliance for fifty miles around; the next it was black against blackness.

To Plat the thousands of screams blended into one thin, lost shriek of fear. He fled, and the shock vibrations of Atlantis's crash to Earth caught his ship and hurled it far.

He never stopped hearing that scream.

Fulton was staring at Plat. He said, "Have you ever told this to anyone?"

Plat shook his head.

Fulton's mind went back a quarter century, too. "We got your message, of course. It was hard to believe, as you expected. Many feared a trap even after report of the Fall arrived. But—well, it's history. The Higher Ones that remained, those on the Surface, were demoralized and before they could recover, they were done.

"But tell me," he turned to Plat with sudden, hard curiosity. "What was it you did? We've always assumed you sabotaged the power stations."

"I know. The truth is so much less romantic, Fulton. The world would prefer to believe its myth. Let it."

"May *I* have the truth?"

"If you will. As I told you, the Higher Ones built and built to saturation. The antigrav energy beams had to support a weight in buildings, guns, and enclosing shell that doubled and tripled as the years went on. Any requests the technicians might have made for newer or bigger motors were turned down, since the Higher Ones would rather have the room and money for their mansions and there was always enough power for the moment.

"The technicians, as I said, had already reached the stage where they were disturbed at the construction of single buildings. I questioned them and found exactly how little margin of safety remained. They were waiting only for the completion of the new theater to make a new request. They did *not* realize, however, that, at my suggestion, Atlantis would be called upon to support the sudden additional burden of a division of Wave cavalry in their ships. Seven thousand five hundred ships, fully rigged!

"When the Waves landed, by then almost two thousand tons, the antigrav power supply was overloaded. The motors failed and Atlantis was only a vast rock, ten miles above the ground. What could such a rock do but fall."

Plat arose. Together they turned back toward their ship.

Fulton laughed harshly. "You know, there is a fatality in names."

"What do you mean?"

"Why, that once more in history Atlantis sank beneath the Waves."

———◄◆►———

Now that you've read the story, you'll notice that the whole thing is for the purpose of that final lousy pun, right? In fact, one person came up to me and, in tones of deep disgust, said, "Why, SHAH GUIDO G. is nothing but a shaggy-dog story."

"Right," I said, "and if you divide the title into two parts instead of three, you get SHAHGUI DOG, so don't you think I know it?"

In other words, the title is a pun, too.

With David on his way, we obviously couldn't remain in that impossible Somerville apartment. Since I could now drive a car, we were no longer bound to the bus lines and could look farther afield. In the spring of 1951 we moved into an apartment in Waltham, Massachusetts, therefore. It was a great improvement over the earlier apartment, though it, too, was pretty hot in the summer.

There were two very small built-in bookcases in the living room of the apartment and I began using that for a collection of my own books in chronological order. I got up to seventeen books while I was in that apartment. When my biochemistry textbook came out in 1952 I placed it with the rest in its proper order. It received no preferential treatment. I saw no way in which a scientific textbook could lay claim to greater respectability than a science fiction novel.

If I had ambitions, in fact, it was not toward respectability. I kept wanting to write funny material.

Humor is a funny thing, however—

All right, humor is a *peculiar* thing, if you have a prejudice against a witty play on words. There is no way of being almost funny or mildly funny or fairly funny or tolerably funny. You are either funny or not funny and there is nothing in between. And usually it is the writer who thinks he is funny and the reader who thinks he isn't.

Naturally, then, humor isn't something a man should lightly undertake; especially in the early days of his career when he has not yet learned to handle his tools. —And yet almost every beginning writer tries his hand at humor, convinced that it is an easy thing to do.

I was no exception. By the time I had written and submitted four stories, and had, as yet, sold none, I already felt it was time to write a funny story. I did. It was *Ring Around the Sun,* something I actually managed to sell and which was eventually incuded in THE EARLY ASIMOV.

I didn't think it was successfully funny even at the time it was written. Nor did I think several other funny stories I tried my hand at, such as *Christmas on Ganymede* (also in THE EARLY ASIMOV) and *Robot AL-76 Goes Astray* (included in THE REST OF THE ROBOTS, Doubleday, 1964) were really funny.

It wasn't till 1952 that (in my own mind only; I say nothing about yours) I succeeded. I wrote two stories, BUTTON, BUTTON and THE MONKEY'S FINGER, in which I definitely thought I had managed to do it right. I was giggling all the way through each one, and I managed to unload both on *Startling Stories,* where they appeared in successive issues, BUTTON, BUTTON in the January 1953 issue and THE MONKEY'S FINGER in the February 1953 issue.

And, Gentle Reader, if you don't think they're funny, do your best not to tell me so. Leave me to my illusions.

BUTTON, BUTTON

It was the tuxedo that fooled me and for two seconds I didn't recognize him. To me, he was just a possible client, the first that had whiffed my way in a week—and he looked beautiful.

Even wearing a tuxedo at 9:45 A.M. he looked beautiful. Six inches of bony wrist and ten inches of knobby hand continued on where his sleeve left off; the top of his socks and the bottom of his trousers did not quite join forces; still he looked beautiful.

Then I looked at his face and it wasn't a client at all. It was my uncle Otto. Beauty ended. As usual, my uncle Otto's face looked like that of a bloodhound that had just been kicked in the rump by his best friend.

I wasn't very original in my reaction. I said, "Uncle Otto!"

You'd know him too, if you saw that face. When he was featured on the cover of *Time* about five years ago (it was either '57 or '58), 204 readers by count wrote in to say that they would never forget that face. Most added comments concerning nightmares. If you want my uncle Otto's full name, it's Otto Schlemmelmayer. But don't jump to conclusions. He's my mother's brother. My own name is Smith.

He said, "Harry, my boy," and groaned.

Interesting, but not enlightening. I said, "Why the tuxedo?"

He said, "It's rented."

"All right. But why do you wear it in the morning?"

"Is it morning already?" He stared vaguely about him, then went to the window and looked out.

That's my uncle Otto Schlemmelmayer.

I assured him it was morning and with an effort he deduced that he must have been walking the city streets all night.

He took a handful of fingers away from his forehead to say, "But I was so upset, Harry. At the banquet—"

The fingers waved about for a minute and then folded into a quart of fist that came down and pounded holes in my desk top. "But it's the end. From now on I do things my own way."

My uncle Otto had been saying that since the business of the "Schlemmelmayer Effect" first started up. Maybe that surprises you.

Maybe you think it was the Schlemmelmayer Effect that made my uncle Otto famous. Well, it's all how you look at it.

He discovered the Effect back in 1952 and the chances are that you know as much about it as I do. In a nutshell, he devised a germanium relay of such a nature as to respond to thoughtwaves, or anyway to the electromagnetic fields of the brain cells. He worked for years to build such a delay into a flute, so that it would play music under the pressure of nothing but thought. It was his love, his life, it was to revolutionize music. Everyone would be able to play; no skill necessary—only thought.

Then, five years ago, this young fellow at Consolidated Arms, Stephen Wheland, modified the Schlemmelmayer Effect and reversed it. He devised a field of supersonic waves that could activate the brain via a germanium relay, fry it, and kill a rat at twenty feet. Also, they found out later, men.

After that, Wheland got a bonus of ten thousand dollars and a promotion, while the major stockholders of Consolidated Arms proceeded to make millions when the government bought the patents and placed its orders.

My uncle Otto? He made the cover of *Time*.

After that, everyone who was close to him, say within a few miles, knew he had a grievance. Some thought it was the fact that he had received no money; others, that his great discovery had been made an instrument of war and killing.

Nuts! It was his flute! That was the real tack on the chair of his life. Poor Uncle Otto. He loved his flute. He carried it with him always, ready to demonstrate. It reposed in its special case on the back of his chair when he ate, and at the head of his bed when he slept. Sunday mornings in the university physics laboratories were made hideous by the sounds of my uncle Otto's flute, under imperfect mental control, flatting its way through some tearful German folk song.

The trouble was that no manufacturer would touch it. As soon as its existence was unveiled, the musicians' union threatened to silence every demiquaver in the land; the various entertainment industries called their lobbyists to attention and marked them off in brigades for instant action; and even old Pietro Faranini stuck his baton behind his ear and made fervent statements to the newspapers about the impending death of art.

Uncle Otto never recovered.

He was saying, "Yesterday were my final hopes. Consolidated informs me they will in my honor a banquet give. Who knows, I say to myself. Maybe they will my flute buy." Under stress, my uncle Otto's word order tends to shift from English to Germanic.

The picture intrigued me.

"What an idea," I said. "A thousand giant flutes secreted in key spots in enemy territories blaring out singing commercials just flat enough to—"

"Quiet! Quiet!" My uncle Otto brought down the flat of his hand on my desk like a pistol shot, and the plastic calendar jumped in fright and fell down dead. "From you also mockery? Where is your respect?"

"I'm sorry, Uncle Otto."

"Then listen. I attended the banquet and they made speeches about the Schlemmelmayer Effect and how it harnessed the power of mind. Then when I thought they would announce they would my flute buy, they give me this!"

He took out what looked like a two-thousand-dollar gold piece and threw it at me. I ducked.

Had it hit the window, it would have gone through and brained a pedestrian, but it hit the wall. I picked it up. You could tell by the weight that it was only gold-plated. On one side it said: "The Elias Bancroft Sudford Award" in big letters, and "to Dr. Otto Schlemmelmayer for his contributions to science" in small letters. On the other side was a profile, obviously not of my uncle Otto. In fact, it didn't look like any breed of dog; more like a pig.

"That," said my uncle Otto, "is Elias Bancroft Sudford, chairman of Consolidated Arms!"

He went on, "So when I saw that was all, I got up and very politely said: 'Gentlemen, dead drop!' and walked out."

"Then you walked the streets all night," I filled in for him, "and came here without even changing your clothes. You're still in your tuxedo."

My uncle Otto stretched out an arm and looked at its covering. "A tuxedo?" he said.

"A tuxedo!" I said.

His long, jowled cheeks turned blotchy red and he roared, "I come here on something of first-rate importance and you insist on about nothing but tuxedos talking. My own nephew!"

I let the fire burn out. My uncle Otto is the brilliant one in the family, so except for trying to keep him from falling into sewers and walking out of windows, we morons try not to bother him.

I said, "And what can I do for you, Uncle?"

I tried to make it sound businesslike; I tried to introduce the lawyer-client relationship.

He waited impressively and said, "I need money."

He had come to the wrong place. I said, "Uncle, right now I don't have—"

"Not from you," he said.

I felt better.

He said, "There is a new Schlemmelmayer Effect; a better one. This one I do *not* in scientific journals publish. My big mouth shut I keep. It entirely my own is." He was leading a phantom orchestra with his bony fist as he spoke.

"From this new Effect," he went on, "I will make money and my own flute factory open."

"Good," I said, thinking of the factory and lying.

"But I don't know how."

"Bad," I said, thinking of the factory and lying.

"The trouble is my mind is brilliant. I can conceive concepts beyond ordinary people. Only, Harry, I can't conceive ways of making money. It's a talent I do not have."

"Bad," I said, not lying at all.

"So I come to you as a lawyer."

I sniggered a little deprecating snigger.

"I come to you," he went on, "to make you help me with your crooked, lying, sneaking, dishonest lawyer's brain."

I filed the remark, mentally, under unexpected compliments and said, "I love you, too, Uncle Otto."

He must have sensed the sarcasm because he turned purple with rage and yelled, "Don't be touchy. Be like me, patient, understanding, and easygoing, lumphead. Who says anything about you as a man? As a man, you are an honest dunderkopf, but as a lawyer, you have to be a crook. Everyone knows that."

I sighed. The Bar Association warned me there would be days like this.

"What's your new Effect, Uncle Otto?" I asked.

He said, "I can reach back into Time and bring things out of the past."

I acted quickly. With my left hand I snatched my watch out of the lower left vest pocket and consulted it with all the anxiety I could work up. With my right hand I reached for the telephone.

"Well, Uncle," I said heartily, "I just remembered an extremely important appointment I'm already hours late for. Always glad to see you. And now, I'm afraid I must say good-bye. Yes, sir, seeing you has been a pleasure, a real pleasure. Well, good-bye. Yes, sir—"

I failed to lift the telephone out of its cradle. I was pulling up all right, but my uncle Otto's hand was on mine and pushing down. It was no contest. Have I said my uncle Otto was once on the Heidelberg wrestling team in '32?

He took hold of my elbow gently (for him) and I was standing. It was a great saving of muscular effort (for me).

"Let's," he said, "to my laboratory go."

He to his laboratory went. And since I had neither the knife nor the inclination to cut my left arm off at the shoulder, I to his laboratory went also. . . .

My uncle Otto's laboratory is down a corridor and around a corner in one of the university buildings. Ever since the Schlemmelmayer Effect had turned out to be a big thing, he had been relieved of all course work and left entirely to himself. His laboratory looked it.

I said, "Don't you keep the door locked anymore?"

He looked at me slyly, his huge nose wrinkling into a sniff. "It *is* locked. With a Schlemmelmayer relay, it's locked. I think a word— and the door opens. Without it, nobody can get in. Not even the president of the university. Not even the *janitor*."

I got a little excited, "Great guns, Uncle Otto. A thought-lock could bring you—"

"Hah! I should sell the patent for someone else rich to get? After last night? Never. In a while, I will myself rich become."

One thing about my uncle Otto. He's not one of these fellows you have to argue and argue with before you can get him to see the light. You know in advance he'll never see the light.

So I changed the subject. I said, "And the time machine?"

My uncle Otto is a foot taller than I am, thirty pounds heavier, and strong as an ox. When he puts his hands around my throat and shakes, I have to confine my own part in the conflict to turning blue.

I turned blue accordingly.

He said, *"Ssh!"*

I got the idea.

He let go and said, "Nobody knows about Project X." He repeated, heavily, "Project X. You understand?"

I nodded. I couldn't speak anyway with a larynx that was only slowly healing.

He said, "I do not ask you to take my word for it. I will for you a demonstration make."

I tried to stay near the door.

He said, "Do you have a piece of paper with your own handwriting on it?"

I fumbled in my inner jacket pocket. I had notes for a possible brief for a possible client on some possible future day.

Uncle Otto said, "Don't show it to me. Just tear it up. In little pieces tear it up and in this beaker the fragments put."

I tore it into one hundred and twenty-eight pieces.

He considered them thoughtfully and began adjusting knobs on a —well, on a machine. It had a thick opal-glass slab attached to it that looked like a dentist's tray.

There was a wait. He kept adjusting.

Then he said, *"Aha!"* and I made a sort of queer sound that doesn't translate into letters.

About two inches above the glass tray there was what seemed to be a fuzzy piece of paper. It came into focus while I watched and —oh, well, why make a big thing out of it? It was my notes. My handwriting. Perfectly legible. Perfectly legitimate.

"Is it all right to touch it?" I was a little hoarse, partly out of astonishment and partly because of my uncle Otto's gentle ways of enforcing secrecy.

"You can't," he said, and passed his hand through it. The paper remained behind, untouched. He said, "It's only an image at one focus of a four-dimensional paraboloid. The other focus is at a point in time before you tore it up."

I put my hand through it, too. I didn't feel a thing.

"Now watch," he said. He turned a knob on the machine and the image of the paper vanished. Then he took out a pinch of paper from the pile of scrap, dropped them in an ashtray, and set a match to it. He flushed the ash down the sink. He turned a knob again and the paper appeared, but with a difference. Ragged patches in it were missing.

"The burned pieces?" I asked.

"Exactly. The machine must trace in time along the hypervectors of the molecules on which it is focused. If certain molecules are in the air dispersed—*pff-f-ft!*"

I had an idea. "Suppose you just had the ash of a document."

"Only those molecules would be traced back."

"But they'd be so well distributed," I pointed out, "that you could get a hazy picture of the entire document."

"Hmm. Maybe."

The idea became more exciting. "Well, then, look, Uncle Otto. Do you know how much police departments would pay for a machine like this. It would be a boon to the legal—"

I stopped. I didn't like the way he was stiffening. I said, politely, "You were saying, Uncle?"

He was remarkably calm about it. He spoke in scarcely more than a shout. "Once and for all, nephew. All my inventions I will myself from now on develop. First I must some initial capital obtain. Capital from some source other than my ideas selling. After that, I will for my flutes a factory to manufacture open. That comes first. Afterward, afterward, with my profits I can time-vector machinery manufacture. But first my flutes. Before anything, my flutes. Last night, I so swore.

"Through selfishness of a few the world of great music is being deprived. Shall my name in history as a murderer go down? Shall the Schlemmelmayer Effect a way to fry men's brains be? Or shall it beautiful music to mind bring? Great, wonderful, enduring music?"

He had a hand raised oracularly and the other behind his back. The windows gave out a shrill hum as they vibrated to his words.

I said quickly, "Uncle Otto, they'll hear you."

"Then stop shouting," he retorted.

"But look," I protested, "how do you plan to get your initial capital, if you won't exploit this machinery?"

"I haven't told you. I can make an image real. What if the image is valuable?"

That did sound good. "You mean, like some lost document, manuscript, first edition—things like that?"

"Well, no. There's a catch. Two catches. Three catches."

I waited for him to stop counting, but three seemed the limit.

"What are they?" I asked.

He said, "First, I must have the object in the present to focus on or I can't locate it in the past."

"You mean you can't get anything that doesn't exist right now where you can see it?"

"Yes."

"In that case, catches two and three are purely academic. But what are they, anyway?"

"I can only remove about a gram of material from the past."

A gram! A thirtieth of an ounce!

"What's the matter? Not enough power?"

My uncle Otto said impatiently, "It's an inverse exponential relationship. All the power in the universe more than maybe two grams couldn't bring."

This left things cloudy. I said, "The third catch?"

"Well." He hesitated. "The further the two foci separated are, the more flexible the bond. It must a certain length be before into the present it can be drawn. In other words, I must at least one hundred fifty years into the past go."

"I see," I said (not that I really did). "Let's summarize."

I tried to sound like a lawyer. "You want to bring something from the past out of which you can coin a little capital. It's got to be something that exists and which you can see, so it can't be a lost object of historical or archaeological value. It's got to weigh less than a thirtieth of an ounce, so it can't be the Kullinan diamond or anything like that. It's got to be at least one hundred and fifty years old, so it can't be a rare stamp."

"Exactly," said my uncle Otto. "You've got it."

"Got what?" I thought two seconds. "Can't think of a thing," I said. "Well, good-bye, Uncle Otto."

I didn't think it would work, but I tried to go.

It didn't work. My uncle Otto's hands came down on my shoulders and I was standing tiptoe on an inch of air.

"You'll wrinkle my jacket, Uncle Otto."

"Harold," he said. "As a lawyer to a client, you owe me more than a quick good-bye."

"I didn't take a retainer," I managed to gargle. My shirt collar was beginning to fit very tightly about my neck. I tried to swallow and the top button pinged off.

He reasoned, "Between relatives a retainer is a formality. As a client and as an uncle, you owe me absolute loyalty. And besides, if you do not help me out I will tie your legs behind your neck and dribble you like a basketball."

Well, as a lawyer, I am always susceptible to logic. I said, "I give up. I surrender. You win."

He let me drop.

And then—this is the part that seems most unbelievable to me when I look back at it all—I got an idea.

It was a whale of an idea. A piperoo. The one in a lifetime that everyone gets once in a lifetime.

I didn't tell Uncle Otto the whole thing at the time. I wanted a few days to think about it. But I told him what to do. I told him he would have to go to Washington. It wasn't easy to argue him into it, but, on the other hand, if you know my uncle Otto, there are ways.

I found two ten-dollar bills lurking pitifully in my wallet and gave them to him.

I said, "I'll make out a check for the train fare and you can keep the two tens if it turns out I'm being dishonest with you."

He considered. "A fool to risk twenty dollars for nothing you aren't," he admitted.

He was right, too. . . .

He was back in two days and pronounced the object focused. After all, it was on public view. It's in a nitrogen-filled, air-tight case, but my uncle Otto said that didn't matter. And back in the laboratory, four hundred miles away, the focusing remained accurate. My uncle Otto assured me of that, too.

I said, "Two things, Uncle Otto, before we do anything."

"What? What? What?" He went on at greater length, "What? What? What?"

I gathered he was growing anxious. I said, "Are you sure that if we bring into the present a piece of something out of the past, that piece won't disappear out of the object as it now exists?"

My uncle Otto cracked his large knuckles and said, "We are creating new matter, not stealing old. Why else should we enormous energy need?"

I passed on to the second point. "What about my fee?"

You may not believe this, but I hadn't mentioned money till then. My uncle Otto hadn't either, but then, that follows.

His mouth stretched in a bad imitation of an affectionate smile. "A fee?"

"Ten per cent of the take," I explained, "is what I'll need."

His jowls drooped. "But how much is the take?"

"Maybe a hundred thousand dollars. That would leave you ninety."

"Ninety thousand— Himmel! Then why do we wait?"

He leaped at his machine and in half a minute the space above the dentist's tray was agleam with an image of parchment.

It was covered with neat script, closely spaced, looking like an entry for an old-fashioned penmanship prize. At the bottom of the sheet there were names: one large one and fifty-five small ones.

Funny thing! I choked up. I had seen many reproductions, but this was the real thing. The real Declaration of Independence!

I said, "I'll be damned. You did it."

"And the hundred thousand?" asked my uncle Otto, getting to the point.

Now was the time to explain. "You see, Uncle, at the bottom of the document there are signatures. These are the names of great Americans, fathers of their country, whom we all reverence. Anything about them is of interest to all true Americans."

"All right," grumbled my uncle Otto, "I will accompany you by playing the 'Stars and Stripes Forever' on my flute."

I laughed quickly to show that I took that remark as a joke. The alternative to a joke would not bear thinking of. Have you ever heard my uncle Otto playing the "Stars and Stripes Forever" on his flute?

I said, "But one of these signers, from the state of Georgia, died in 1777, the year after he signed the Declaration. He didn't leave much behind him and so authentic examples of his signature are about the most valuable in the world. His name was Button Gwinnett."

"And how does this help us cash in?" asked my uncle Otto, his mind still fixed grimly on the eternal verities of the universe.

"Here," I said, simply, "is an authentic, real-life signature of Button Gwinnett, right on the Declaration of Independence."

My uncle Otto was stunned into absolute silence, and to bring absolute silence out of my uncle Otto, he's really got to be stunned!

I said, "Now you see him right here on the extreme left of the signature space along with the two other signers for Georgia, Lyman Hall and George Walton. You'll notice they crowded their names although there's plenty of room above and below. In fact, the capital G of Gwinnett runs down into practical contact with Hall's name. So we won't try to separate them. We'll get them all. Can you handle that?"

Have you ever seen a bloodhound that looked happy? Well, my uncle Otto managed it.

A spot of brighter light centered about the names of the three Georgian signers.

My uncle Otto said, a little breathlessly, "I have this never tried before."

"What!" I screamed. *Now* he told me.

"It would have too much energy required. I did not wish the university to inquire what was in here going on. But don't worry! My mathematics cannot wrong be."

I prayed silently that his mathematics not wrong were.

The light grew brighter and there was a humming that filled the laboratory with raucous noise. My uncle Otto turned a knob, then another, then a third.

Do you remember the time a few weeks back when all of upper Manhattan and the Bronx were without electricity for twelve hours because of the damndest overload cut-off in the main power house? I won't say we did that, because I am in no mood to be sued for damages. But I will say this: The electricity went off when my uncle Otto turned the third knob.

Inside the lab, all the lights went out and I found myself on the floor with a terrific ringing in my ears. My uncle Otto was sprawled across me.

We worked each other to our feet and my uncle Otto found a flashlight.

He howled his anguish. "Fused. Fused. My machine in ruins is. It has to destruction devoted been."

"But the signatures?" I yelled at him. "Did you get them?"

He stopped in mid-cry. "I haven't looked."

He looked, and I closed my eyes. The disappearance of a hundred thousand dollars is not an easy thing to watch.

He cried, "Ah, ha!" and I opened my eyes quickly. He had a

square of parchment in his hand some two inches on a side. It had three signatures on it and the top one was that of Button Gwinnett.

Now, mind you, the signature was absolutely genuine. It was no fake. There wasn't an atom of fraud about the whole transaction. I want that understood. Lying on my uncle Otto's broad hand was a signature indited with the Georgian hand of Button Gwinnett himself on the authentic parchment of the honest-to-God, real-life Declaration of Independence.

It was decided that my uncle Otto would travel down to Washington with the parchment scrap. I was unsatisfactory for the purpose. I was a lawyer. I would be expected to know too much. He was merely a scientific genius, and wasn't expected to know anything. Besides, who could suspect Dr. Otto Schlemmelmayer of anything but the most transparent honesty.

We spent a week arranging our story. I bought a book for the occasion, an old history of colonial Georgia, in a secondhand shop. My uncle Otto was to take it with him and claim that he had found a document among its leaves; a letter to the Continental Congress in the name of the state of Georgia. He had shrugged his shoulders at it and held it out over a Bunsen flame. Why should a physicist be interested in letters? Then he became aware of the peculiar odor it gave off as it burned and the slowness with which it was consumed. He beat out the flames but saved only the piece with the signatures. He looked at it and the name Button Gwinnett had stirred a slight fiber of memory.

He had the story cold. I burnt the edges of the parchment so that the lowest name, that of George Walton, was slightly singed.

"It will make it more realistic," I explained. "Of course, a signature, without a letter above it, loses value, but here we have three signatures, all signers."

My uncle Otto was thoughtful. "And if they compare the signatures with those on the Declaration and notice it is all even microscopically the same, won't they fraud suspect?"

"Certainly. But what can they do? The parchment is authentic. The ink is authentic. The signatures are authentic. They'll have to concede that. No matter how they suspect something queer, they can't prove anything. Can they conceive of reaching through time for it? In fact, I hope they do try to make a fuss about it. The publicity will boost the price."

The last phrase made my uncle Otto laugh.

The next day he took the train to Washington with visions of flutes in his head. Long flutes, short flutes, bass flutes, flute tremolos, massive flutes, micro flutes, flutes for the individual and flutes for the orchestra. A world of flutes for mind-drawn music.

"Remember," his last words were, "the machine I have no money to rebuild. This must work."

And I said, "Uncle Otto, it can't miss."

Ha!

He was back in a week. I had made long-distance calls each day and each day he told me they were investigating.

Investigating.

Well, wouldn't you investigate? But what good would it do them?

I was at the station waiting for him. He was expressionless. I didn't dare ask anything in public. I wanted to say, "Well, yes or no?" but I thought, let *him* speak.

I took him to my office. I offered him a cigar and a drink. I hid my hands under the desk but that only made the desk shake too, so I put them in my pocket and shook all over.

He said, "They investigated."

"Sure! I told you they would. Ha, ha, ha! Ha, ha?"

My uncle Otto took a slow drag at the cigar. He said, "The man at the Bureau of Documents came to me and said, 'Professor Schlemmelmayer,' he said, 'you are the victim of a clever fraud.' I said, 'So? And how can it a fraud be? The signature a forgery is?' So he answered, 'It certainly doesn't look like a forgery, but it must be!' 'And why must it be?' I asked."

My uncle Otto put down his cigar, put down his drink, and leaned across the desk toward me. He had me so in suspense, I leaned forward toward him, so in a way I deserved everything I got.

"Exactly," I babbled, "why must it be? They can't prove a thing wrong with it, because it's genuine. Why must it be a fraud, eh? *Why?*"

My uncle Otto's voice was terrifyingly saccharine. He said, "We got the parchment from the past?"

"Yes. Yes. You know we did."

"Well in the past."

"Over a hundred fifty years in the past. You said—"

"And a hundred fifty years ago the parchment on which the Declaration of Independence was written pretty new was. No?"

I was beginning to get it, but not fast enough.

My uncle Otto's voice switched gears and became a dull, throbbing roar, "And if Button Gwinnett in 1777 died, you Godforsaken dunderlump, how can an authentic signature of his on a new piece of parchment be found?"

After that it was just a case of the whole world rushing backward and forward about me.

I expect to be on my feet soon. I still ache, but the doctors tell me no bones were broken.

Still, my uncle Otto didn't have to make me swallow the damned parchment.

If I had hoped to be recognized as a master of humor as a result of these stories, I think I failed.

L. Sprague de Camp, one of the most successful writers of humorous science fiction and fantasy, had this to say about me in his *Science Fiction Handbook* (Hermitage House, 1953), which, as you see, appeared not long after these (in my opinion) successful forays into humor:

"Asimov is a stoutish, youngish-looking man with wavy brown hair, blue eyes, and a bouncing, jovial, effervescent manner, esteemed among his friends for his generous, warm-hearted nature. Extremely sociable, articulate, and witty, he is a perfect toastmaster. This vein of oral humor contrasts with the sobriety of his stories."

Sobriety!

On the other hand, twelve years later, Groff Conklin included BUTTON, BUTTON in his anthology *13 Above the Night* (Dell, 1965) and he said, in part, "When the Good Doctor . . . decides to take a day off and be funny, he can be very funny indeed. . . ."

Now, although Groff and Sprague were both very dear friends of mine (Groff is now dead, alas), there is no question but that in this particular case I think Groff shows good taste and Sprague is nowhere.

Incidentally, before I pass on I had better explain that "generous, warm-hearted nature" crack by Sprague, which may puzzle those who know me as a vicious, rotten brute.

Sprague's prejudice in my favor is, I think, all based on a single incident.

It was back in 1942, when Sprague and I were working at the Philadelphia Navy Yard. It was wartime and we needed badges to get in. Anyone who forgot his badge had to buck the bureaucracy for an hour to get a temporary, was docked an hour's pay, and had the heinous misdeed entered on his record.

As we walked up to the gate on this particular day Sprague turned a pastel shade of green and said, "I forgot my badge!" He was up for a lieutenancy in the Navy and he was afraid that even a slight flaw in his civilian record might have an adverse effect on the whole thing.

Well, I wasn't up for anything at all, and I was so used to being sent to the principal's office during my school days that being yelled at by the authorities had no terrors for me.

So I handed him my badge and said, "Go in, Sprague, and pin this on your lapel. They'll never look at it." He went in, and they didn't, and I reported myself as having forgotten my badge and took my lumps.

Sprague has never forgotten. To this day, he goes around telling people what a great guy I am, despite the fact that everyone just stares at him in disbelief. That one impulsive action has given rise to a lifetime of fervent pro-Asimov propaganda. Cast your bread upon the waters—

But, let's move onward.

THE MONKEY'S FINGER

"Yes. Yes. Yes. Yes. Yes. Yes. Yes. Yes. Yes. Yes. Yes. Yes. Yes. Yes. Yes. Yes," said Marmie Tallinn, in sixteen different inflections and pitches, while the Adam's apple in his long neck bobbed convulsively. He was a science fiction writer.

"No," said Lemuel Hoskins, staring stonily through his steel-rimmed glasses. He was a science fiction editor.

"Then you won't accept a scientific test. You won't listen to me. I'm outvoted, eh?" Marmie lifted himself on his toes, dropped down, repeated the process a few times, and breathed heavily. His dark hair was matted into tufts, where fingers had clutched.

"One to sixteen," said Hoskins.

"Look," said Marmie, "what makes you always right? What makes me always wrong?"

"Marmie, face it. We're each judged in our own way. If magazine circulation were to drop, I'd be a flop. I'd be out on my ear. The president of Space Publishers would ask no questions, believe me. He would just look at the figures. But circulation doesn't go down; it's going up. That makes me a good editor. And as for you—when editors accept you, you're a talent. When they reject you, you're a bum. At the moment, you are a bum."

"There are other editors, you know. You're not the only one." Marmie held up his hands, fingers outspread. "Can you count? That's how many science fiction magazines on the market would gladly take a Tallinn yarn, sight unseen."

"Gesundheit," said Hoskins.

"Look," Marmie's voice sweetened, "you wanted two changes, right? You wanted an introductory scene with the battle in space. Well, I gave that to you. It's right here." He waved the manuscript under Hoskin's nose and Hoskin moved away as though at a bad smell.

"But you also wanted the scene on the spaceship's hull cut into with a flashback into the interior," went on Marmie, "and that you can't get. If I make that change, I ruin an ending which, as it stands, has pathos and depth and feeling."

Editor Hoskins sat back in his chair and appealed to his secretary, who throughout had been quietly typing. She was used to these scenes.

Hoskins said, "You hear that, Miss Kane? *He* talks of pathos, depth, and feeling. What does a writer know about such things? Look, if you insert the flashback, you increase the suspense; you tighten the story; you make it more valid."

"*How* do I make it more valid?" cried Marmie in anguish. "You mean to say that having a bunch of fellows in a spaceship start talking politics and sociology when they're liable to be blown up makes it more *valid*? Oh, my God."

"There's nothing else you can do. If you wait till the climax is past and then discuss your politics and sociology, the reader will go to sleep on you."

"But I'm trying to tell you that you're wrong and I can prove it. What's the use of talking when I've arranged a scientific experiment—"

"What scientific experiment?" Hoskins appealed to his secretary again. "How do you like that, Miss Kane. He thinks he's one of his own characters."

"It so happens I know a scientist."

"Who?"

"Dr. Arndt Torgesson, professor of psychodynamics at Columbia."

"Never heard of him."

"I suppose that means a lot," said Marmie, with contempt. "*You* never heard of him. You never heard of Einstein until your writers started mentioning him in their stories."

"Very humorous. A yuk. What about this Torgesson?"

"He's worked out a system for determining scientifically the value of a piece of writing. It's a tremendous piece of work. It's—it's—"

"And it's secret?"

"Certainly it's secret. He's not a science fiction professor. In science fiction, when a man thinks up a theory, he announces it to the newspapers right away. In real life, that's not done. A scientist spends years on experimentation sometimes before going into print. Publishing is a serious thing."

"Then how do *you* know about it? Just a question."

"It so happens that Dr. Torgesson is a fan of mine. He happens to like my stories. He happens to think I'm the best fantasy writer in the business."

"And he shows you his work?"

"That's right. I was counting on you being stubborn about this yarn and I've asked him to run an experiment for us. He said he would do it if we don't talk about it. He said it would be an interesting experiment. He said—"

"What's so secret about it?"

"Well—" Marmie hesitated. "Look, suppose I told you he had a monkey that could type *Hamlet* out of its head."

Hoskins stared at Marmie in alarm. "What are you working up here, a practical joke?" He turned to Miss Kane. "When a writer writes science fiction for ten years he just isn't safe without a personal cage."

Miss Kane maintained a steady typing speed.

Marmie said, "You heard me; a common monkey, even funnier-looking than the average editor. I made an appointment for this afternoon. Are you coming with me or not?"

"Of course not. You think I'd abandon a stack of manuscripts this high"—and he indicated his larynx with a cutting motion of the hand—"for your stupid jokes? You think I'll play straight man for you?"

"If this is in any way a joke, Hoskins, I'll stand you dinner in any restaurant you name. Miss Kane's the witness."

Hoskins sat back in his chair. "You'll buy me dinner? You, Marmaduke Tallinn, New York's most widely known tapeworm-on-credit, are going to pick up a check?"

Marmie winced, not at the reference to his agility in overlooking a dinner check, but at the mention of his name in all its horrible trysyllabicity. He said, "I repeat. Dinner on me wherever you want and whatever you want. Steaks, mushrooms, breast of guinea hen, Martian alligator, anything."

Hoskins stood up and plucked his hat from the top of the filing cabinet.

"For a chance," he said, "to see you unfold some of the old-style, large-size dollar bills you've been keeping in the false heel of your left shoe since nineteen-two-eight, I'd walk to Boston. . . ."

Dr. Torgesson was honored. He shook Hoskins's hand warmly and said, "I've been reading *Space Yarns* ever since I came to this country, Mr. Hoskins. It is an excellent magazine. I am particularly fond of Mr. Tallinn's stories."

"You hear?" asked Marmie.

"I hear. Marmie says you have a monkey with talent, Professor."

"Yes," Torgesson said, "but of course this must be confidential. I am not yet ready to publish, and premature publicity could be my professional ruin."

"This is strictly under the editorial hat, Professor."

"Good, good. Sit down, gentlemen, sit down." He paced the floor before them. "What have you told Mr. Hoskins about my work, Marmie?"

"Not a thing, Professor."

"So. Well, Mr. Hoskins, as the editor of a science fiction magazine, I don't have to ask you if you know anything about cybernetics."

Hoskins allowed a glance of concentrated intellect to ooze out past his steel-rims. He said, "Ah, yes. Computing machines—M.I.T.— Norbert Weiner—" He mumbled some more.

"Yes. Yes." Torgesson paced faster. "Then you must know that chess-playing computers have been constructed on cybernetic principles. The rules of chess moves and the object of the game are built into its circuits. Given any position on the chess board, the machine can then compute all possible moves together with their consequence and choose that one which offers the highest probability of winning the game. It can even be made to take the temperament of its opponent into account."

"Ah, yes," said Hoskins, stroking his chin profoundly.

Torgesson said, "Now imagine a similar situation in which a computing machine can be given a fragment of a literary work to which the computer can then add words from its stock of the entire vocabulary such that the greatest literary values are served. Naturally, the machine would have to be taught the significance of the various keys of a typewriter. Of course, such a computer would have to be much, much more complex than any chess player."

Hoskins stirred restlessly. "The monkey, Professor. Marmie mentioned a monkey."

"But that is what I am coming to," said Torgesson. "Naturally, no machine built is sufficiently complex. But the human brain—ah. The human brain is itself a computing machine. Of course, I couldn't use a human brain. The law, unfortunately, would not permit me. But even a monkey's brain, properly managed, can do more than any machine ever constructed by man. Wait! I'll go get little Rollo."

He left the room. Hoskins waited a moment, then looked cautiously at Marmie. He said, "Oh, brother!"

Marmie said, "What's the matter?"

"What's the matter? The man's a phony. Tell me, Marmie, where did you hire this faker?"

Marmie was outraged. "Faker? This is a genuine professor's office in Fayerweather Hall, Columbia. You recognize Columbia, I hope. You saw the statue of Alma Mater on 116th Street. I pointed out Eisenhower's office."

"Sure, but—"

"And this is Dr. Torgesson's office. Look at the dust." He blew at a textbook and stirred up clouds of it. "The dust alone shows it's the real thing. And look at the title of the book: *Psychodynamics of Human Behavior,* by Professor Arndt Rolf Torgesson."

"Granted, Marmie, granted. There is a Torgesson and this is his office. How you knew the real guy was on vacation and how you managed to get the use of his office, I don't know. But are you trying to tell me that this comic with his monkeys and computers is the real thing? Hah!"

"With a suspicious nature like yours, I can only assume you had a very miserable, rejected type of childhood."

"Just the result of experience with writers, Marmie. I have my restaurant all picked out and this will cost you a pretty penny."

Marmie snorted, "This won't cost me even the ugliest penny you ever paid me. Quiet, he's coming back."

With the professor, and clinging to his neck, was a very melancholy capuchin monkey.

"This," said Torgesson, "is little Rollo. Say hello, Rollo."

The monkey tugged at his forelock.

The professor said, "He's tired, I'm afraid. Now, I have a piece of his manuscript right here."

He put the monkey down and let it cling to his finger while he brought out two sheets of paper from his jacket pocket and handed them to Hoskins.

Hoskins read, " 'To be or not to be; that is the question: Whether 'tis nobler in the mind to suffer the slings and arrows of outrageous fortune, or to take arms against a host of troubles, and by opposing end them? To die: to sleep; No more: and, by a sleep to say we—' "

He looked up. "Little Rollo typed this?"

"Not exactly. It's a copy of what he typed."

"Oh, a copy. Well, little Rollo doesn't know his Shakespeare. It's 'to take arms against a sea of troubles.'"

Torgesson nodded. "You are quite correct, Mr. Hoskins. Shakespeare *did* write 'sea.' But you see that's a mixed metaphor. You don't fight a sea with arms. You fight a host or army with arms. Rollo chose the monosyllable and typed 'host.' It's one of Shakespeare's rare mistakes."

Hoskins said, "Let's see him type."

"Surely." The professor trundled out a typewriter on a little table. A wire trailed from it. He explained, "It is necessary to use an electric typewriter as otherwise the physical effort would be too great. It is also necessary to wire little Rollo to this transformer."

He did so, using as leads two electrodes that protruded an eighth of an inch through the fur on the little creature's skull.

"Rollo," he said, "was subjected to a very delicate brain operation in which a nest of wires were connected to various regions of his brain. We can short his voluntary activities and, in effect, use his brain simply as a computer. I'm afraid the details would be—"

"Let's see him type," said Hoskins.

"What would you like?"

Hoskins thought rapidly. "Does he know Chesterton's 'Lepanto'?"

"He knows nothing by heart. His writing is purely computation. Now, you simply recite a little of the piece so that he will be able to estimate the mood and compute the consequences of the first words."

Hoskins nodded, inflated his chest, and thundered, "White founts falling in the courts of the sun, and the Soldan of Byzantium is smiling as they run. There is laughter like the fountains in that face of all men feared; it stirs the forest darkness, the darkness of his beard; it curls the blood-red crescent, the crescent of his lips; for the inmost sea of all the world is shaken by his ships—"

"That's enough," said Torgesson.

There was silence as they waited. The monkey regarded the typewriter solemnly.

Torgesson said, "The process takes time, of course. Little Rollo has to take into account the romanticism of the poem, the slightly archaic flavor, the strong sing-song rhythm, and so on."

And then a black little finger reached out and touched a key. It was a *t*.

"He doesn't capitalize," said the scientist, "or punctuate, and his spacing isn't very reliable. That's why I usually retype his work when he's finished."

Little Rollo touched an *h,* then an *e* and a *y.* Then, after a long-ish pause, he tapped the space bar.

"They," said Hoskins.

The words typed themselves out: "they have dared thewhite repub lics upthe capes of italy they have dashed the adreeatic round-the lion of the sea; and the popehas throw n his arms abroa dfor agoni and loss and called the kings of chrissndom for sords about the cross."

"My God!" said Hoskins.

"That's the way the piece goes then?" asked Torgesson.

"For the love of Pete!" said Hoskins.

"If it is, then Chesterton must have done a good, consistent job."

"Holy smokes!" said Hoskins.

"You see," said Marmie, massaging Hoskins's shoulder, "you see, you see, you see. You see," he added.

"I'll be damned," said Hoskins.

"Now look," said Marmie, rubbing his hair till it rose in clusters like a cockatoo's crest, "let's get to business. Let's tackle my story."

"Well, but—"

"It will not be beyond little Rollo's capacity," Torgesson assured him. "I frequently read little Rollo parts of some of the better science fiction, including many of Marmie's tales. It's amazing how some of the yarns are improved."

"It's not that," said Hoskins. "Any monkey can write better SF than some of the hacks we've got. But the Tallinn story is thirteen thousand words long. It'll take forever for the monk to type it."

"Not at all, Mr. Hoskins, not at all. I shall read the story to him, and at the crucial point we will let him continue."

Hoskins folded his arms. "Then shoot. I'm ready."

"I," said Marmie, "am more than ready." And he folded his arms.

Little Rollo sat there, a furry little bundle of cataleptic misery, while Dr. Torgesson's soft voice rose and fell in cadence with a space-ship battle and the subsequent struggles of Earthmen captives to re-capture their lost ship.

One of the characters made his way out to the spaceship hull, and Dr. Torgesson followed the flamboyant events in mild rapture. He read:

". . . Stalny froze in the silence of the eternal stars. His aching knee tore at his consciousness as he waited for the monsters to hear the thud and—"

Marmie yanked desperately at Dr. Torgesson's sleeve. Torgesson looked up and disconnected little Rollo.

"That's it," said Marmie. "You see, Professor, it's just about here that Hoskins is getting his sticky little fingers into the works. I continue the scene outside the spaceship till Stalny wins out and the ship is back in Earth hands. Then I go into explanations. Hoskins wants me to break that outside scene, get back inside, halt the action for two thousand words, then get back out again. Ever hear such crud?"

"Suppose we let the monk decide," said Hoskins.

Dr. Torgesson turned little Rollo on, and a black shriveled finger reached hesitantly out to the typewriter. Hoskins and Marmie leaned forward simultaneously, their heads coming softly together just over little Rollo's brooding body. The typewriter punched out the letter *t*.

"T," encouraged Marmie, nodding.

"T," agreed Hoskins.

The typewriter made an *a*, then went on at a more rapid rate: "take action stalnee waited in helpless hor ror forair locks toyawn and suited laroos to emerge relentlessly—"

"Word for word," said Marmie in raptures.

"He certainly has your gooey style."

"The readers like it."

"They wouldn't if their average mental age wasn't—" Hoskins stopped.

"Go on," said Marmie, "say it. Say it. Say their IQ is that of a twelve-year-old child and I'll quote you in every fan magazine in the country."

"Gentlemen," said Torgesson, "gentlemen. You'll disturb little Rollo."

They turned to the typewriter, which was still tapping steadily: "—the stars whelled in ther mightie orb its as stalnees earthbound senses insis ted the rotating ship sto od still."

The typewriter carriage whipped back to begin a new line. Marmie held his breath. Here, if anywhere, would come—

And the little finger moved out and made: *

Hoskins yelled, "Asterisk!"

Marmie muttered, "Asterisk."

Torgesson said, "Asterisk?"

A line of nine more asterisks followed.

"That's all, brother," said Hoskins. He explained quickly to the staring Torgesson, "With Marmie, it's a habit to use a line of asterisks when he wants to indicate a radical shift of scene. And a radical shift of scene is exactly what I wanted."

The typewriter started a new paragraph: "within the ship—"

"Turn it off, Professor," said Marmie.

Hoskins rubbed his hands. "When do I get the revision, Marmie?"

Marmie said coolly, "What revision?"

"You said the monk's version."

"I sure did. It's what I brought you here to see. That little Rollo is a machine; a cold, brutal, logical machine."

"Well?"

"And the point is that a good writer is not a machine. He doesn't write with his mind, but with his heart. His heart." Marmie pounded his chest.

Hoskins groaned. "What are you doing to me, Marmie? If you give me that heart-and-soul-of-a-writer routine, I'll just be forced to turn sick right here and right now. Let's keep all this on the usual I'll-write-anything-for-money basis."

Marmie said, "Just listen to me for a minute. Little Rollo corrected Shakespeare. You pointed that out yourself. Little Rollo wanted Shakespeare to say, 'host of troubles,' and he was right from his machine standpoint. A 'sea of troubles' under the circumstances is a mixed metaphor. But don't you suppose Shakespeare knew that, too? Shakespeare just happened to know when to *break* the rules, that's all. Little Rollo is a machine that can't break the rules, but a good writer can, and *must*. 'Sea of troubles' is more impressive; it has roll and power. The hell with the mixed metaphor.

"Now, when you tell me to shift the scene, you're following mechanical rules on maintaining suspense, so of course little Rollo agrees with you. But I know that I must break the rules to maintain the profound emotional impact of the ending as I see it. Otherwise I have a mechanical product that a computer can turn out."

Hoskins said, "But—"

"Go on," said Marmie, "vote for the mechanical. Say that little Rollo is all the editor you'll ever be."

Hoskins said, with a quiver in his throat, "All right, Marmie, I'll take the story as is. No, don't give it to me; mail it. I've got to find a bar, if you don't mind."

He forced his hat down on his head and turned to leave. Torgesson called after him, "Don't tell anyone about little Rollo, please."

The parting answer floated back over a slamming door, "Do you think I'm crazy? . . ."

Marmie rubbed his hands ecstatically when he was sure Hoskins was gone.

"Brains, that's what it was," he said, and probed one finger as deeply into his temple as it would go. "This sale I enjoyed. This sale, Professor, is worth all the rest I've ever made. All the rest of them together." He collapsed joyfully on the nearest chair.

Torgesson lifted little Rollo to his shoulder. He said mildly, "But, Marmaduke, what would you have done if little Rollo had typed your version instead?"

A look of grievance passed momentarily over Marmie's face. "Well, damn it," he said, "that's what I *thought* it was going to do."

----------◄◆►----------

In the MONKEY'S FINGER, by the way, the writer and editor were modeled on a real pair, arguing over a real story in a real way.

The story involved was *C-Chute,* which had appeared in the October 1951 *Galaxy* (after the argument) and which was eventually included in my book NIGHTFALL AND OTHER STORIES. I was the writer, of course, and Horace Gold was the editor.

Though the argument and the story are authentic, the people are caricatured. I am nothing at all like the writer in the story and Horace is certainly nothing at all like the editor in the story. Horace has his own peculiarities which are far more interesting than the ones I made up for fictional purposes, and so have I—but never mind that.

Of all the stories I have written that have appeared once and then never again, this next is the one I talk about most. I have discussed it in dozens of talks and mentioned it in print occasionally, for a very good reason which I'll come to later.

In April 1953 I was in Chicago. I'm not much of a traveler and that was the first time I was ever in Chicago (and I have returned since then only once). I was there to attend an American Chemical Society convention at which I was supposed to present a small paper. That was little fun, so I thought I would liven things up by going to

Evanston, a northern suburb, and visiting the offices of *Universe Science Fiction.*

This magazine was then edited by Bea Mahaffey, an extraordinarily good-looking young woman. (The way I usually put it is that science fiction writers had voted her, two years running, the editor to whom they would most like to submit.)

When I arrived in the office on April 7, 1953, Bea greeted me with great glee and at once asked why I had not brought a story for her with me.

"You want a story?" I said, basking in her beauty. "I'll write you a story. Bring me a typewriter."

Actually, I was just trying to impress her, hoping that she would throw herself into my arms in a spasm of wild adoration. She didn't. She brought me a typewriter.

I had to come through. Since the task of climbing Mount Everest was much in the news those days (men had been trying to scale it for thirty years and the seventh attempt to do so had just failed) I thought rapidly and wrote EVEREST.

Bea read it, liked it, and offered me thirty dollars, which I accepted with alacrity. I promptly spent half of it on a fancy dinner for the two of us, and labored with so much success to be charming, debonair, and suave that the waitress said to me, longingly, that she wished her son-in-law were like me.

That seemed hopeful and with a light heart I took Bea home to her apartment. I am not sure what I had in mind, but if I did have anything in mind that was not completely proper (surely not!) I was foiled. Bea managed to get into that apartment, leaving me standing in the hallway, without my ever having seen the door open.

EVEREST

In 1952 they were about ready to give up trying to climb Mount Everest. It was the photographs that kept them going.

As photographs go, they weren't much; fuzzy, streaked, and with just dark blobs against the white to be interested in. But those dark blobs were living creatures. The men swore to it.

I said, "What the hell, they've been talking about creatures skidding along the Everest glaciers for forty years. It's about time we did something about it."

Jimmy Robbons (pardon me, James Abram Robbons) was the one who pushed me into that position. He was always nuts on mountain climbing, you see. He was the one who knew all about how the Tibetans wouldn't go near Everest because it was the mountain of the gods. He could quote me every mysterious manlike footprint ever reported in the ice twenty-five thousand feet up; he knew by heart every tall story about the spindly white creatures, speeding along the crags just over the last heart-breaking camp which the climbers had managed to establish.

It's good to have one enthusiastic creature of the sort at Planetary Survey headquarters.

The last photographs put bite into his words, though. After all, you *might* just barely think they were men.

Jimmy said, "Look, boss, the point isn't that they're there, the point is that they move fast. Look at that figure. It's blurred."

"The camera might have moved."

"The crag here is sharp enough. And the men swear it was running. Imagine the metabolism it must have to run at that oxygen pressure. Look, boss, would you have believed in deep-sea fish if you'd never heard of them? You have fish which are looking for new niches in environment which they can exploit, so they go deeper and deeper into the abyss until one day they find they can't return. They've adapted so thoroughly they can live only under tons of pressure."

"Well—"

"Damn it, can't you reverse the picture? Creatures can be forced up a mountain, can't they? They can learn to stick it out in thinner air and colder temperatures. They can live on moss or on occasional birds, just as the deep-sea fish in the last analysis live on the upper fauna that slowly go filtering down. Then, someday, they find they can't go down again. I don't even say they're men. They can be chamois or mountain goats or badgers or anything."

I said stubbornly, "The witnesses said they were vaguely man-like, and the reported footprints are certainly manlike."

"Or bearlike," said Jimmy. "You can't tell."

So that's when I said, "It's about time we did something about it."

Jimmy shrugged and said, "They've been trying to climb Mount Everest for forty years." And he shook his head.

"For gossake," I said. "All you mountain climbers are nuts. That's for sure. You're not interested in getting to the top. You're just interested in getting to the top in a certain way. It's about time we stopped fooling around with picks, ropes, camps, and all the paraphernalia of the Gentlemen's Club that sends suckers up the slopes every five years or so."

"What are you getting at?"

"They invented the airplane in 1903, you know?"

"You mean fly over Mount Everest!" He said it the way an English lord would say, "Shoot a fox!" or an angler would say, "Use worms!"

"Yes," I said, "fly over Mount Everest and let someone down on the top. Why not?"

"He won't live long. The fellow you let down, I mean."

"Why not?" I asked again. "You drop supplies and oxygen tanks, and the fellow wears a spacesuit. Naturally."

It took time to get the Air Force to listen and to agree to send a plane and by that time Jimmy Robbons had swiveled his mind to the point where he volunteered to be the one to land on Everest's peak. "After all," he said in a half whisper, "I'd be the first man ever to stand there."

That's the beginning of the story. The story itself can be told very simply, and in far fewer words.

The plane waited two weeks during the best part of the year (as far as Everest was concerned, that is) for a siege of only moderately nasty flying weather, then took off. They made it. The pilot reported by radio to a listening group exactly what the top of Mount

Everest looked like when seen from above and then he described exactly how Jimmy Robbons looked as his parachute got smaller and smaller.

Then another blizzard broke and the plane barely made it back to base and it was another two weeks before the weather was bearable again.

And all that time Jimmy was on the roof of the world by himself and I hated myself for a murderer.

The plane went back up two weeks later to see if they could spot his body. I don't know what good it would have done if they had, but that's the human race for you. How many dead in the last war? Who can count that high? But money or anything else is no object to the saving of one life, or even the recovering of one body.

They didn't find his body, but they did find a smoke signal; curling up in the thin air and whipping away in the gusts. They let down a grapple and Jimmy came up, still in his spacesuit, looking like hell, but definitely alive.

The p.s. to the story involves my visit to the hospital last week to see him. He was recovering very slowly. The doctors said shock, they said exhaustion, but Jimmy's eyes said a lot more.

I said, "How about it, Jimmy, you haven't talked to the reporters, you haven't talked to the government. All right. How about talking to me?"

"I've got nothing to say," he whispered.

"Sure you have," I said. "You lived on top of Mount Everest during a two-week blizzard. You didn't do that by yourself, not with all the supplies we dumped along with you. Who helped you, Jimmy boy?"

I guess he knew there was no use trying to bluff. Or maybe he was anxious to get it off his mind.

He said, "They're intelligent, boss. They compressed air for me. They set up a little power pack to keep me warm. They set up the smoke signal when they spotted the airplane coming back."

"I see." I didn't want to rush him. "It's like we thought. They've adapted to Everest life. They can't come down the slopes."

"No, they can't. And we can't go up the slopes. Even if the weather didn't stop us, they would!"

"They sound like kindly creatures, so why should they object? They helped *you*."

"They have nothing against us. They spoke to me, you know. Telepathy."

I frowned. "Well, then."

"But they don't intend to be interfered with. They're watching us, boss. They've got to. We've got atomic power. We're about to have rocket ships. They're worried about us. And Everest is the only place they can watch us from!"

I frowned deeper. He was sweating and his hands were shaking.

I said, "Easy, boy. Take it easy. What on Earth are these creatures?"

And he said, "What do you suppose would be so adapted to thin air and subzero cold that Everest would be the only livable place on Earth to them. That's the whole point. They're nothing at all on Earth. They're Martians."

And that's it.

———————◄◆►————————

And now let me explain the reason I so frequently discuss EVEREST.

Naturally, I did not actually believe that there were Martians on Mount Everest or that anything would long delay the eventual conquest of the mountain. I just thought that people would have the decency to refrain from climbing it until the story was published.

But no! On May 29, 1953, less than two months after I had written and sold EVEREST, Edmund Hillary and Tenzing Norgay stood upon Everest's highest point and saw neither Martians nor Abominable Snowmen.

Of course, *Universe* might have sacrificed thirty dollars and left the story unpublished; or I might have offered to buy back the story. Neither of us made the gesture and EVEREST appeared in the December 1953 issue of *Universe*.

Since I am frequently called on to discuss the future of man, I can't help using EVEREST to point out what an expert futurist I am. After all, I predicted that Mount Everest would never be climbed, five months *after* it was climbed.

Nowadays it is quite fashionable to publish anthologies of original science fiction stories, and I rather disapprove of this. It drains off some of the stories and readers that might otherwise go to the magazines. I don't want that to happen. I think that magazines are essential to science fiction.

Is my feeling born of mere nostalgia? Does it arise out of the memory of what science fiction magazines meant to me in my childhood and of how they gave me my start as a writer? In part, yes, I suppose; but in part it is the result of an honest feeling that they do play a vital role.

Where can a young writer get a start? Magazines, appearing six or twelve times a year, simply *must* have stories. An anthology can delay publication till the desired stories come in; a magazine cannot. Driven by unswervable deadlines, a magazine must accept an occasional substandard story, and an occasional young writer gets a start while he is still perhaps of only marginal quality. That was how I got my start, in fact.

It means, to be sure, that the reader is subjected to an occasional amateurish story in the magazine, but the amateur writer who wrote it gets enough encouragement to continue working and to become (just possibly) a great writer.

When the anthologies of original science fiction first appeared, however, they were novelties. I never really thought they would come to much, and had no feeling of contributing to an impending doom when I wrote for them. In fact, since they paid better than the magazines usually did, I felt good about writing for them.

The first of the breed was *New Tales of Space and Time*, edited by Raymond J. Healy (Henry Holt, 1951), and for it I wrote *In a Good Cause*—a story that was eventually included in NIGHTFALL AND OTHER STORIES.

A few years later, August Derleth was editing an anthology of originals, and for it I wrote THE PAUSE.

THE PAUSE

The white powder was confined within a thin-walled, transparent capsule. The capsule in turn was heat-sealed into a double strip of parafilm. Along that strip of parafilm were other capsules at six-inch intervals.

The strip moved. Each capsule in the course of events rested for one minute on a metal jaw immediately beneath a mica window. On another portion of the face of the radiation counter a number clicked out upon an unrolling cylinder of paper. The capsule moved on; the next took its place.

The number printed at 1:45 P.M. was 308. A minute later 256 appeared. A minute later, 391. A minute later, 477. A minute later, 202. A minute later, 251. A minute later, 000. A minute later, 000. A minute later, 000. A minute later, 000.

Shortly after 2 P.M. Mr. Alexander Johannison passed by the counter and the corner of one eye stubbed itself over the row of figures. Two steps past the counter he stopped and returned.

He ran the paper cylinder backward, then restored its position and said, "Nuts!"

He said it with vehemence. He was tall and thin, with big-knuckled hands, sandy hair, and light eyebrows. He looked tired and, at the moment, perplexed.

Gene Damelli wandered his way with the same easy carelessness he brought to all his actions. He was dark, hairy, and on the short side. His nose had once been broken and it made him look curiously unlike the popular conception of the nuclear physicist.

Damelli said, "My damned Geiger won't pick up a thing, and I'm not in the mood to go over the wiring. Got a cigarette?"

Johannison held out a pack. "What about the others in the building?"

"I haven't tried them, but I guess they haven't all gone."

"Why not? My counter isn't registering either."

"No kidding. You see? All the money invested, too. It doesn't mean a thing. Let's step out for a Coke."

Johannison said with greater vehemence than he intended, "No! I'm going to see George Duke. I want to see his machine. If *it's* off—"

Damelli tagged along. "It won't be off, Alex. Don't be an ass."

George Duke listened to Johannison and watched him disapprovingly over rimless glasses. He was an old-young man with little hair and less patience.

He said, "I'm busy."

"Too busy to tell me if your rig is working, for heaven's sake?"

Duke stood up. "Oh, hell, when does a man have time to work around here?" His slide rule fell with a thud over a scattering of ruled paper as he rounded his desk.

He stepped to a cluttered lab table and lifted the heavy gray leaden top from a heavier gray leaden container. He reached in with a two-foot-long pair of tongs and took out a small silvery cylinder.

Duke said grimly, "Stay where you are."

Johannison didn't need the advice. He kept his distance. He had not been exposed to any abnormal dosage of radioactivity over the past month but there was no sense getting any closer than necessary to "hot" cobalt.

Still using the tongs, and with arms held well away from his body, Duke brought the shining bit of metal that contained the concentrated radioactivity up to the window of his counter. At two feet, the counter should have chattered its head off. It didn't.

Duke said, "Guk!" and let the cobalt container drop. He scrabbled madly for it and lifted it against the window again. Closer.

There was no sound. The dots of light on the scaler did not show. Numbers did not step up and up.

Johannison said, "Not even background noise."

Damelli said, "Holy jumping Jupiter!"

Duke put the cobalt tube back into its leaden sheath, as gingerly as ever, and stood there, glaring.

Johannison burst into Bill Everard's office, with Damelli at his heels. He spoke for excited minutes, his bony hands knuckly white on Everard's shiny desk. Everard listened, his smooth, fresh-shaven cheeks turning pink and his plump neck bulging out a bit over his stiff, white collar.

Everard looked at Damelli and pointed a questioning thumb at

Johannison. Damelli shrugged, bringing his hands forward, palms upward, and corrugating his forehead.

Everard said, "I don't see how they can all go wrong."

"They *have,* that's all," insisted Johannison. "They all went dead at about two o'clock. That's over an hour ago now and none of them is back in order. Even George Duke can't do anything about it. I'm telling you, it isn't the counters."

"You're saying it is."

"I'm saying they're not working. But that's not their fault. There's nothing for them to work on."

"What do you mean?"

"I mean there isn't any radioactivity in this place. In this whole building. Nowhere."

"I don't believe you."

"Listen, if a hot cobalt cartridge won't start up a counter, maybe there's something wrong with every counter we try. But when that same cartridge won't discharge a gold-leaf electroscope and when it won't even fog a photographic film, then there's something wrong with the cartridge."

"All right," said Everard, "so it's a dud. Somebody made a mistake and never filled it."

"The same cartridge was working this morning, but never mind that. Maybe cartridges can get switched somehow. But I got that hunk of pitchblende from our display box on the fourth floor and that doesn't register either. You're not going to tell me that someone forgot to put the uranium in it."

Everard rubbed his ear. "What do you think, Damelli?"

Damelli shook his head. "I don't know, boss. Wish I did."

Johannison said, "It's not the time for thinking. It's a time for doing. You've got to call Washington."

"What about?" asked Everard.

"About the A-bomb supply."

"What?"

"That might be the answer, boss. Look, someone has figured out a way to stop radioactivity, all of it. It might be blanketing the country, the whole U.S.A. If that's being done, it can only be to put our A-bombs out of commission. They don't know where we keep them, so they have to blank out the nation. And if *that's* right, it means an attack is due. Any minute, maybe. Use the phone, boss!"

Everard's hand reached for the phone. His eyes and Johannison's met and locked.

He said into the mouthpiece, "An outside call, please."

It was five minutes to four. Everard put down the phone.

"Was that the commissioner?" asked Johannison.

"Yes," said Everard. He was frowning.

"All right. What did he say?"

"'Son,'" said Everard, "he said to me, 'What A-bombs?'"

Johannison looked bewildered. "What the devil does he mean, 'What A-bombs?' I know! They've already found out they've got duds on their hands, and they won't talk. Not even to us. Now what?"

"Now nothing," said Everard. He sat back in his chair and glowered at the physicist. "Alex, I know the kind of strain you're under; so I'm not going to blow up about this. What bothers me is, how did you get *me* started on this nonsense?"

Johannison paled. "This isn't nonsense. Did the commissioner say it was?"

"He said I was a fool, and so I am. What the devil do you mean coming here with your stories about A-bombs? What *are* A-bombs? I never heard of them."

"You never heard of atom bombs? What is this? A gag?"

"I never heard of them. It sounds like something from a comic strip."

Johannison turned to Damelli, whose olive complexion had seemed to deepen with worry. "Tell him, Gene."

Damelli shook his head. "Leave me out of this."

"All right." Johannison leaned forward, looking at the line of books in the shelves about Everard's head. "I don't know what this is all about, but I can go along with it. Where's Glasstone?"

"Right there," said Everard.

"No. Not the *Textbook of Physical Chemistry*. I want his *Sourcebook on Atomic Energy*."

"Never heard of it."

"What are you talking about? It's been here in your shelf since I've been here."

"Never heard of it," said Everard stubbornly.

"I suppose you haven't heard of Kamen's *Radioactive Tracers in Biology* either?"

"No."

Johannison shouted, "All right. Let's use Glasstone's *Textbook* then. It will do."

He brought down the thick book and flipped the pages. First once, then a second time. He frowned and looked at the copyright page. It said: Third Edition, 1956. He went through the first two chapters page by page. It was there, atomic structure, quantum numbers, electrons and their shells, transition series—but no radioactivity, nothing about that.

He turned to the table of elements on the inside front cover. It took him only a few seconds to see that there were only eighty-one listed, the eighty-one nonradioactive ones.

Johannison's throat felt bricky-dry. He said huskily to Everard. "I suppose you never heard of uranium."

"What's that?" asked Everard coldly. "A trade name?"

Desperately, Johannison dropped Glasstone and reached for the *Handbook of Chemistry and Physics*. He used the index. He looked up radioactive series, uranium, plutonium, isotopes. He found only the last. With fumbling, jittery fingers he turned to the table of isotopes. Just a glance. Only the stable isotopes were listed.

He said pleadingly, "All right. I give up. Enough's enough. You've set up a bunch of fake books just to get a rise out of me, haven't you?" He tried to smile.

Everard stiffened. "Don't be a fool, Johannison. You'd better go home. See a doctor."

"There's nothing wrong with me."

"You may not think so, but there is. You need a vacation, so take one. Damelli, do me a favor. Get him into a cab and see that he gets home."

Johannison stood irresolute. Suddenly he screamed, "Then what are all the counters in this place for? What do they do?"

"I don't know what you mean by counters. If you mean computers, they're here to solve our problems for us."

Johannison pointed to a plaque on the wall. "All right, then. See those initials. A! E! C! Atomic! Energy! Commission!" He spaced the words, staccato.

Everard pointed in turn. "Air! Experimental! Commission! Get him home, Damelli."

Johannison turned to Damelli when they reached the sidewalk. Urgently he whispered, "Listen, Gene, don't be a setup for that guy.

Everard's sold out. They got to him some way. Imagine them setting up the faked books and trying to make me think I'm crazy."

Damelli said levelly, "Cool down, Alex boy. You're just jumping a little. Everard's all right."

"You heard him. He never heard of A-bombs. Uranium's a trade name. How can he be all right?"

"If it comes to that, I never heard of A-bombs *or* uranium."

He lifted a finger. "Taxi!" It whizzed by.

Johannison got rid of the gagging sensation. "Gene! You were there when the counters quit. You were there when the pitchblende went dead. You came with me to Everard to get the thing straightened out."

"If you want the straight truth, Alex, you said you had something to discuss with the boss and you asked me to come along, and that's all I know about it. Nothing went wrong as far as I know, and what the devil would we be doing with this pitchblende? We don't use any tar in the place. —Taxi!"

A cab drew up to the curb.

Damelli opened the door, motioned Johannison in. Johannison entered, then, with red-eyed fury, turned, snatched the door out of Damelli's hand, slammed it closed, and shouted an address at the cab driver. He leaned out the window as the cab pulled away, leaving Damelli stranded and staring.

Johannison cried, "Tell Everard it won't work. I'm wise to all of you."

He fell back into the upholstery, exhausted. He was sure Damelli had heard the address he gave. Would they get to the FBI first with some story about a nervous breakdown? Would they take Everard's word against his? They couldn't deny the stopping of the radio-activity. They couldn't deny the faked books.

But what was the good of it? An enemy attack was on its way and men like Everard and Damelli— How rotten with treason was the country?

He stiffened suddenly. "Driver!" he cried. Then louder, *"Driver!"*

The man at the wheel did not turn around. The traffic passed smoothly by them.

Johannison tried to struggle up from his seat, but his head was swimming.

"Driver!" he muttered. This wasn't the way to the FBI. He was being taken home. But how did the driver know where he lived?

A planted driver, of course. He could scarcely see and there was a roaring in his ears.

Lord, what organization! There was no use fighting! He blacked out!

He was moving up the walk toward the small, two-story, brick-fronted house in which Mercedes and he lived. He didn't remember getting out of the cab.

He turned. There was no taxicab in sight. Automatically, he felt for his wallet and keys. They were there. Nothing had been touched.

Mercedes was at the door, waiting. She didn't seem surprised at his return. He looked at his watch quickly. It was nearly an hour before his usual homecoming.

He said, "Mercy, we've got to get out of here and—"

She said huskily, "I know all about it, Alex. Come in."

She looked like heaven to him. Straight hair, a little on the blond side, parted in the middle and drawn into a horse tail; wide-set blue eyes with that slight Oriental tilt, full lips, and little ears set close to the head. Johannison's eyes devoured her.

But he could see she was doing her best to repress a certain tension.

He said, "Did Everard call you? Or Damelli?"

She said, "We have a visitor."

He thought, They've got to *her*.

He might snatch her out of the doorway. They would run, try to make it to safety. But how could they? The visitor would be standing in the shadows of the hallway. It would be a sinister man, he imagined, with a thick, brutal voice and foreign accent, standing there with a hand in his jacket pocket and a bulge there that was bigger than his hand.

Numbly he stepped inside.

"In the living room," said Mercedes. A smile flashed momentarily across her face. "I think it's all right."

The visitor was standing. He had an unreal look about him, the unreality of perfection. His face and body were flawless and carefully devoid of individuality. He might have stepped off a billboard.

His voice had the cultured and unimpassioned sound of the professional radio announcer. It was entirely free of accent.

He said, "It was quite troublesome getting you home, Dr. Johannison."

Johannison said, "Whatever it is, whatever you want, I'm not co-operating."

Mercedes broke in. "No, Alex, you don't understand. We've been talking. He says all radioactivity has been stopped."

"Yes, it has, and how I wish this collar-ad could tell me how it was done! Look here, you, are you an American?"

"You still don't understand, Alex," said his wife. "It's stopped all over the world. This man isn't from anywhere on Earth. Don't look at me like that, Alex. It's true. I know it's true. Look at him."

The visitor smiled. It was a perfect smile. He said, "This body in which I appear is carefully built up according to specification, but it is only matter. It's under complete control." He held out a hand and the skin vanished. The muscles, the straight tendons, and crooked veins were exposed. The walls of the veins disappeared and blood flowed smoothly without the necessity of containment. All dissolved to the appearance of smooth gray bone. That went also.

Then all reappeared.

Johannison muttered, "Hypnotism!"

"Not at all," said the visitor, calmly.

Johannison said, "Where are you from?"

The visitor said, "That's hard to explain. Does it matter?"

"I've got to understand what's going on," cried Johannison. "Can't you see that?"

"Yes. I can. It's why I'm here. At this moment I am speaking to a hundred and more of your people all over your planet. In different bodies, of course, since different segments of your people have different preferences and standards as far as bodily appearance is concerned!"

Fleetingly, Johannison wondered if he was mad after all. He said, "Are you from—from Mars? Any place like that? Are you taking over? Is this war?"

"You see," said the visitor, "that sort of attitude is what we're trying to correct. Your people are sick, Dr. Johannison, very sick. For tens of thousands of your years we have known that your particular species has great possibilities. It has been a great disappointment to us that your development has taken a pathological pathway. Definitely pathological." He shook his head.

Mercedes interrupted, "He told me before you came that he was trying to cure us."

"Who asked him?" muttered Johannison.

The visitor only smiled. He said, "I was assigned the job a long time ago, but such illnesses are always hard to treat. For one thing, there is the difficulty in communication."

"We're communicating," said Johannison stubbornly.

"Yes. In a manner of speaking, we are. I'm using your concepts, your code system. It's quite inadequate. I couldn't even explain to you the true nature of the disease of your species. By your concepts, the closest approach I can make is that it is a disease of the spirit."

"Huh."

"It's a kind of social ailment that is very ticklish to handle. That's why I've hesitated for so long to attempt a direct cure. It would be sad if, through accident, so gifted a potentiality as that of your race were lost to us. What I've tried to do for millennia has been to work indirectly through the few individuals in each generation who had natural immunity to the disease. Philosophers, moralists, warriors, and politicians. All those who had a glimpse of world brotherhood. All those who—"

"All right. You failed. Let it go at that. Now suppose you tell me about your people, not mine."

"What can I tell you that you would understand?"

"Where are you from? Begin with that."

"You have no proper concept. I'm not from anywhere in the yard."

"What yard?"

"In the universe, I mean. I'm from outside the universe."

Mercedes interrupted again, leaning forward. "Alex, don't you see what he means? Suppose you landed on the New Guinea coast and talked to some natives through television somehow. I mean to natives who had never seen or heard of anyone outside their tribe. Could you explain how television worked or how it made it possible for you to speak to many men in many places at once? Could you explain that the image wasn't you yourself but merely an illusion that you could make disappear and reappear? You couldn't even explain where you came from if all the universe they knew was their own island."

"Well, then, we're savages to him. Is that it?" demanded Johannison.

The visitor said, "Your wife is being metaphorical. Let me finish. I can no longer try to encourage your society to cure itself. The disease has progressed too far. I am going to have to alter the temperamental makeup of the race."

"How?"

"There are neither words nor concepts to explain that either. You must see that our control of physical matter is extensive. It was quite simple to stop all radioactivity. It was a little more difficult to see to it that all things, including books, now suited a world in which radioactivity did not exist. It was still more difficult, and took more time, to wipe out all thought of radioactivity from the minds of men. Right now, uranium does not exist on Earth. No one ever heard of it."

"I have," said Johannison. "How about you, Mercy?"

"I remember, too," said Mercedes.

"You two are omitted for a reason," said the visitor, "as are over a hundred others, men and women, all over the world."

"No radioactivity," muttered Johannison. "Forever?"

"For five of your years," said the visitor. "It is a pause, nothing more. Merely a pause, or call it a period of anesthesia, so that I can operate on the species without the interim danger of atomic war. In five years the phenomenon of radioactivity will return, together with all the uranium and thorium that currently do not exist. The knowledge will not return, however. That is where you will come in. You and the others like you. You will re-educate the world gradually."

"That's quite a job. It took fifty years to get us to this point. Even allowing for less the second time, why not simply restore knowledge? You can do that, can't you?"

"The operation," said the visitor, "will be a serious one. It will take anywhere up to a decade to make certain there are no complications. So we want re-education slowly, on purpose."

Johannison said, "How do we know when the time comes? I mean when the operation's over."

The visitor smiled. "When the time comes, you will know. Be assured of that."

"Well, it's a hell of a thing, waiting five years for a gong to ring in your head. What if it never comes? What if your operation isn't successful?"

The visitor said seriously, "Let us hope that it is."

"But if it isn't? Can't you clear our minds temporarily, too? Can't you let us live normally till it's time?"

"No. I'm sorry. I need your minds untouched. If the operation *is* a failure, if the cure does not work out, I will need a small reservoir of normal, untouched minds out of which to bring about the growth of a new population on this planet on whom a new variety of cure may be attempted. At all costs, your species must be preserved. It is valuable to us. It is why I am spending so much time trying to explain the situation to you. If I had left you as you were an hour ago, five days, let alone five years, would have completely ruined you."

And without another word he disappeared.

Mercedes went through the motions of preparing supper and they sat at the table almost as though it had been any other day.

Johannison said, "Is it true? Is it all real?"

"I saw it, too," said Mercedes. "I heard it."

"I went through my own books. They're all changed. When this— pause is over, we'll be working strictly from memory, all of us who are left. We'll have to build instruments again. It will take a long time to get it across to those who won't remember." Suddenly he was angry, "And what for, I want to know. What for?"

"Alex," Mercedes began timidly, "he may have been on Earth before and spoken to people. He's lived for thousands and thousands of years. Do you suppose he's what we've been thinking of for so long as—as—"

Johannison looked at her. "As God? Is that what you're trying to say? How should I know? All I know is that his people, whatever they are, are infinitely more advanced than we, and that he's curing us of a disease."

Mercedes said, "Then I think of him as a doctor or what's equivalent to it in his society."

"A doctor? All he kept saying was that the difficulty of communication was the big problem. What kind of a doctor can't communicate with his patients? A vet! An animal doctor!"

He pushed his plate away.

His wife said, "Even so. If he brings an end to war—"

"Why should he want to? What are we to him? We're animals. We *are* animals to him. Literally. He as much as said so. When I asked him where he was from, he said he didn't come from the 'yard' at all. Get it? The *barnyard*. Then he changed it to the 'universe.' He didn't come from the 'universe' at all. His difficulty in communication gave him away. He used the concept for what our universe was to him rather than what it was to us. So the universe is a barnyard and we're—horses, chickens, sheep. Take your choice."

Mercedes said softly, " 'The Lord is my Shepherd. I shall not want . . .' "

"Stop it, Mercy. That's a metaphor; this is reality. If he's a shepherd, then we're sheep with a queer, unnatural desire, and ability, to kill one another. Why stop us?"

"He said—"

"I know what he said. He said we have great potentialities. We're very valuable. Right?"

"Yes."

"But what are the potentialities and values of sheep to a shepherd? The sheep wouldn't have any idea. They couldn't. Maybe if they knew why they were coddled so, they'd prefer to live their own lives. They'd take their own chances with wolves or with themselves."

Mercedes looked at him helplessly.

Johannison cried, "It's what I keep asking myself now. Where are we going? Where are we going? Do sheep know? Do we know? Can we know?"

They sat staring at their plates, not eating.

Outside, there was the noise of traffic and the calling of children at play. Night was falling and gradually it grew dark.

———◆———

One memory I have concerning THE PAUSE reinforces my constant delight that I am at the writing end of things and am not part of any other facet of the literary game.

I was in the offices of Farrar, Straus & Young at a time when the anthology was in the early stage of production and the woman who was the in-house editor was agonizing over the title of the anthology. It was supposed to be *In Time To Come,* but she thought that lacked something and was wondering about alternatives.

"What do you think, Dr. Asimov?" she asked and looked at me pleadingly. (People often think I have the answers, when sometimes I don't even have the questions.)

I thought desperately and said, "Leave out the first word and make it *Time to Come*. That strengthens the concept 'time' and makes the title seem more science-fictional."

She cried out at once, *"Just* the thing," and *Time to Come* was indeed the title of the anthology when it appeared.

Well, did the change in title improve sales? How would they ever know? How could they be sure it didn't actually hurt sales?

I'm very glad I'm not an editor.

While all this writing was going on, my professional labors at the medical school were doing very well. In 1951 I had been promoted to assistant professor of biochemistry, and I now had the professorial status to add to my doctorate. This double dose of title didn't seem to add to my dignity in the least, however. I continued to have a "bouncing, jovial, effervescent manner," as Sprague would say, and I still do to this day, as anyone who meets me will testify, despite the fact that my "wavy brown hair," while still wavy, is longer and less brown that it used to be.

All that effervescing made it possible for me to get along very well with the students, but perhaps not always so well with a few of the faculty members. Fortunately, everyone was quite aware that I was a science fiction writer. It helped! It seemed to reconcile them to the fact that I was an eccentric and they thereupon forgave me a great deal.

As for myself, I made no attempt to conceal the fact. Some people in the more staid callings use pseudonyms when they succumb to the temptation to write what they fear is trash. Since I never thought of science fiction as trash, and since I was writing and selling long before I had become a faculty member, I had no choice but to use my own peculiar name on my stories.

Nor did I intend to get the school itself into anything that would hurt *its* dignity.

I had sold my first book, PEBBLE IN THE SKY, some six weeks before I had accepted the job at the medical school. What I did not know was that Doubleday was going to exploit my new professional position in connection with the book. It was only when I saw the book jacket, toward the end of 1949, that I saw what was to be on the back cover.

Along with a very good likeness of myself at the age of twenty-five (which breaks my heart now when I look at it) there was a final sentence, which read: "Dr. Asimov lives in Boston, where he is engaged in cancer research at Boston University School of Medicine."

I thought about that for quite a while, then decided to do the straightforward thing. I asked to see Dean James Faulkner, and I put it to him frankly. I was a science fiction writer, I said, and had been for years. My first book was coming out under my own name, and my association with the medical school would be mentioned. Did he want my resignation?

The dean, a Boston Brahmin with a sense of humor, said, "Is it a good book?"

Cautiously, I said, "The publishers think so."

And he said, "In that case the medical school will be glad to be identified with it."

That took care of that and never, in my stay at the medical school, did I get into trouble over my science fiction. In fact, it occurred to some of the people at the school to put me to use. In October 1954 the people running the *Boston University Graduate Journal* asked me for a few hundred words of science fiction with which to liven up one of their issues. I obliged with LET'S NOT, which then appeared in the December 1954 issue.

LET'S NOT

Professor Charles Kittredge ran in long, unsteady strides. He was in time to bat the glass from the lips of Associate Professor Heber Vandermeer. It was almost like an exercise in slow motion.

Vandermeer, whose absorption had apparently been such that he had not heard the thud of Kittredge's approach, looked at once startled and ashamed. His glance sank to the smashed glass and the puddling liquid that surrounded it.

"What was it?" asked Kittredge grimly.

"Potassium cyanide. I'd kept a bit, when we left. Just in case . . ."

"How would that have helped? And it's one glass gone, too. Now it's got to be cleaned up. . . . No, I'll do it."

Kittredge found a precious fragment of cardboard to scoop up the glass fragments and an even more precious scrap of cloth to soak up the poisonous fluid. He left to discard the glass and, regretfully, the cardboard and cloth into one of the chutes that would puff them to the surface, a half mile up.

He returned to find Vandermeer sitting on the cot, eyes fixed glassily on the wall. The physicist's hair had turned quite white and he had lost weight, of course. There were no fat men in the Refuge. Kittredge, who had been long, thin, and gray to begin with, had, in contrast, scarcely changed.

Vandermeer said, "Remember the old days, Kitt."

"I try not to."

"It's the only pleasure left," said Vandermeer. "Schools were schools. There were classes, equipment, students, air, light, and people. People."

"A school's a school as long as there is one teacher and one student."

"You're almost right," mourned Vandermeer. "There are two teachers. You, chemistry. I, physics. The two of us, everything else we can get out of the books. And one graduate student. He'll be the first man ever to get his Ph.D. down here. Quite a distinction. Poor Jones."

Kittredge put his hands behind his back to keep them steady. "There are twenty other youngsters who will live to be graduate students someday."

Vandermeer looked up. His face was gray. "What do we teach them meanwhile? History? How man discovered what makes hydrogen go boom and was happy as a lark while it went boom and boom and boom? Geography? We can describe how the winds blew the shining dust everywhere and the water currents carried the dissolved isotopes to all the deeps and shallows of the ocean."

Kittredge found it very hard. He and Vandermeer were the only qualified scientists who got away in time. The responsibility of the existence of a hundred men, women, and children was theirs as they hid from the dangers and rigors of the surface and from the terror Man had created here in this bubble of life half a mile below the planet's crust.

Desperately, he tried to put nerve into Vandermeer. He said, as forcefully as he could, "You know what we must teach them. We must keep science alive so that someday we can repopulate the Earth. Make a new start."

Vandermeer did not answer that. He turned his face to the wall.

Kittredge said, "Why not? Even radioactivity doesn't last forever. Let it take a thousand years, five thousand. Someday the radiation level on Earth's surface will drop to bearable amounts."

"Someday."

"Of course. Someday. Don't you see that what we have here is the most important school in the history of man? If we succeed, you and I, our descendants will have open sky and free-running water again. They'll even have," and he smiled wryly, "graduate schools such as those we remember."

Vandermeer said, "I don't believe any of it. At first, when it seemed better than dying, I would have believed anything. But now, it just doesn't make sense. So we'll teach them all we know, down here, and then we die . . . *down here.*"

"But before long Jones will be teaching with us, and then there'll be others. The youngsters who hardly remember the old ways will become teachers, and then the youngsters who were born here will teach. This will be the critical point. Once the native-born are in charge, there will be no memories to destroy morale. This will be their life and they will have a goal to strive for, something to fight for . . . a whole world to win once more. *If,* Van, *if* we keep alive the knowledge of physical science on the graduate level. You understand why, don't you?"

"Of course I understand," said Vandermeer irritably, "but that doesn't make it possible."

"Giving up will make it impossible. That's for sure."

"Well, I'll try," said Vandermeer in a whisper.

So Kittredge moved to his own cot and closed his eyes and wished desperately that he might be standing in his protective suit on the planet's surface. Just for a little while. Just for a little while. He would stand beside the shell of the ship that had been dismantled and cannibalized to create the bubble of life here below. Then he could rouse his own courage just after sunset by looking up and seeing once more, just once more as it gleamed through the thin, cold atmosphere of Mars, the bright, dead evening star that was Earth.

Some people accuse me of getting every last bit of mileage out of everything I write. It's not a deliberate policy of mine, actually, but I must admit that the mileage does seem to mount up. Even as long ago as 1954 it was happening.

I had written LET'S NOT for my school, and, of course, I was not paid for it and didn't expect to be. Shortly thereafter, though, Martin Greenberg of Gnome Press asked me for an introduction for a new anthology he was planning, *All About the Future*, which was slated for publication in 1955.

I did not really like to refuse because I liked Martin Greenberg, even though he was years behind in his royalty payments. On the other hand, I did not wish to reward him with more material, so I compromised.

"How about a little story instead?" I said, and offered him LET'S NOT. He ran it as one of the introductions (the other, a more conventional one, was by Robert A. Heinlein) and, wonder of wonders, paid me ten dollars.

In that same year another turning point was hitting me. (Odd how many turning points there are in one's life, and how difficult it is to recognize them when they come.)

I had been writing nonfiction to a small extent ever since the days of my doctoral dissertation. There were scientific papers dealing with my research, for instance. These were not many, because I was not long in finding out that I was not really an enthusiastic researcher. Then, too, writing the papers was a dreadful chore, since scientific writing is abhorrently stylized and places a premium on poor quality.

The textbook was more enjoyable but in writing it I had been constantly hampered and tied down because of my two collaborators—wonderful men, both, but with styles different from my own. My frustration led me to a desire to write a biochemistry book on my own, not for medical students but for the general public. I looked upon it as only a dream, however, for I could not really see past my own science fiction.

However, my collaborator, Bill Boyd, had written a popular book on genetics, *Genetics and the Races of Man* (Little-Brown, 1950), and in 1953 there came from New York one Henry Schuman, owner of a small publishing house named after himself. He tried to persuade Bill to write a book for him but Bill was busy and, being a kind-hearted soul, tried to let Mr. Schuman down easily by introducing him to me, with the suggestion that he get *me* to write a book.

Of course, I agreed and wrote the book promptly. When publication time rolled around, however, Henry Schuman had sold his firm to another small firm, Abelard. When my book appeared, then, it was THE CHEMICALS OF LIFE (Abelard-Schuman, 1954).

It was the first nonfiction book that ever appeared with my name on it and no other; the first nonfiction book I ever wrote for the general public.

What's more, it had turned out to be a very easy task, much easier than my science fiction. I took only ten weeks to write the book, never spending more than an hour or two a day on it, and it was intense *fun*. I instantly began to think of other, similar nonfiction books I could do, and that began a course of action that was to fill my life—though I did not have any inkling at the time that this would happen.

That same year, too, it began to look as though a second offspring was on its way. This one also caught us by surprise and created a serious problem.

When we had first moved into our Waltham apartment, in the spring of 1951, there were just the two of us. We slept in one bedroom, and the other bedroom was the office. My book THE CURRENTS OF SPACE (Doubleday, 1952) was written in that second bedroom.

After David was born and grew large enough to need a room of his own, he got the second bedroom and my office was moved into the master bedroom, and that's where THE CAVES OF STEEL (Double-day, 1953) was written.

Then, on February 19, 1955, my daughter, Robyn Joan, was born, and I moved into the corridor in anticipation. It was the only place left to me. The fourth of my Lucky Starr novels was begun on the very day she was brought home from the hospital. It was LUCKY STARR AND THE BIG SUN OF MERCURY (Doubleday, 1956) and it was dedicated "To Robyn Joan, who did her best to interfere."

The interfering was entirely too efficient. With a child in each bedroom and me in the corridor it was bad enough, but eventually Robyn Joan would be large enough to need a room of her own, so we made up our mind to look for a house.

That was traumatic. I had never lived in a house. For all my thirty-five years of life, I had lived in a series of rented apartments. What had to be, however, had to be. In January 1956 we found a house in Newton, Massachusetts, just west of Boston, and on March 12, 1956, we moved in.

On March 16, 1956, Boston had one of its worst blizzards in memory, and three feet of snow fell. Having never had to shovel snow before, I found myself starting with a lulu in a deep, broad driveway. I had barely dug myself out when, on March 20, 1956, a second blizzard struck and four more feet fell.

The melting snow packed against the outer walls of the house found its way past the wood and into the basement and we had a small flood. —Heavens, how we wished ourselves back in the apartment.

But we survived that, and then came a graver worry—for me at least. My life had changed so radically, what with two children, a house, and a mortgage, that I began to wonder if I would still be able to write. (My novel THE NAKED SUN, Doubleday, 1957, had been finished two days *before* the move.)

You know, one gets such a feeling that a writer is a delicate plant who must be carefully nurtured or he will wither, that any traumatic change in one's way of life is bound to give the feeling of all the blossoms being lopped off.

What with the blizzards and the snow-shoveling and the basement pumping and everything else, I didn't get a chance to try to write for a while.

But then Bob Lowndes asked me to do a story for *Future,* and in June 1956 I began my first writing job in the new house. It was the first heat wave of the season but the basement was cool, so I set up my typewriter there in the unique luxury of being able to feel cool in a heat wave.

There was no trouble. I could still write. I turned out EACH AN EXPLORER and it appeared in issue ※30 of *Future* (the issues of this magazine were so irregular at this time that it was not felt safe to put a month-designation on the issues).

EACH AN EXPLORER

Herman Chouns was a man of hunches. Sometimes he was right; sometimes he was wrong—about fifty-fifty. Still, considering that one has the whole universe of possibilities from which to pull a right answer, fifty-fifty begins to look pretty good.

Chouns wasn't always as pleased with the matter as might be expected. It put too much of a strain on him. People would huddle around a problem, making nothing of it, then turn to him and say, "What do you think, Chouns? Turn on the old intuition."

And if he came up with something that fizzled, the responsibility for that was made clearly his.

His job, as field explorer, rather made things worse.

"Think that planet's worth a closer look?" they would say. "What do you think, Chouns?"

So it was a relief to draw a two-man spot for a change (meaning that the next trip would be to some low-priority place, and the pressure would be off) and, on top of it, to get Allen Smith as partner.

Smith was as matter-of-fact as his name. He said to Chouns the first day out, "The thing about you is that the memory files in your brain are on extraspecial call. Faced with a problem, you remember enough little things that maybe the rest of us don't come up with to make a decision. Calling it a hunch just makes it mysterious, and it isn't."

He rubbed his hair slickly back as he said that. He had light hair that lay down like a skull cap.

Chouns, whose hair was very unruly, and whose nose was snub and a bit off-center, said softly (as was his way), "I think maybe it's telepathy."

"What!"

"Just a trace of it."

"Nuts!" said Smith, with loud derision (as was *his* way). "Scientists have been tracking psionics for a thousand years and gotten nowhere. There's no such thing: no precognition; no telekinesis; no clairvoyance; *and* no telepathy."

"I admit that, but consider this. If I get a picture of what each of a group of people are thinking—even though I might not be aware of what was happening—I could integrate the information and come up with an answer. I would know more than any single individual in the group, so I could make a better judgment than the others—sometimes."

"Do you have any evidence at all for that?"

Chouns turned his mild brown eyes on the other. "Just a hunch."

They got along well. Chouns welcomed the other's refreshing practicality, and Smith patronized the other's speculations. They often disagreed but never quarreled.

Even when they reached their objective, which was a globular cluster that had never felt the energy thrusts of a human-designed nuclear reactor before, increasing tension did not worsen matters.

Smith said, "Wonder what they do with all this data back on Earth. Seems a waste sometimes."

Chouns said, "Earth is just beginning to spread out. No telling how far humanity will move out into the galaxy, given a million years or so. All the data we can get on any world will come in handy someday."

"You sound like a recruiting manual for the Exploration Teams. Think there'll be anything interesting in that thing?" He indicated the visi-plate on which the no-longer distant cluster was centered like spilled talcum powder.

"Maybe. I've got a hunch—" Chouns stopped, gulped, blinked once or twice, and then smiled weakly.

Smith snorted. "Let's get a fix on the nearest stargroups and make a random pass through the thickest of it. One gets you ten, we find a McKomin ratio under 0.2."

"You'll lose," murmured Chouns. He felt the quick stir of excitement that always came when new worlds were about to be spread beneath them. It was a most contagious feeling, and it caught hundreds of youngsters each year. Youngsters, such as he had been once, flocked to the Teams, eager to see the worlds their descendants someday would call their own, each an explorer—

They got their fix, made their first close-quarters hyperspatial jump into the cluster, and began scanning stars for planetary systems. The computers did their work; the information files grew steadily, and all proceeded in satisfactory routine—until at system 23, shortly after completion of the jump, the ship's hyperatomic motors failed.

Chouns muttered, "Funny. The analyzers don't say what's wrong."

He was right. The needles wavered erratically, never stopping once for a reasonable length of time, so that no diagnosis was indicated. And, as a consequence, no repairs could be carried through.

"Never saw anything like it," growled Smith. "We'll have to shut everything off and diagnose manually."

"We might as well do it comfortably," said Chouns, who was already at the telescopes. "Nothing's wrong with the ordinary spacedrive, and there are two decent planets in this system."

"Oh? How decent and which ones?"

"The first and second out of four: Both water-oxygen. The first is a bit warmer and larger than Earth; the second a bit colder and smaller. Fair enough?"

"Life?"

"Both. Vegetation, anyway."

Smith grunted. There was nothing in that to surprise anyone; vegetation occurred more often than not on water-oxygen worlds. And, unlike animal life, vegetation could be seen telescopically—or, more precisely, spectroscopically. Only four photochemical pigments had ever been found in any plant form, and each could be detected by the nature of the light it reflected.

Chouns said, "Vegetation on both planets is chlorophyll type, no less. It'll be just like Earth; real homey."

Smith said, "Which is closer?"

"Number two, and we're on our way. I have a feeling it's going to be a nice planet."

"I'll judge that by the instruments, *if* you don't mind," said Smith.

But this seemed to be one of Chouns's correct hunches. The planet was a tame one with an intricate ocean network that insured a climate of small temperature range. The mountain ranges were low and rounded, and the distribution of vegetation indicated high and widespread fertility.

Chouns was at the controls for the actual landing.

Smith grew impatient. "What are you picking and choosing for? One place is like another."

"I'm looking for a bare spot," said Chouns. "No use burning up an acre of plant life."

"What if you do?"

"What if I don't?" said Chouns, and found his bare spot.

It was only then, after landing, that they realized a small part of what they had tumbled into.

"Jumping space-warps," said Smith.

Chouns felt stunned. Animal life was much rarer than vegetation, and even the glimmerings of intelligence were far rarer still; yet here, not half a mile away from landing point, was a clustering of low, thatched huts that were obviously the product of a primitive intelligence.

"Careful," said Smith dazedly.

"I don't think there's any harm," said Chouns. He stepped out onto the surface of the planet with firm confidence; Smith followed.

Chouns controlled his excitement with difficulty. "This is terrific. No one's ever reported anything better than caves or woven tree-branches before."

"I hope they're harmless."

"It's too peaceful for them to be anything else. Smell the air."

Coming down to landing, the terrain—to all points of horizon, except where a low range of hills broke the even line—had been colored a soothing pale pink, dappled against the chlorophyll green. At closer quarters the pale pink broke up into individual flowers, fragile and fragrant. Only the areas in the immediate neighborhood of the huts were amber with something that looked like a cereal grain.

Creatures were emerging from the huts, moving closer to the ship with a kind of hesitating trust. They had four legs and a sloping body which stood three feet high at the shoulders. Their heads were set firmly on those shoulders, with bulging eyes (Chouns counted six) set in a circle and capable of the most disconcertingly independent motion. (*That makes up for the immovability of the head,* thought Chouns.)

Each animal had a tail that forked at the end, forming two sturdy fibrils that each animal held high. The fibrils maintained a rapid tremor that gave them a hazy, blurred look.

"Come on," said Chouns. "They won't hurt us; I'm sure of it."

The animals surrounded the men at a cautious distance. Their tails made a modulated humming noise.

"They might communicate that way," said Chouns. "And I think it's obvious they're vegetarians." He pointed toward one of the huts, where a small member of the species sat on its haunches, plucking at the amber grain with his tails, and flickering an ear of it through his mouth like a man sucking a series of maraschino cherries off a toothpick.

"Human beings eat lettuce," said Smith, "but that doesn't prove anything."

More of the tailed creatures emerged, hovered about the men for a moment, then vanished off into the pink and green.

"Vegetarians," said Chouns firmly. "Look at the way they cultivate the main crop."

The main crop, as Chouns called it, consisted of a coronet of soft green spikes, close to the ground. Out of the center of the coronet grew a hairy stem which, at two-inch intervals, shot out fleshy, veined buds that almost pulsated, they seemed so vitally alive. The stem ended at the tip with the pale pink blossoms that, except for the color, were the most Earthly thing about the plants.

The plants were laid out in rows and files with geometric precision. The soil about each was well loosened and powdered with a foreign substance that could be nothing but fertilizer. Narrow passageways, just wide enough for an animal to pass along, crisscrossed the field, and each passageway was lined with narrow sluiceways, obviously for water.

The animals were spread through the fields now, working diligently, heads bent. Only a few remained in the neighborhood of the two men.

Chouns nodded. "They're good farmers."

"Not bad," agreed Smith. He walked briskly toward the nearest of the pale pink blooms and reached for one; but six inches short of it he was stopped by the sound of tail vibrations keening to shrillness, and by the actual touch of a tail upon his arm. The touch was delicate but firm, interposing itself between Smith and the plants.

Smith fell back. "What in Space—"

He had half reached for his blaster when Chouns said, "No cause for excitement; take it easy."

Half a dozen of the creatures were now gathering about the two, offering stalks of grain humbly and gently, some using their tails, some nudging it forward with their muzzles.

Chouns said, "They're friendly enough. Picking a bloom might be against their customs; the plants probably have to be treated according to rigid rules. Any culture that has agriculture probably has fertility rites, and Lord knows what that involves. The rules governing the cultivation of the plants must be strict, or there wouldn't be those accurate measured rows. . . . Space, won't they sit up back home when they hear this?"

The tail humming shot up in pitch again, and the creatures near them fell back. Another member of the species was emerging from a larger hut in the center of the group.

"The chief, I suppose," muttered Chouns.

The new one advanced slowly, tail high, each fibril encircling a small black object. At a distance of five feet its tail arched forward.

"He's giving it to us," said Smith in astonishment, "and Chouns, for God's sake, *look* at it."

Chouns was doing so, feverishly. He choked out, "They're Gamow hyperspatial sighters. Those are ten-thousand-dollar instruments."

Smith emerged from the ship again, after an hour within. He shouted from the ramp in high excitement, "They work. They're perfect. We're rich."

Chouns called back, "I've been checking through their huts. I can't find any more."

"Don't sneeze at just two. Good Lord, these are as negotiable as a handful of cash."

But Chouns still looked about, arms akimbo, exasperated. Three of the tailed creatures had dogged him from hut to hut—patiently, never interfering, but remaining always between him and the geometrically cultivated pale pink blossoms. Now they stared multiply at him.

Smith said, "It's the latest model, too. Look here." He pointed to the raised lettering which said *Model X-20, Gamow Products, Warsaw, European Sector.*

Chouns glanced at it and said impatiently, "What interests me is getting more. I *know* there are more Gamow sighters somewhere, I want them." His cheeks were flushed and his breathing heavy.

The sun was setting; the temperature dropped below the comfortable point. Smith sneezed twice, then Chouns.

"We'll catch pneumonia," snuffled Smith.

"I've got to make them understand," said Chouns stubbornly. He had eaten hastily through a can of pork sausage, had gulped down a can of coffee, and was ready to try again.

He held the sighter high. "More," he said, "more," making encircling movements with his arms. He pointed to one sighter, then to the other, then to the imaginary additional ones lined up before him. "More."

Then, as the last of the sun dipped below the horizon, a vast hum arose from all parts of the field as every creature in sight ducked its head, lifted its forked tail, and vibrated it into screaming invisibility in the twilight.

"What in Space," muttered Smith uneasily. "Hey, look at the blooms!" He sneezed again.

The pale pink flowers were shriveling visibly.

Chouns shouted to make himself heard above the hum, "It may be a reaction to sunset. You know, the blooms close at night. The noise may be a religious observance of the fact."

A soft flick of a tail across his wrist attracted Chouns's instant attention. The tail he had felt belonged to the nearest creature; and now it was raised to the sky, toward a bright object low on the western horizon. The tail bent downward to point to the sighter, then up again to the star.

Chouns said excitedly, "Of course—the inner planet; the other habitable one. These must have come from there." Then, reminded by the thought, he cried in sudden shock, "Hey, Smith, the hyper-atomic motors are still out."

Smith looked shocked, as though he had forgotten, too; then he mumbled, "Meant to tell you—they're all right."

"You fixed them?"

"Never touched them. But when I was testing the sighters I used the hyperatomics and they worked. I didn't pay any attention at the time; I forgot there was anything wrong. Anyway, they worked."

"Then let's go," said Chouns at once. The thought of sleep never occurred to him.

Neither one slept through the six-hour trip. They remained at the controls in an almost drug-fed passion. Once again they chose a bare spot on which to land.

It was hot with an afternoon subtropical heat; and a broad, muddy river moved placidly by them. The near bank was of hardened mud, riddled with large cavities.

The two men stepped out onto planetary surface and Smith cried hoarsely, "Chouns, look at that!"

Chouns shook off the other's grasping hand. He said, "The same plants! I'll be damned."

There was no mistaking the pale pink blossoms, the stalk with its veined buds, and the coronet of spikes below. Again there was the geometric spacing, the careful planting and fertilization, the irrigation canals.

Smith said, "We haven't made a mistake and circled—"

"Oh, look at the sun; it's twice the diameter it was before. And look there."

Out of the nearest burrows in the river bank smoothly tan and sinuous objects, as limbless as snakes, emerged. They were a foot in diameter, ten feet in length. The two ends were equally featureless, equally blunt. Midway along their upper portions were bulges. All the bulges, as though on signal, grew before their eyes to fat ovals, split in two to form lipless, gaping mouths that opened and closed with a sound like a forest of dry sticks clapping together.

Then, just as on the outer planet, once their curiosities were satisfied and their fears calmed, most of the creatures drifted away toward the carefully cultivated field of plants.

Smith sneezed. The force of expelled breath against the sleeve of his jacket raised a powdering of dust.

He stared at that with amazement, then slapped himself and said, "Damn it, I'm dusty." The dust rose like a pale pink fog. "You, too," he added, slapping Chouns.

Both men sneezed with abandon.

"Picked it up on the other planet, I suppose," said Chouns.

"We can work up an allergy."

"Impossible." Chouns held up one of the sighters and shouted at the snake-things, "Do you have any of these?"

For a while there was nothing in answer but the splashing of water, as some of the snake things slid into the river and emerged with silvery clusters of water life, which they tucked beneath their bodies toward some hidden mouth.

But then one snake-thing, longer than the others, came thrusting along the ground, one blunt end raised questingly some two inches, weaving blindly side to side. The bulb in its center swelled gently at first, then alarmingly, splitting in two with an audible pop. There, nestling within the two halves, were two more sighters, the duplicates of the first two.

Chouns said ecstatically, "Lord in heaven, isn't that beautiful?"

He stepped hastily forward, reaching out for the objects. The swelling that held them thinned and lengthened, forming what were almost tentacles. They reached out toward him.

Chouns was laughing. They were Gamow sighters all right; duplicates, absolute duplicates, of the first two. Chouns fondled them.

Smith was shouting, "Don't you hear me? Chouns, damn it, listen to me."

Chouns said, "What?" He was dimly aware that Smith had been yelling at him for over a minute.

"Look at the flowers, Chouns."

They were closing, as had those on the other planet, and among the rows the snake-things reared upward, balancing on one end and swaying with a queer, broken rhythm. Only the blunt ends of them were visible above the pale pink.

Smith said, "You can't say they're closing up because of nightfall. It's broad day."

Chouns shrugged. "Different planet, different plant. Come on! We've only got two sighters here; there must be more."

"Chouns, let's go home." Smith firmed his legs into two stubborn pillars and the grip he held on Chouns's collar tightened.

Chouns's reddened face turned back toward him indignantly. "What are you doing?"

"I'm getting ready to knock you out if you don't come back with me at once, into the ship."

For a moment Chouns stood irresolute; then a certain wildness about him faded, a certain slackening took place, and he said, "All right."

They were halfway out of the starcluster. Smith said, "How are you?"

Chouns sat up in his bunk and rumpled his hair. "Normal, I guess; sane again. How long have I been sleeping?"

"Twelve hours."

"What about you?"

"I've catnapped." Smith turned ostentatiously to the instruments and made some minor adjustments. He said self-consciously, "Do you know what happened back there on those planets?"

Chouns said slowly, "Do you?"

"I think so."

"Oh? May I hear?"

Smith said, "It was the same plant on both planets. You'll grant that?"

"I most certainly do."

"It was transplanted from one planet to the other, somehow. It grows on both planets perfectly well; but occasionally—to maintain vigor, I imagine—there must be crossfertilization, the two strains mingling. That sort of thing happens on Earth often enough."

"Crossfertilization for vigor? Yes."

"But *we* were the agents that arranged for the mingling. We landed on one planet and were coated with pollen. Remember the blooms closing? That must have been just after they released their pollen; and that's what was making us sneeze, too. Then we landed on the other planet and knocked the pollen off our clothes. A new hybrid strain will start up. We were just a pair of two-legged bees, Chouns, doing our duty by the flowers."

Chouns smiled tentatively. "An inglorious role, in a way."

"Hell, that's not it. Don't you see the danger? Don't you see why we have to get back home *fast?*"

"Why?"

"Because organisms don't adapt themselves to nothing. Those plants seem to be adapted to interplanetary fertilization. We even got paid off, the way bees are; not with nectar, but with Gamow sighters."

"Well?"

"Well, you can't have interplanetary fertilization unless something or someone is there to do the job. *We* did it this time, but we were the first humans ever to enter the cluster. So, before this, it must be nonhumans who did it; maybe the same nonhumans who transplanted the blooms in the first place. That means that somewhere in this cluster there is an intelligent race of beings; intelligent enough for space travel. And Earth must know about that."

Slowly Chouns shook his head.

Smith frowned. "You find flaws somewhere in the reasoning?"

Chouns put his head between his own palms and looked miserable. "Let's say you've missed almost everything."

"What have I missed?" demanded Smith angrily.

"Your crossfertilization theory is good, as far as it goes, but you haven't considered a few points. When we approached that stellar system our hyperatomic motor went out of order in a way the automatic controls could neither diagnose nor correct. After we landed we made no effort to adjust them. We forgot about them, in fact; and when you handled them later you found they were in perfect order, and were so unimpressed by that that you didn't even mention it to me for another few hours.

"Take something else: How conveniently we chose landing spots near a grouping of animal life on both planets. Just luck? And our incredible confidence in the good will of the creatures. We never even bothered checking atmospheres for trace poisons before exposing ourselves.

"And what bothers me most of all is that I went completely crazy over the Gamow sighters. Why? They're valuable, yes, but not *that* valuable—and I don't generally go overboard for a quick buck."

Smith had kept an uneasy silence during all that. Now he said, "I don't see that any of that adds up to anything."

"Get off it, Smith; you know better than that. Isn't it obvious to you that we were under mental control from the outside?"

Smith's mouth twisted and caught halfway between derision and doubt. "Are you on the psionic kick again?"

"Yes; facts are facts. I told you that my hunches might be a form of rudimentary telepathy."

"Is that a fact, too? You didn't think so a couple of days ago."

"I think so now. Look, I'm a better receiver than you, and I was more strongly affected. Now that it's over, I understand more about what happened because I received more. Understand?"

"No," said Smith harshly.

"Then listen further. You said yourself the Gamov sighters were the nectar that bribed us into pollination. *You* said that."

"All right."

"Well, then, where did they come from? They were Earth products; we even read the manufacturer's name and model on them, letter by letter. Yet, if no human beings have ever been in the cluster, where did the sighters come from? Neither one of us worried about that, then; and you don't seem to worry about it even now."

"Well—"

"What did you do with the sighters after we got on board ship, Smith? You took them from me; I remember that."

"I put them in the safe," said Smith defensively.

"Have you touched them since?"

"No."

"Have I?"

"Not as far as I know."

"You have my word I didn't. Then why not open the safe now?"

Smith stepped slowly to the safe. It was keyed to his fingerprints, and it opened. Without looking he reached in. His expression altered and with a sharp cry he first stared at the contents, then scrabbled them out.

He held four rocks of assorted color, each of them roughly rectangular.

"They used our own emotions to drive us," said Chouns softly, as though insinuating the words into the other's stubborn skull one at a time. "They made us think the hyperatomics were wrong so we could land on one of the planets; it didn't matter which, I suppose. They made us think we had precision instruments in our hand after we landed on one so we would race to the other."

"Who are 'they'?" groaned Smith. "The tails or the snakes? Or both?"

"Neither," said Chouns. "It was the plants."

"The plants? The *flowers?*"

"Certainly. We saw two different sets of animals tending the same species of plant. Being animals ourselves, we assumed the animals were the masters. But why should we assume that? It was the plants that were being taken care of."

"We cultivate plants on Earth, too, Chouns."

"But we eat those plants," said Chouns.

"And maybe those creatures eat their plants, too."

"Let's say I know they don't," said Chouns. "They maneuvered us well enough. Remember how careful I was to find a bare spot on which to land."

"*I* felt no such urge."

"You weren't at the controls; they weren't worried about you. Then, too, remember that we never noticed the pollen, though we were covered with it—not till we were safely on the second planet. Then we dusted the pollen off, on order."

"I never heard anything so impossible."

"Why is it impossible? We don't associate intelligence with plants, because plants have no nervous systems; but these might have. Remember the fleshy buds on the stems? Also, plants aren't free-moving; but they don't have to be if they develop psionic powers and can make use of free-moving animals. They get cared for, fertilized, irrigated, pollinated, and so on. The animals tend them with single-minded devotion and are happy over it because the plants make them feel happy."

"I'm sorry for you," said Smith in a monotone. "If you try to tell this story back on Earth, I'm sorry for you."

"I have no illusions," muttered Chouns, "yet—what can I do but try to warn Earth. You see what they do to animals."

"They make slaves of them, according to you."

"Worse than that. Either the tailed creatures or the snake-things, or both, must have been civilized enough to have developed space travel once; otherwise the plants couldn't be on both planets. But once the plants developed psionic powers (a mutant strain, perhaps), that came to an end. Animals at the atomic stage are dangerous. So they were made to forget; they were reduced to what they are. —Damn it, Smith, those plants are the most dangerous things in the universe. Earth must be informed about them, because some other Earthmen may be entering that cluster."

Smith laughed. "You know, you're completely off base. If those plants really had us under control, why would they let us get away to warn the others?"

Chouns paused. "I don't know."

Smith's good humor was restored. He said, "For a minute you had me going, I don't mind telling you."

Chouns rubbed his skull violently. Why *were* they let go? And for that matter, why did he feel this horrible urgency to warn Earth about a matter with which Earthmen would not come into contact for millennia perhaps?

He thought desperately and something came glimmering. He fumbled for it, but it drifted away. For a moment he thought desperately that it was as though the thought had been *pushed* away; but then that feeling, too, left.

He knew only that the ship had to remain at full thrust, that they had to hurry.

So, after uncounted years, the proper conditions had come about again. The protospores from two planetary strains of the mother plant met and mingled, sifting together into the clothes and hair and ship of the new animals. Almost at once the hybrid spores formed; the hybrid spores that alone had all the capacity and potentiality of adapting themselves to a new planet.

The spores waited quietly, now, on the ship which, with the last impulse of the mother plant upon the minds of the creatures aboard, was hurtling them at top thrust toward a new and ripe world where free-moving creatures would tend their needs.

The spores waited with the patience of the plant (the all-conquering patience no animal can ever know) for their arrival on a new world—each, in its own tiny way, an explorer—

———◆———

The stories in this book have not been much anthologized. That is the very reason I have chosen them, and it was one of the points Doubleday urged on me. EACH AN EXPLORER has, however, been anthologized twice, once by Judith Merril in 1957 and once by Vic Ghidalia in 1973.

That still isn't much, though. Some of my stories tend to appear many times. A little story I wrote called THE FUN THEY HAD has appeared, to date, at least forty-two times since it was first published, in 1951, and is currently in press for eight more appearances. It may have appeared in other places, too, but I only have forty-two in my library.

You can find the story, if you wish, in my book EARTH IS ROOM ENOUGH (Doubleday, 1957). That's one of the forty-two places.

Editors are always trying to think up gimmicks. Sometimes I am the victim.

On November 14, 1956, I was in the office of *Infinity Science Fiction,* talking to the editor, Larry Shaw. We got along well together, he and I,* and I often dropped in to see him when I visited New York.

That day he had an idea. He was to give me the title for a story —the least inspirational title he could think of—and I was to write a short-short, on the spot, based on that title. Then he would give the same title to two other writers and they would do the same.

I asked, cautiously, what the title was, and he said, "Blank."

"Blank?" I said.

"Blank," he said.

So I thought a little and wrote the following story, with the title of BLANK! (with an exclamation point).

Randall Garrett wrote a story entitled *Blank?* with a question mark, and Harlan Ellison wrote one called *Blank* with no punctuation at all.

---

* I mustn't make that sound exceptional. I get along with nearly everyone.

BLANK!

"Presumably," said August Pointdexter, "there is such a thing as overweening pride. The Greeks called it *hubris,* and considered it to be defiance of the gods, to be followed always by *ate,* or retribution." He rubbed his pale blue eyes uneasily.

"Very pretty," said Dr. Edward Barron impatiently. "Has that any connection with what I said?" His forehead was high and had horizontal creases in it that cut in sharply when he raised his eyebrows in contempt.

"Every connection," said Pointdexter. "To construct a time machine is itself a challenge to fate. You make it worse by your flat confidence. How can you be *sure* that your time-travel machine will operate through all of time without the possibility of paradox?"

Barron said, "I didn't know you were superstitious. The simple fact is that a time machine is a machine like any other machine, no more and no less sacrilegious. Mathematically, it is analogous to an elevator moving up and down its shaft. What danger of retribution lies in that?"

Pointdexter said energetically, "An elevator doesn't involve paradoxes. You can't move from the fifth floor to the fourth and kill your grandfather as a child."

Dr. Barron shook his head in agonized impatience. "I was waiting for that. For *exactly* that. Why couldn't you suggest that I would meet myself or that I would change history by telling McClellan that Stonewall Jackson was going to make a flank march on Washington, or anything else? Now I'm asking you point blank. Will you come into the machine with me?"

Pointdexter hesitated. "I . . . I don't think so."

"Why do you make things difficult? I've explained already that time is invariant. If I go into the past it will be because I've already been there. Anything I decided to do and proceed to do, I will have already done in the past all along, so I'll be changing nothing and no paradoxes will result. If I decided to kill my grandfather as a baby, and *did* it, I would not be here. But I *am* here. Therefore I did not kill my grandfather. No matter how I try to kill him and plan to kill him, the fact is I didn't kill him and so I won't kill him. Nothing would change that. Do you understand what I'm explaining?"

"I understand what you say, but are you right?"

"Of course I'm right. For God's sake, why couldn't you have been a mathematician instead of a machinist with a college education?" In his impatience, Barron could scarcely hide his contempt. "Look, this machine is only possible because certain mathematical relationships between space and time hold true. You understand that, don't you, even if you don't follow the details of the mathematics? The machine exists, so the mathematical relations I worked out have some correspondence in reality. Right? You've seen me send rabbits a week into the future. You've seen them appear out of nothing. You've watched me send a rabbit a week into the past one week after it appeared. And they were unharmed."

"All right. I admit all that."

"Then will you believe me if I tell you that the equations upon which this machine is based assume that time is composed of particles that exist in an unchanging order; that time is invariant. If the order of the particles could be changed in any way—any way at all—the equations would be invalid and this machine wouldn't work; this particular method of time travel would be impossible."

Pointdexter rubbed his eyes again and looked thoughtful. "I wish I knew mathematics."

Barron said, "Just consider the facts. You tried to send the rabbit *two* weeks into the past when it had arrived only one week in the past. That would have created a paradox, wouldn't it? But what happened? The indicator stuck at one week and wouldn't budge. You *couldn't* create a paradox. Will you come?"

Pointdexter shuddered at the edge of the abyss of agreement and drew back. He said, "No."

Barron said, "I wouldn't ask you to help if I could do this alone, but you know it takes two men to operate the machine for intervals of more than a month. I need someone to control the Standards so that we can return with precision. And you're the one I want to use. We share the—the glory of this thing now. Do you want to thin it out, cut in a third person? Time enough for that after we've established ourselves as the first time travelers in history. Good Lord, man, don't you want to see where we'll be a hundred years from now, or a thousand; don't you want to see Napoleon, or Jesus, for that matter? We'll be like—like"—Barron seemed carried away —"like gods."

"Exactly," mumbled Pointdexter. *"Hubris.* Time travel isn't godlike enough to risk being stranded out of my own time."

"Hubris. Stranded. You keep making up fears. We're just moving along the particles of time like an elevator along the floors of a building. Time travel is actually safer because an elevator cable can break, whereas in the time machine there'll be no gravity to pull us down destructively. Nothing wrong can possibly happen. I guarantee it," said Barron, tapping his chest with the middle finger of his right hand. "I guarantee it."

"Hubris," muttered Pointdexter, but fell into the abyss of agreement nevertheless, overborne at last.

Together they entered the machine.

Pointdexter did not understand the controls in the sense Barron did, for he was no mathematician, but he knew how they were supposed to be handled.

Barron was at one set, the Propulsions. They supplied the drive that forced the machine along the time axis. Pointdexter was at the Standards that kept the point of origin fixed so that the machine could move back to the original starting point at any time.

Pointdexter's teeth chattered as the first motion made itself felt in his stomach. Like an elevator's motion it was, but not quite. It was something more subtle, yet very real. He said, "What if—"

Barron snapped out, "Nothing can go wrong. Please!"

And at once there was a jar and Pointdexter fell heavily against the wall.

Barron said, "What the devil!"

"What happened?" demanded Pointdexter breathlessly.

"I don't know, but it doesn't matter. We're only twenty-two hours into the future. Let's step out and check."

The door of the machine slid into its recessed panel and the breath went out of Pointdexter's body in a panting whoosh. He said, "There's nothing there."

Nothing. No matter. No light. Blank!

Pointdexter screamed. "The Earth moved. We forgot that. In twenty-two hours, it moved thousands of miles through space, traveling around the sun."

"No," said Barron faintly, "I didn't forget that. The machine is designed to follow the time path of Earth wherever that leads. Besides, even if Earth moved, where is the sun? Where are the stars?"

Barron went back to the controls. Nothing budged. Nothing worked. The door would no longer slide shut. Blank!

Pointdexter found it getting difficult to breathe, difficult to move. With effort he said, "What's wrong, then?"

Barron moved slowly toward the center of the machine. He said painfully, "The particles of time. I think we happened to stall . . . between two . . . particles."

Pointdexter tried to clench a fist but couldn't. "Don't understand."

"Like an elevator. Like an elevator." He could no longer sound the words, but only move his lips to shape them. "Like an elevator, after all . . . stuck between the floors."

Pointdexter could not even move his lips. He thought: Nothing can proceed in nontime. All motion is suspended, all consciousness, all everything. There was an inertia about themselves that had carried them along in time for a minute or so, like a body leaning forward when an automobile comes to a sudden halt—but it was dying fast.

The light within the machine dimmed and went out. Sensation and awareness chilled into nothing.

One last thought, one final, feeble, mental sigh: *Hubris, ate!*

Then thought stopped, too.

Stasis! Nothing! For all eternity, where even eternity was meaningless, there would only be—blank!

All three *Blanks* were published in the June 1957 issue of *Infinity* and the idea of the gimmick, I suppose, was to let the reader compare them and note how three different imaginations took off from a single, nondescript title.

Perhaps you wish you could have all three stories here, so that you could make the comparison yourself. Well, you can't.

In the first place, I'd have to get permissions from Randall and from Harlan and I don't want to have to go through that. In the second place, you underestimate my self-centered nature. I don't want their stories included with mine!

Then, too, I must explain that I always dismantle magazines with my stories in them, because I just can't manage to keep intact those magazines containing my stories. There are too many magazines and not enough room. I take out my own particular stories and bind them into volumes for future reference (as in the preparation of this book). Actually, I am running out of room for the volumes.

Anyway, when it came to dismantling the June 1957 *Infinity* I abstracted only BLANK! and discarded *Blank?* and *Blank*.

Or, perhaps, you don't underestimate my self-centered nature and expect me, as a matter of course, to do that sort of thing.

Back in the middle 1950s, when some of the less affluent science fiction magazines (not that any of them were really *affluent*) asked me for a story, it was my practice to request the rates that *Astounding* and *Galaxy* paid if any magazine expected a story written especially for them. They would do so, quite confident that if I said a story was written especially for them, it was, and that it had not been slipped out of the bottom of the barrel. (There are times when having a reputation as being too dumb to be crooked comes in handy.)

The corollary of that, of course, is that if a story of mine is ever rejected by EDITOR A, it is incumbent upon me to tell this to EDITOR B when I offer it anew. In the first place, a rejection of a story with my name on it must give rise to thoughts such as "Wow! This story *must* be a stinker!" and it's only fair to give the second editor a chance to agree. Secondly, even if the second editor accepts the story he need not feel called upon to pay me more than his own standard fees. It meant an occasional loss of a few dollars but it made me more comfortable inside my wizened little soul.

Anyway, DOES A BEE CARE? was written in October 1956, after I had discussed it with Robert P. Mills, of *Fantasy and Science Fiction,* who had taken over the editorship of a new sister magazine of *F & SF,* which was to be called *Venture Science Fiction.*

I guess the execution fell short of the promise, because Mills rejected it and it was deemed unworthy both for *Venture* and for *F & SF.* So I passed it on to *If: Worlds of Science Fiction* with the word of the rejection and I got less than top rates for it. It appeared in the June 1957 issue.

Now the sad part is that I can never tell what there is about a story that makes the difference between acceptance and rejection, or which editor, the rejecting one or the accepting one, is correct. That's why I'm not an editor and never intend to be.

But you can judge for yourself.

DOES A BEE CARE?

The ship began as a metal skeleton. Slowly a shining skin was layered on without and odd-shaped vitals were crammed within.

Thornton Hammer, of all the individuals (but one) involved in the growth, did the least physically. Perhaps that was why he was most highly regarded. He handled the mathematical symbols that formed the basis for lines on drafting paper, which, in turn, formed the basis for the fitting together of the various masses and different forms of energy that went into the ship.

Hammer watched now through close-fitting spectacles somberly. Their lenses caught the light of the fluorescent tubes above and sent them out again as highlights. Theodore Lengyel, representing Personnel of the corporation that was footing the bill for the project, stood beside him and said, as he pointed with a rigid, stabbing finger:

"There he is. That's the man."

Hammer peered. "You mean Kane?"

"The fellow in the green overalls, holding a wrench."

"That's Kane. Now what is this you've got against him?"

"I want to know what he does. The man's an idiot." Lengyel had a round, plump face and his jowls quivered a bit.

Hammer turned to look at the other, his spare body assuming an air of displeasure along every inch. "Have you been bothering him?"

"*Bothering* him? I've been talking to him. It's my job to talk to the men, to get their viewpoints, to get information out of which I can build campaigns for improved morale."

"How does Kane disturb that?"

"He's insolent. I asked him how it felt to be working on a ship that would reach the moon. I talked a little about the ship being a pathway to the stars. Perhaps I made a little speech about it, built it up a bit, when he turned away in the rudest possible manner. I called him back and said, 'Where are you going?' And he said, 'I get tired of that kind of talk. I'm going out to look at the stars.' "

Hammer nodded. "All right. Kane likes to look at the stars."

"It was daytime. The man's an idiot. I've been watching him since and he doesn't do any work."

"I know that."

"Then why is he kept on?"

Hammer said with a sudden, tight fierceness, "Because I want him around. Because he's my luck."

"Your luck?" faltered Lengyel. "What the hell does that mean?"

"It means that when he's around I think better. When he passes me, holding his damned wrench, I get ideas. It's happened three times. I don't explain it; I'm not interested in explaining it. It's happened. He stays."

"You're joking."

"No, I'm not. Now leave me alone."

Kane stood there in his green overalls, holding his wrench.

Dimly he was aware that the ship was almost ready. It was not designed to carry a man, but there was space for a man. He knew that the way he knew a lot of things; like keeping out of the way of most people most of the time; like carrying a wrench until people grew used to him carrying a wrench and stopped noticing it. Protective coloration consisted of little things, really—like carrying the wrench.

He was full of drives he did not fully understand, like looking at the stars. At first, many years back, he had just looked at the stars with a vague ache. Then, slowly, his attention had centered itself on a certain region of the sky, then to a certain pinpointed spot. He didn't know why that certain spot. There were no stars in that spot. There was nothing to see.

That spot was high in the night sky in the late spring and in the summer months and he sometimes spent most of the night watching the spot until it sank toward the southwestern horizon. At other times in the year he would stare at the spot during the day.

There was some thought in connection with that spot which he couldn't quite crystallize. It had grown stronger, come nearer to the surface as the years passed, and it was almost bursting for expression now. But still it had not quite come clear.

Kane shifted restlessly and approached the ship. It was almost complete, almost whole. Everything fitted just so. Almost.

For within it, far forward, was a hole a little larger than a man; and leading to that hole was a pathway a little wider than a man. Tomorrow that pathway would be filled with the last of the vitals, and before that was done the hole had to be filled, too. But not with anything *they* planned.

Kane moved still closer and no one paid any attention to him. They were used to him.

There was a metal ladder that had to be climbed and a catwalk that had to be moved along to enter the last opening. He knew where the opening was as exactly as if he had built the ship with his own hands. He climbed the ladder and moved along the catwalk. There was no one there at the mo——

He was wrong. One man.

That one said sharply, "What are you doing here?"

Kane straightened and his vague eyes stared at the speaker. He lifted his wrench and brought it down on the speaker's head lightly. The man who was struck (and who had made no effort to ward off the blow) dropped, partly from the effect of the blow.

Kane let him lie there, without concern. The man would not remain unconscious for long, but long enough to allow Kane to wriggle into the hole. When the man revived he would recall nothing about Kane or about the fact of his own unconsciousness. There would simply be five minutes taken out of his life that he would never find and never miss.

It was dark in the hole and, of course, there was no ventilation, but Kane paid no attention to that. With the sureness of instinct, he clambered upward toward the hold that would receive him, then lay there, panting, fitting the cavity neatly, as though it were a womb.

In two hours they would begin inserting the last of the vitals, close the passage, and leave Kane there, unknowingly. Kane would be the sole bit of flesh and blood in a thing of metal and ceramics and fuel.

Kane was not afraid of being prematurely discovered. No one in the project knew the hole was there. The design didn't call for it. The mechanics and construction men weren't aware of having put it in.

Kane had arranged that entirely by himself.

He didn't know how he had arranged it but he knew he had.

He could watch his own influence without knowing how it was exerted. Take the man Hammer, for instance, the leader of the project and the most clearly influenced. Of all the indistinct figures about Kane, he was the least indistinct. Kane would be very aware of him at times, when he passed near him in his slow and hazy journeys about the grounds. It was all that was necessary—passing near him.

Kane recalled it had been so before, particularly with theoreticians. When Lise Meitner decided to test for barium among the products of the neutron bombardment of uranium, Kane had been there, an unnoticed plodder along a corridor nearby.

He had been picking up leaves and trash in a park in 1904 when the young Einstein had passed by, pondering. Einstein's steps had quickened with the impact of sudden thought. Kane felt it like an electric shock.

But he didn't know how it was done. Does a spider know architectural theory when it begins to construct its first web?

It went further back. The day the young Newton had stared at the moon with the dawn of a certain thought, Kane had been there. And further back still.

The panorama of New Mexico, ordinarily deserted, was alive with human ants crawling about the metal shaft lancing upward. This one was different from all the similar structures that had preceded it.

This would go free of Earth more nearly than any other. It would reach out and circle the moon before falling back. It would be crammed with instruments that would photograph the moon and measure its heat emissions, probe for radioactivity, and test by microwave for chemical structure. It would, by automation, do almost everything that could be expected of a manned vehicle. And it would learn enough to make certain that the next ship sent out *would* be a manned vehicle.

Except that, in a way, this first one was a manned vehicle after all.

There were representatives of various governments, of various industries, of various social and economic groupings. There were television cameras and feature writers.

Those who could not be there watched in their homes and heard numbers counted backward in painstaking monotone in the manner grown traditional in a mere three decades.

At zero the reaction motors came to life and ponderously the ship lifted.

Kane heard the noise of the rushing gases, as though from a distance, and felt the gathering acceleration press against him.

He detached his mind, lifting it up and outward, freeing it from direct connection with his body in order that he might be unaware of the pain and discomfort.

Dizzily, he knew his long journey was nearly over. He would no longer have to maneuver carefully to avoid having people realize he was immortal. He would no longer have to fade into the background, no longer wander eternally from place to place, changing names and personality, manipulating minds.

It had not been perfect, of course. The myths of the Wandering Jew and the Flying Dutchman had arisen, but he was still here. He had not been disturbed.

He could see his spot in the sky. Through the mass and solidity of the ship he could see it. Or not "see" really. He didn't have the proper word.

He knew there was a proper word, though. He could not say how he knew a fraction of the things he knew, except that as the centuries had passed he had gradually grown to know them with a sureness that required no reason.

He had begun as an ovum (or as something for which "ovum" was the nearest word he knew), deposited on Earth before the first cities had been built by the wandering hunting creatures since called "men." Earth had been chosen carefully by his progenitor. Not every world would do.

What world would? What was the criterion? That he still didn't know.

Does an ichneumon wasp study ornithology before it finds the one species of spider that will do for her eggs, and stings it just so in order that it may remain alive?

The ovum spilt him forth at length and he took the shape of a man and lived among men and protected himself against men. And his one purpose was to arrange to have men travel along a path that would end with a ship and within the ship a hole and within the hole, himself.

It had taken eight thousand years of slow striving and stumbling.

The spot in the sky became sharper now as the ship moved out of the atmosphere. That was the key that opened his mind. That was the piece that completed the puzzle.

Stars blinked within that spot that could not be seen by a man's eye unaided. One in particular shone brilliantly and Kane yearned toward it. The expression that had been building within him for so long burst out now.

"Home," he whispered.

He knew? Does a salmon study cartography to find the head-waters of the fresh-water stream in which years before it had been born?

The final step was taken in the slow maturing that had taken eight thousand years, and Kane was no longer larval, but adult.

The adult Kane fled from the human flesh that had protected the larva, and fled the ship, too. It hastened onward, at inconceivable speeds, toward home, from which someday it, too, might set off on wanderings through space to fertilize some planet with its ovum.

It sped through Space, giving no thought to the ship carrying an empty chrysalis. It gave no thought to the fact that it had driven a whole world toward technology and space travel in order only that the thing that had been Kane might mature and reach its fulfillment.

Does a bee care what has happened to a flower when the bee has done and gone its way?

----×◆×----

Going through DOES A BEE CARE? makes me think of the many editors with whom I have dealt, and with the way in which they sometimes vanish into limbo.

There have been editors whom, for a period of time, I saw frequently, and with whom I felt quite close. Then, for one reason or another, they left their positions and vanished out of my ken. I haven't seen Horace Gold for many years, for instance—and I haven't seen James L. Quinn, who bought DOES A BEE CARE? and a few other stories of mine.

He had a southern accent, I remember, and was a delightful person—and now I don't know where he is or even if he is still alive.

The next story, SILLY ASSES, is one that I had better say very little about or the commentary will be longer than the story. I wrote it on July 29, 1957, and it was rejected by two different magazines before Bob Lowndes kindly made a home for it. It appeared in the February 1958 issue of *Future*.

SILLY ASSES

Naron of the long-lived Rigellian race was the fourth of his line to keep the galactic records.

He had the large book which contained the list of the numerous races throughout the galaxies that had developed intelligence, and the much smaller book that listed those races that had reached maturity and had qualified for the Galactic Federation. In the first book, a number of those listed were crossed out; those that, for one reason or another, had failed. Misfortune, biochemical or biophysical shortcomings, social maladjustment took their toll. In the smaller book, however, no member listed had yet blanked out.

And now Naron, large and incredibly ancient, looked up as a messenger approached.

"Naron," said the messenger. "Great One!"

"Well, well, what is it? Less ceremony."

"Another group of organisms has attained maturity."

"Excellent. Excellent. They are coming up quickly now. Scarcely a year passes without a new one. And who are these?"

The messenger gave the code number of the galaxy and the co-ordinates of the world within it.

"Ah, yes," said Naron. "I know the world." And in flowing script he noted it in the first book and transferred its name into the second, using, as was customary, the name by which the planet was known to the largest fraction of its populace. He wrote: Earth.

He said, "These new creatures have set a record. No other group has passed from intelligence to maturity so quickly. No mistake, I hope."

"None, sir," said the messenger.

"They have attained to thermonuclear power, have they?"

"Yes, sir."

"Well, that's the criterion." Naron chuckled. "And soon their ships will probe out and contact the Federation."

"Actually, Great One," said the messenger, reluctantly, "the Observers tell us they have not yet penetrated space."

Naron was astonished. "Not at all? Not even a space station?"

"Not yet, sir."

"But if they have thermonuclear power, where then do they conduct their tests and detonations?"

"On their own planet, sir."

Naron rose to his full twenty feet of height and thundered, "On their own planet?"

"Yes, sir."

Slowly Naron drew out his stylus and passed a line though the latest addition in the smaller book. It was an unprecedented act, but, then, Naron was very wise and could see the inevitable as well as anyone in the galaxy.

"Silly asses," he muttered.

——————◆——————

This is another story with a moral, I'm afraid. But, you see, the nuclear danger had escalated when both the United States and the Soviet Union developed the fusion H-bomb, and I was bitter again.

As 1957 ended another turning point was upon me. It came about in this wise:

When Walker, Boyd, and I wrote our textbook we all spent school time freely on it (though naturally much of the work overflowed into evenings and weekends). It was a scholarly endeavor and part of our job.

When I wrote THE CHEMICALS OF LIFE I felt that that, too, was a scholarly endeavor, and worked on it during school hours without any qualms. I worked on other books of the sort during school hours, too.* By the end of 1957 I had in this fashion written seven nonfiction books for the general public.

Meanwhile, though, James Faulkner, the sympathetic dean, and Burnham S. Walker, the sympathetic department head, had resigned their positions and there had come replacements—who viewed me without sympathy.

Dean Faulkner's replacement did not approve of my activities, and he had a point, I suppose. In my eagerness to write nonfiction I had completely abandoned research, and he thought it was research on which the school's reputation depended. To an extent that is true, but it is not *always* true, and in my case it wasn't.

* I must stress, again, that I *never* worked on science fiction during school hours.

We had a conference and I presented my view in a frank and straightforward manner, as my unworldly father had always taught me to do.

"Sir," I said, "as a writer I am outstanding and my work will reflect luster on the school. As a researcher, however, I am merely competent, and if there is one thing Boston University School of Medicine does not need, it is another merely competent researcher."

I suppose I might have been more diplomatic, for that seemed to end the discussion. I was taken off the payroll and the spring semester of 1958 was the last in which I taught regular classes, after nine years at that game.

It didn't bother me very much. Concerning the school salary I cared nothing. Even after two pay raises it only came to sixty-five hundred dollars a year, and my writing earned me considerably more than that already.

Nor did I worry about losing the chance to do research; I had abandoned that already. As for teaching, my nonfiction books (and even my science fiction) were forms of teaching that satisfied me with their great variety far more than teaching a limited subject matter could. I didn't even fear missing the personal interaction of lecturing, since from 1950 onward I had been establishing myself as a professional lecturer and was beginning to earn respectable fees in that manner.

However, it was the new dean's intention to deprive me of my title, too, and kick me out of the school altogether. *That* I would not allow. I maintained that I had earned tenure, for I had become an associate professor in 1955, and could not be deprived of the title without cause. The fight went on for two years and I won. I retained the title, and I *still* retain the title right now. I am still associate professor of biochemistry at Boston University School of Medicine.

What's more, the school is now happy about it. My adversary retired at last and has since died. (He wasn't really a bad fellow; we just didn't see eye to eye.) And lest I give a false impression, let me state emphatically that, except for that one period involving just one or two people, the school, and everyone in it, has always treated me with perfect kindness.

I still do not teach and am not on the payroll, but that is my own choice. I have been asked to come back in one way or another a number of times, but have explained why I cannot. I do give lectures at the school when requested, and on May 19, 1974, I gave the commencement address at the medical school—so all is well, you see.

Nevertheless, when I found I had time on my hands, with no classes to take care of and no commuting to do, I found that my impulse was to put that extra time into nonfiction, with which I had fallen completely and helplessly and hopelessly in love.

Remember, too, that on October 4, 1957, *Sputnik I* had gone into orbit, and in the excitement that followed I grew very fervent concerning the importance of writing science for the layman. What's more, the publishers were now fiercely interested in it as well, and in no time at all I found I had been hounded into so many projects that it became difficult and even impossible to find time to work on major science fiction projects, and, alas, it has continued so to the present day.

Mind you, I didn't quit science fiction altogether. No year has passed that hasn't seen me write something, even if only a couple of short pieces. On January 14, 1958, as I was getting ready to start my last semester and before the full impact of my decision had struck home, I wrote the following story for Bob Mills and his (alas) short-lived *Venture*. It appeared in the May 1958 issue.

BUY JUPITER

He was a simulacron, of course, but so cleverly contrived that the human beings dealing with him had long since given up thinking of the real energy-entities, waiting in white-hot blaze in their field-enclosure "ship" miles from Earth.

The simulacron, with a majestic golden beard and deep brown, wide-set eyes, said gently, "We understand your hesitations and suspicions, and we can only continue to assure you we mean you no harm. We have, I think, presented you with proof that we inhabit the coronal haloes of O-spectra stars; that your own sun is too weak for us; while your planets are of solid matter and therefore completely and eternally alien to us."

The Terrestrial Negotiator (who was Secretary of Science and, by common consent, had been placed in charge of negotiations with the aliens) said, "But you have admitted we are now on one of your chief trade routes."

"Now that our new world of Kimmonoshek has developed new fields of protonic fluid, yes."

The Secretary said, "Well, here on Earth, positions on trade routes can gain military importance out of proportion to their intrinsic value. I can only repeat, then, that to gain our confidence you must tell us exactly why you need Jupiter."

And as always, when that question or a form of it was asked, the simulacron looked pained. "Secrecy is important. If the Lamberj people—"

"Exactly," said the Secretary. "To us it sounds like war. You and what you call the Lamberj people—"

The simulacron said hurriedly, "But we are offering you a most generous return. You have only colonized the inner planets of your system and we are not interested in those. We ask for the world you call Jupiter, which, I understand, your people can never expect to live on, or even land on. Its size" (he laughed indulgently) "is too much for you."

The Secretary, who disliked the air of condescension, said stiffly, "The Jovian satellites are practical sites for colonization, however, and we intend to colonize them shortly."

"But the satellites will not be disturbed in any way. They are yours in every sense of the word. We ask only Jupiter itself, a completely useless world to you, and for that the return we offer is generous. Surely you realize that we could take your Jupiter, if we wished, without your permission. It is only that we prefer payment and a legal treaty. It will prevent disputes in the future. As you see, I'm being completely frank."

The Secretary said stubbornly, "Why do you need Jupiter?"

"The Lamberj—"

"Are you at war with the Lamberj?"

"It's not quite—"

"Because you see that if it is war and you establish some sort of fortified base on Jupiter, the Lamberj may, quite properly, resent that, and retaliate against us for granting you permission. We cannot allow ourselves to be involved in such a situation."

"Nor would I ask you to be involved. My word that no harm would come to you. Surely" (he kept coming back to it) "the return is generous. Enough power boxes each year to supply your world with a full year of power requirement."

The Secretary said, "On the understanding that future increases in power consumption will be met."

"Up to a figure five times the present total. Yes."

"Well, then, as I have said, I am a high official of the government and have been given considerable powers to deal with you—but not infinite power. I, myself, am inclined to trust you, but I could not accept your terms without understanding exactly why you want Jupiter. If the explanation is plausible and convincing, I could perhaps persuade our government and, through them, our people, to make the agreement. If I tried to make an agreement without such an explanation, I would simply be forced out of office and Earth would refuse to honor the agreement. You could then, as you say, take Jupiter by force, but you would be in illegal possession and you have said you don't wish that."

The simulacron clicked its tongue impatiently. "I cannot continue forever in this petty bickering. The Lamberj—" Again he stopped, then said, "Have I your word of honor that this is all not a device inspired by the Lamberj people to delay us until—"

"My word of honor," said the Secretary.

The Secretary of Science emerged, mopping his forehead and looking ten years younger. He said softly, "I told him his people could have it as soon as I obtained the President's formal approval. I don't think he'll object, or Congress, either. Good Lord, gentlemen, think of it; free power at our fingertips in return for a planet we could never use in any case."

The Secretary of Defense, growing purplish with objection, said, "But we had agreed that only a Mizzarett-Lamberj war could explain their need for Jupiter. Under those circumstances, and comparing their military potential with ours, a strict neutrality is essential."

"But there is no war, sir," said the Secretary of Science. "The simulacron presented an alternate explanation of their need for Jupiter so rational and plausible that I accepted at once. I think the President will agree with me, and you gentlemen, too, when you understand. In fact, I have here their plans for the new Jupiter, as it will soon appear."

The others rose from their seats, clamoring. "A new Jupiter?" gasped the Secretary of Defense.

"Not so different from the old, gentlemen," said the Secretary of Science. "Here are the sketches provided in form suitable for observation by matter beings such as ourselves."

He laid them down. The familiar banded planet was there before them on one of the sketches: yellow, pale green, and light brown with curled white streaks here and there and all against the speckled velvet background of space. But across the bands were streaks of blackness as velvet as the background, arranged in a curious pattern.

"That," said the Secretary of Science, "is the day side of the planet. The night side is shown in this sketch." (There, Jupiter was a thin crescent enclosing darkness, and within that darkness were the same thin streaks arranged in similar pattern, but in a phosphorescent glowing orange this time.)

"The marks," said the Secretary of Science, "are a purely optical phenomenon, I am told, which will not rotate with the planet, but will remain static in its atmospheric fringe."

"But what is it?" asked the Secretary of Commerce.

"You see," said the Secretary of Science, "our solar system is now on one of their major trade routes. As many as seven of their ships pass within a few hundred million miles of the system in a single day, and each ship has the major planets under telescopic observation as they pass. Tourist curiosity, you know. Solid planets of any size are a marvel to them."

"What has that to do with these marks?"

"That is one form of their writing. Translated, those marks read: 'Use Mizzarett Ergone Vertices For Health and Glowing Heat.' "

"You mean Jupiter is to be an advertising billboard?" exploded the Secretary of Defense.

"Right. The Lamberj people, it seems, produce a competing ergone tablet, which accounts for the Mizzarett anxiety to establish full legal ownership of Jupiter—in case of Lamberj lawsuits. Fortunately, the Mizzaretts are novices at the advertising game, it appears."

"Why do you say that?" asked the Secretary of the Interior.

"Why, they neglected to set up a series of options on the other planets. The Jupiter billboard will be advertising our system, as well as their own product. And when the competing Lamberj people come storming in to check on the Mizzarett title to Jupiter, we will have Saturn to sell to *them. With* its rings. As we will be easily able to explain to them, the rings will make Saturn much the better spectacle."

"And therefore," said the Secretary of the Treasury, suddenly beaming, "worth a *much* better price."

And they all suddenly looked very cheerful.

———————◄◆►———————

BUY JUPITER was not my original title for the story. I am usually indignant when an editor changes the title I have given a story, and change it back when it appears in one of my own collections and then mutter about it in the commentary. —But not this time.

I called the story *It Pays,* an utterly undistinguished title. Bob Mills, without even consulting me, quietly changed it to BUY JUPITER and I fell in love with that as soon as the change came to my attention. To a punster like myself, it is the perfect title for the story—so perfect that I have given it to this entire collection, which, as you know, is BUY JUPITER AND OTHER STORIES.

Bob Mills gets the credit.

During those early years in which, with a certain amount of uneasy horror, I was watching my science fiction writing begin to fall off, I would occasionally get into a state of blue funk.

Could it be that I could no longer write science fiction at all? Suppose I *wanted* to write science fiction—could I?

I was driving down to Marshfield, Massachusetts, on July 23, 1958, to begin a three-week vacation which I dreaded (I dread all vacations). I deliberately set about thinking up a plot to keep my mind off that vacation—and to see if I could. A STATUE FOR FATHER was the result. I sold it to a new magazine, *Satellite Science Fiction,* and it appeared in the February 1959 issue.

A STATUE FOR FATHER

First time? Really? But of course you have heard of it. Yes, I was sure you had.

If you're really interested in the discovery, believe me, I'll be delighted to tell you. It's a story I've always liked to tell, but not many people give me the chance. I've even been advised to keep the story under wraps. It interferes with the legends growing up about my father.

Still, I think the truth is valuable. There's a moral to it. A man can spend his life devoting his energies solely to the satisfaction of his own curiosity and then, quite accidentally, without ever intending anything of the sort, find himself a benefactor of humanity.

Dad was just a theoretical physicist, devoted to the investigation of time travel. I don't think he ever gave a thought to what time travel might mean to *Homo sapiens*. He was just curious about the mathematical relationships that governed the universe, you see.

Hungry? All the better. I imagine it will take nearly half an hour. They will do it properly for an official such as yourself. It's a matter of pride.

To begin with, Dad was poor as only a university professor can be poor. Eventually, though, he became wealthy. In the last years before his death he was fabulously rich, and as for myself and my children and grandchildren—well, you can see for yourself.

They've put up statues to him, too. The oldest is on the hillside right here where the discovery was made. You can just see it out the window. Yes. Can you make out the inscription? Well, we're standing at a bad angle. No matter.

By the time Dad got into time-travel research the whole problem had been given up by most physicists as a bad job. It had begun with a splash when the Chrono-funnels were first set up.

Actually, they're not much to see. They're completely irrational and uncontrollable. What you see is distorted and wavery, two feet across at the most, and it vanishes quickly. Trying to focus on the past is like trying to focus on a feather caught in a hurricane that has gone mad.

They tried poking grapples into the past but that was just as un-predictable. Sometimes it was carried off successfully for a few seconds with one man leaning hard against the grapple. But more often a pile driver couldn't push it through. Nothing was ever obtained out of the past until— Well, I'll get to that.

After fifty years of no progress, physicists just lost interest. The operational technique seemed a complete blind alley; a dead end. I can't honestly say I blame them as I look back on it. Some of them even tried to show that the funnels didn't actually expose the past, but there had been too many sightings of living animals through the funnels—animals now extinct.

Anyway, when time travel was almost forgotten, Dad stepped in. He talked the government into giving him a grant to set up a Chrono-funnel of his own, and tackled the matter all over again.

I helped him in those days. I was fresh out of college, with my own doctorate in physics.

However, our combined efforts ran into bad trouble after a year or so. Dad had difficulty in getting his grant renewed. Industry wasn't interested, and the university decided he was besmirching their reputation by being so single-minded in investigating a dead field. The dean of the graduate school, who understood only the financial end of scholarship, began by hinting that he switch to more lucrative fields and ended by forcing him out.

Of course, the dean—still alive and still counting grant-dollars when Dad died—probably felt quite foolish, I imagine, when Dad left the school a million dollars free and clear in his will, with a codicil canceling the bequest on the ground that the dean lacked vision. But that was merely posthumous revenge. For years before that—

I don't wish to dictate, but please *don't have any more of the breadsticks. The clear soup, eaten slowly to prevent a too-sharp appetite, will do.*

Anyway, we managed somehow. Dad kept the equipment we had bought with the grant money, moved it out of the university and set it up here.

Those first years on our own were brutal, and I kept urging him to give up. He never would. He was indomitable, always managing to find a thousand dollars somewhere when we needed it.

Life went on, but he allowed nothing to interfere with his research. Mother died; Dad mourned and returned to his task. I married, had a son, then a daughter, couldn't always be at his side. He carried on without me. He broke his leg and worked with the cast impeding him for months.

So I give him all the credit. I helped, of course. I did consulting work on the side and carried on negotiation with Washington. But *he* was the life and soul of the project.

Despite all that, we weren't getting anywhere. All the money we managed to scrounge might just as well have been poured into one of the Chrono-funnels—not that it would have passed through.

After all, we never once managed to get a grapple through a funnel. We came near on only one occasion. We had the grapple about two inches out the other end when focus changed. It snapped off clean and somewhere in the Mesozoic there is a man-made piece of steel rod rusting on a riverbank.

Then one day, the crucial day, the focus held for ten long minutes —something for which the odds were less than one in a trillion. Lord, the frenzies of excitement we experienced as we set up the cameras. We could see living creatures just the other side of the funnel, moving energetically.

Then, to top it off, the Chrono-funnel grew permeable, until you might have sworn there was nothing but air between the past and ourselves. The low permeability must have been connected with the long holding of focus, but we've never been able to prove that it did.

Of course, we had no grapple handy, wouldn't you know. But the low permeability was clear enough because something just fell through, moving from the *Then* into the *Now*. Thunderstruck, acting simply on blind instinct, I reached forward and caught it.

At that moment we lost focus, but it no longer left us embittered and despairing. We were both staring in wild surmise at what I held. It was a mass of caked and dried mud, shaved off clean where it had struck the borders of the Chrono-funnel, and on the mud cake were fourteen eggs about the size of duck eggs.

I said, "Dinosaur eggs? Do you suppose they really are?"

Dad said, "Maybe. We can't tell for sure."

"Unless we hatch them," I said in sudden, almost uncontrollable excitement. I put them down as though they were platinum. They felt warm with the heat of the primeval sun. I said, "Dad, if we hatch them, we'll have creatures that have been extinct for over a hundred million years. It will be the first case of something actually brought out of the past. If we announce this—"

I was thinking of the grants we could get, of the publicity, of all that it would mean to Dad. I was seeing the look of consternation on the dean's face.

But Dad took a different view of the matter. He said firmly. "Not a word, son. If this gets out, we'll have twenty research teams on the trail of the Chrono-funnels, cutting off my advance. No, once I've solved the riddle of the funnels, you can make all the announcements you want. Until then—we keep silent. Son, don't look like that. I'll have the answer in a year. I'm sure of it."

I was a little less confident, but those eggs, I felt convinced, would arm us with all the proof we'd need. I set up a large oven at blood-heat; I circulated air and moisture. I rigged up an alarm that would sound at the first signs of motion within the eggs.

They hatched at 3 A.M. nineteen days later, and there they were —fourteen wee kangaroos with greenish scales, clawed hindlegs, plump little thighs, and thin, whiplash tails.

I thought at first they were tyrannosauri, but they were too small for that species of dinosaur. Months passed, and I could see they weren't going to grow any larger than moderate-sized dogs.

Dad seemed disappointed, but I held on, hoping he would let me use them for publicity. One died before maturity and one was killed in a scuffle. But the other twelve survived—five males and seven females. I fed them on chopped carrots, boiled eggs, and milk, and grew quite fond of them. They were fearfully stupid and yet gentle. And they were truly beautiful. Their scales—

Oh, well, it's silly to describe them. Those original publicity pictures have made their rounds. Though, come to think of it, I don't know about Mars— Oh, there, too. Well, good.

But it took a long time for the pictures to make an impression on the public, let alone a sight of the creatures in the flesh. Dad remained intransigent. A year passed, two, and finally three. We had no luck whatsoever with the Chrono-funnels. The one break was not repeated, and still Dad would not give in.

Five of our females laid eggs and soon I had over fifty of the creatures on my hands.

"What shall we do with them?" I demanded.

"Kill them off," he said.

Well, I couldn't do that, of course.

Henri, is it almost ready? Good.

We had reached the end of our resources when it happened. No more money was available. I had tried everywhere, and met with consistent rebuffs. I was even glad because it seemed to me that Dad would have to give in now. But with a chin that was firm and indomitably set, he coolly set up another experiment.

I swear to you that if the accident had not happened the truth would have eluded us forever. Humanity would have been deprived of one of its greatest boons.

It happens that way sometimes. Perkin spots a purple tinge in his gunk and comes up with aniline dyes. Remsen puts a contaminated finger to his lips and discovers saccharin. Goodyear drops a mixture on the stove and finds the secret of vulcanization.

With us, it was a half-grown dinosaur wandering into the main research lab. They had become so numerous I hadn't been able to keep track of them.

The dinosaur stepped right across two contact points which happened to be open—just at the point where the plaque immortalizing the event is now located. I'm convinced that such a happenstance couldn't occur again in a thousand years. There was a blinding flash, a blistering short circuit, and the Chrono-funnel which had just been set up vanished in a rainbow of sparks.

Even at the moment, really, we didn't know exactly what we had. All we knew was that the creature had short-circuited and perhaps destroyed two hundred thousand dollars worth of equipment and that we were completely ruined financially. All we had to show for it was one thoroughly roasted dinosaur. We were slightly scorched ourselves, but the dinosaur got the full concentration of field energies. We could smell it. The air was saturated with its aroma. Dad and I looked at each other in amazement. I picked it up gingerly in a pair of tongs. It was black and charred on the outside, but the burnt scales crumbled away at a touch, carrying the skin with it. Under the char was white, firm flesh that resembled chicken.

I couldn't resist tasting it, and it resembled chicken about the way Jupiter resembles an asteroid.

Believe me or not, with our scientific work reduced to rubble about us, we sat there in seventh heaven and devoured dinosaur. Parts were burnt, parts were nearly raw. It hadn't been dressed. But we didn't stop until we had picked the bones clean.

Finally I said, "Dad, we've got to raise them gloriously and systematically for food purposes."

Dad had to agree. We were completely broke.

I got a loan from the bank by inviting the president to dinner and feeding him dinosaur.

It has never failed to work. No one who has once tasted what we now call "dinachicken" can rest content with ordinary fare. A meal without dinachicken is a meal we choke down to keep body and soul together. Only dinachicken is *food*.

Our family still owns the only herd of dinachickens in existence and we are the only suppliers for the worldwide chain of restaurants —this is the first and oldest—which has grown up about it.

Poor Dad! He was never happy, except for those unique moments when he was actually eating dinachicken. He continued working on the Chrono-funnels and so did twenty other research teams which, as he had predicted would happen, jumped in. Nothing ever came of any of it, though, to this day. Nothing *except* dinachicken.

Ah, Pierre, thank you. A superlative job! Now, sir, if you will allow me to carve. No salt, now, and just a trace of the sauce. That's right. . . . Ah, that is precisely the expression I always see on the face of a man who experiences his first taste of the delight.

A grateful humanity contributed fifty thousand dollars to have the statue on the hillside put up, but even that tribute failed to make Dad happy.

All he could see was the inscription: The Man Who Gave Dinachicken to the World.

You see, to his dying day, he wanted only one thing, to find the secret of time travel. For all that he was a benefactor of humanity, he died with his curiosity unsatisfied.

———◆———

My original title had been *Benefactor of Humanity,* which I thought carried a fine flavor of irony, and I chafed when Leo Margulies of *Satellite* changed that title. When *The Saturday Evening Post* asked permission to reprint the story (and it appeared in the March-April 1973 issue of that magazine) I made it a condition that they restore the original title. But then, when I saw my own title in print, I thought about it and decided that Leo's title was better. So it appears here as A STATUE FOR FATHER again.

Bob Mills, by the way, whom I mentioned in connection with BUY JUPITER, was a very close friend of mine when he was working with *F & SF* and with *Venture*. He is not one of those with whom I have lost contact, either. He has sold his soul to the devil and is now an agent, but we see each other now and then and are as friendly as ever.

It was Bob who contributed to my switch to nonfiction, too. Since I hated writing research pieces, I began, in 1953, to write imaginative pieces on chemistry for the *Journal of Chemical Education*. I had done about half a dozen before it occurred to me that I was getting nothing for them and was not reaching my audience.

I began writing nonfiction articles for the science fiction magazines, therefore; articles that gave me far more scope and far more variety than any scholarly journal could. The first of these was *Hemoglobin and the Universe,* which appeared in the February 1955 *Astounding*.

In September 1957, however, Bob Mills called me up and asked if I would do a regular science article for *Venture*. I agreed with alacrity and the first of these, *Fecundity Limited,* appeared in the January 1958 *Venture*. Alas, *Venture* lasted only a very few more issues before folding, but I was then asked to do the same column for *F & SF*. The first of these was *Dust of Ages,* which appeared in the November 1958 issue of that magazine.

The *F & SF* series lasted and flourished. The request had been for a fifteen-hundred-word column at first and that was the length of all those in *Venture* and the first in *F & SF*. The request came quickly to raise the wordage to four thousand and, beginning with *Catching Up With Newton,* in the December 1958 issue of *F & SF,* they were the longer length.

The *F & SF* series has been amazingly successful. My two hundredth article in the series appeared in the June 1975 issue of *F & SF*. So far I have not missed an issue, and it may be the longest series of items by one author (other than the editor) ever to have appeared in a science fiction magazine. These articles are periodically collected by Doubleday into books of essays, of which at this time of writing there have been eleven.

Most important of all, though, is the fun I get out of these monthly articles. To this day I get more pleasure out of them than out of any other writing assignment I get. I am constantly anywhere from one to two months ahead of deadline, because I can't wait, but the editors don't seem to mind.

In a way it was Bob Mills who helped establish my present article-writing style, one of intense informality that has managed to leak across into my fiction collections too (as this book bears witness). While I wrote that column for him he constantly referred to me as "the Good Doctor," while I called him "the Kindly Editor," and we had fun kidding each other in the footnotes till he resigned his post. (No, that was not cause-and-effect.)

Anyway, the articles helped confirm me in my nonfiction and made it even harder to get to fiction. Bob, you must understand, did not approve of my not writing fiction. Sometimes he suggested plots for stories in an attempt to lure me into writing, and sometimes I liked his suggestions. For instance, one of his suggestions ended as UNTO THE FOURTH GENERATION, which appeared in the April 1959 issue of *F & SF* and was then included in NIGHTFALL AND OTHER STORIES. That story is one of my personal favorites.

I thought he had suggested another winner when I wrote up one of his ideas in RAIN, RAIN, GO AWAY. I wrote it on November 1, 1958, submitted to him on November 2, and had it rejected on November 3. Kindly Editor, indeed!

Eventually I found a home for it, though, and it appeared in the September 1959 issue of *Fantastic Universe Science Fiction*.

RAIN, RAIN,
GO AWAY

"There she is again," said Lillian Wright as she adjusted the venetian blinds carefully. "There she is, George."

"There who is?" asked her husband, trying to get satisfactory contrast on the TV so that he might settle down to the ball game.

"Mrs. Sakkaro," she said, and then, to forestall her husband's inevitable "Who's that?" added hastily, "The new neighbors, for goodness sake."

"Oh."

"Sunbathing. Always sunbathing. I wonder where her boy is. He's usually out on a nice day like this, standing in that tremendous yard of theirs and throwing the ball against the house. Did you ever see him, George?"

"I've heard him. It's a version of the Chinese water torture. Bang on the wall, biff on the ground, smack in the hand. Bang, biff, smack, bang, biff—"

"He's a *nice* boy, quiet and well-behaved. I wish Tommie would make friends with him. He's the right age, too, just about ten, I should say."

"I didn't know Tommie was backward about making friends."

"Well, it's hard with the Sakkaros. They keep so to themselves. I don't even know what Mr. Sakkaro does."

"Why should you? It's not really anyone's business what he does."

"It's odd that I never see him go to work."

"No one ever sees me go to work."

"You stay home and write. What does *he* do."

"I dare say Mrs. Sakkaro knows what Mr. Sakkaro does and is all upset because she doesn't know what *I* do."

"Oh, George." Lillian retreated from the window and glanced with distaste at the television. (Schoendienst was at bat.) "I think we should make an effort; the neighborhood should."

"What kind of an effort?" George was comfortable on the couch now, with a king-size Coke in his hand, freshly opened and frosted with moisture.

"To get to know them."

"Well, didn't you, when she first moved in? You said you called."

"I said hello but, well, she'd just moved in and the house was still upset, so that's all it could be, just hello. It's been two months now and it's still nothing more than hello, sometimes. —She's so odd."

"Is she?"

"She's always looking at the sky; I've seen her do it a hundred times and she's never been out when it's the least bit cloudy. Once, when the boy was out playing, she called to him to come in, shouting that it was going to rain. I happened to hear her and I thought, Good Lord, wouldn't you know and me with a wash on the line, so I hurried out and, you know, it was broad sunlight. Oh, there were some clouds, but nothing, really."

"Did it rain, eventually?"

"Of course not. I just had to run out in the yard for nothing."

George was lost amid a couple of base hits and a most embarrassing bobble that meant a run. When the excitement was over and the pitcher was trying to regain his composure, George called out after Lillian, who was vanishing into the kitchen, "Well, since they're from Arizona, I dare say they don't know rainclouds from any other kind."

Lillian came back into the living room with a patter of high heels. "From where?"

"From Arizona, according to Tommie."

"How did Tommie know?"

"He talked to their boy, in between ball chucks, I guess, and he told Tommie they came from Arizona and then the boy was called in. At least, Tommie says it might have been Arizona, or maybe Alabama or some place like that. You know Tommie and his non-total recall. But if they're that nervous about the weather, I guess it's Arizona and they don't know what to make of a good rainy climate like ours."

"But why didn't you ever tell me?"

"Because Tommie only told me this morning and because I thought he must have told you already and, to tell the absolute truth, because I thought you could just manage to drag out a normal existence even if you never found out. Wow—"

The ball went sailing into the right field stands and that was that for the pitcher.

Lillian went back to the venetian blinds and said, "I'll simply just have to make her acquaintance. She looks *very* nice. —Oh, Lord, look at that, George."

George was looking at nothing but the TV.

Lillian said, "I know she's staring at that cloud. And now she'll be going in. Honestly."

George was out two days later on a reference search in the library and came home with a load of books. Lillian greeted him jubilantly.

She said, "Now, you're not doing anything tomorrow."

"That sounds like a statement, not a question."

"It *is* a statement. We're going out with the Sakkaros to Murphy's Park."

"With—"

"With the next-door neighbors, George. *How* can you never remember the name?"

"I'm gifted. How did it happen?"

"I just went up to their house this morning and rang the bell."

"That easy?"

"It wasn't easy. It was hard. I stood there, jittering, with my finger on the doorbell, till I thought that ringing the bell would be easier than having the door open and being caught standing there like a fool."

"And she didn't kick you out?"

"No. She was sweet as she could be. Invited me in, knew who I was, said she was so glad I had come to visit. *You* know."

"And you suggested we go to Murphy's Park."

"Yes. I thought if I suggested something that would let the children have fun, it would be easier for her to go along with it. She wouldn't want to spoil a chance for her boy."

"A mother's psychology."

"But you should see her home."

"Ah. You had a reason for all this. It comes out. You wanted the Cook's tour. But, please, spare me the color-scheme details. I'm not interested in the bedspreads, and the size of the closets is a topic with which I can dispense."

It was the secret of their happy marriage that Lillian paid no attention to George. She went into the color-scheme details, was most meticulous about the bedspreads, and gave him an inch-by-inch description of closet-size.

"And *clean?* I have never seen any place so spotless."

"If you get to know her, then, she'll be setting you impossible standards and you'll have to drop her in self-defense."

"Her kitchen," said Lillian, ignoring him, "was so spanking clean you just couldn't believe she ever used it. I asked for a drink of water and she held the glass underneath the tap and poured slowly so that not one drop fell in the sink itself. It wasn't affectation. She did it so casually that I just knew she always did it that way. And when she gave me the glass she held it with a clean napkin. Just hospital-sanitary."

"She must be a lot of trouble to herself. Did she agree to come with us right off?"

"Well—not right off. She called to her husband about what the weather forecast was, and he said that the newspapers all said it would be fair tomorrow but that he was waiting for the latest report on the radio."

"*All* the newspapers said so, eh?"

"Of course, they all just print the official weather forecast, so they would all agree. But I think they do subscribe to all the newspapers. At least I've watched the bundle the newsboy leaves—"

"There isn't much you miss, is there?"

"Anyway," said Lillian severely, "she called up the weather bureau and had them tell her the latest and she called it out to her husband and they said they'd go, except they said they'd phone us if there were any unexpected changes in the weather."

"All right. Then we'll go."

The Sakkaros were young and pleasant, dark and handsome. In fact, as they came down the long walk from their home to where the Wright automobile was parked, George leaned toward his wife and breathed into her ear, "So *he's* the reason."

"I wish he were," said Lillian. "Is that a handbag he's carrying?"

"Pocket-radio. To listen to weather forecasts, I bet."

The Sakkaro boy came running after them, waving something which turned out to be an aneroid barometer, and all three got into the back seat. Conversation was turned on and lasted, with neat give-and-take on impersonal subjects, to Murphy's Park.

The Sakkaro boy was so polite and reasonable that even Tommie Wright, wedged between his parents in the front seat, was subdued by example into a semblance of civilization. Lillian couldn't recall when she had spent so serenely pleasant a drive.

She was not the least disturbed by the fact that, barely to be heard under the flow of the conversation, Mr. Sakkaro's small radio was on, and she never actually saw him put it occasionally to his ear.

It was a beautiful day at Murphy's Park; hot and dry without being too hot; and with a cheerfully bright sun in a blue, blue sky. Even Mr. Sakkaro, though he inspected every quarter of the heavens with a careful eye and then stared piercingly at the barometer, seemed to have no fault to find.

Lillian ushered the two boys to the amusement section and bought enough tickets to allow one ride for each on every variety of centrifugal thrill that the park offered.

"Please," she had said to a protesting Mrs. Sakkaro, "let this be my treat. I'll let you have your turn next time."

When she returned, George was alone. "Where—" she began.

"Just down there at the refreshment stand. I told them I'd wait here for you and we would join them." He sounded gloomy.

"Anything wrong?"

"No, not really, except that I think he must be independently wealthy."

"What?"

"I don't know what he does for a living. I hinted—"

"Now who's curious?"

"I was doing it for you. He said he's just a student of human nature."

"How philosophical. That would explain all those newspapers."

"Yes, but with a handsome, wealthy man next door, it looks as though I'll have impossible standards set for me, too."

"Don't be silly."

"And he doesn't come from Arizona."

"He doesn't?"

"I said I heard he was from Arizona. He looked so surprised, it was obvious he didn't. Then he laughed and asked if he had an Arizona accent."

Lillian said thoughtfully, "He has some kind of accent, you know. There are lots of Spanish-ancestry people in the Southwest, so he could still be from Arizona. Sakkaro could be a Spanish name."

"Sounds Japanese to me. —Come on, they're waving. Oh, good Lord, look what they've bought."

The Sakkaros were each holding three sticks of cotton candy, hugh swirls of pink foam consisting of threads of sugar dried out of frothy syrup that had been whipped about in a warm vessel. It melted sweetly in the mouth and left one feeling sticky.

The Sakkaros held one out to each Wright, and out of politeness the Wrights accepted.

They went down the midway, tried their hand at darts, at the kind of poker game where balls were rolled into holes, at knocking wooden cylinders off pedestals. They took pictures of themselves and recorded their voices and tested the strength of their hand-grips.

Eventually they collected the youngsters, who had been reduced to a satisfactorily breathless state of roiled-up insides, and the Sakkaros ushered theirs off instantly to the refreshment stand. Tommie hinted the extent of his pleasure at the possible purchase of a hot-dog and George tossed him a quarter. He ran off, too.

"Frankly," said George, "I prefer to stay here. If I see them biting away at another cotton candy stick I'll turn green and sicken on the spot. If they haven't had a dozen apieces, I'll eat a dozen myself."

"I know, and they're buying a handful for the child now."

"I offered to stand Sakkaro a humburger and he just looked grim and shook his head. Not that a hamburger's much, but after enough cotton candy, it ought to be a feast."

"I know. I offered her an orange drink and the way she jumped when she said no, you'd think I'd thrown it in her face. —Still, I suppose they've never been to a place like this before and they'll need time to adjust to the novelty. They'll fill up on cotton candy and then never eat it again for ten years."

"Well, maybe." They strolled toward the Sakkaros. "You know, Lil, it's clouding up."

Mr. Sakkaro had the radio to his ear and was looking anxiously toward the west.

"Uh-oh," said George, "he's seen it. One gets you fifty, he'll want to go home."

All three Sakkaros were upon him, polite but insistent. They were sorry, they had had a wonderful time, a marvelous time, the

Wrights would have to be their guests as soon as it could be managed, but now, really, they had to go home. It looked stormy. Mrs. Sakkaro wailed that all the forecasts had been for fair weather.

George tried to console them. "It's hard to predict a local thunderstorm, but even if it were to come, and it mightn't, it wouldn't last more than half an hour on the outside."

At which comment, the Sakkaro youngster seemed on the verge of tears, and Mrs. Sakkaro's hand, holding a handkerchief, trembled visibly.

"Let's go home," said George in resignation.

The drive back seemed to stretch interminably. There was no conversation to speak of. Mr. Sakkaro's radio was quite loud now as he switched from station to station, catching a weather report every time. They were mentioning "local thundershowers" now.

The Sakkaro youngster piped up that the barometer was falling, and Mrs. Sakkaro, chin in the palm of her hand, stared dolefully at the sky and asked if George could not drive faster, please.

"It does look rather threatening, doesn't it?" said Lillian in a polite attempt to share their guests' attitude. But then George heard her mutter, "Honestly!" under her breath.

A wind had sprung up, driving the dust of the weeks-dry road before it, when they entered the street on which they lived, and the leaves rustled ominously. Lightning flickered.

George said, "You'll be indoors in two minutes, friends. We'll make it."

He pulled up at the gate that opened onto the Sakkaro's spacious front yard and got out of the car to open the back door. He thought he felt a drop. They were *just* in time.

The Sakkaros tumbled out, faces drawn with tension, muttering thanks, and started off toward their long front walk at a dead run.

"Honestly," began Lillian, "you would think they were—"

The heavens opened and the rain came down in giant drops as though some celestial dam had suddenly burst. The top of their car was pounded with a hundred drum sticks, and halfway to their front door the Sakkaros stopped and looked despairingly upward.

Their faces blurred as the rain hit; blurred and shrank and ran together. All three shriveled, collapsing within their clothes, which sank down into three sticky-wet heaps.

And while the Wrights sat there, transfixed with horror, Lillian found herself unable to stop the completion of her remark: "—made of sugar and afraid they would melt."

———◆———

My book THE EARLY ASIMOV did sufficiently well for Doubleday to decide to do other, similar books by other writers who have been writing long enough to have had an early period of some worth. The next book in the series is THE EARLY DEL REY (Doubleday, 1975) by my good old friend Lester del Rey.

Lester doesn't have his book filled with autobiographical minutiae, as I do, but has meant his book to be a more sober device for describing his views on how to write science fiction.

I would cheerfully do the same except that I don't know how to write science fiction, or anything else. What I do, I do by blind instinct.

However, something does occasionally occur to me, and one little tiny rule comes up in connection with RAIN, RAIN, GO AWAY. If you're going to write a story, avoid contemporary references. They date a story and they have no staying power. The story mentions Schoendienst as having been at bat during a baseball game. Well, who the heck was Schoendienst? Do you remember? Does the name have meaning to you a decade and a half later?

And if it does, is there any point in reminding the reader that the story is a decade and a half old? —Of course, I spend pages telling you how old my stories are and everything else about them, but that's different. You're all friends of mine.

The drift to nonfiction continued. In the spring of 1959 Leon Svirsky of Basic Books, Inc., persuaded me to do a large book to be called THE INTELLIGENT MAN'S GUIDE TO SCIENCE, which was published in 1960. It was my first real success in the nonfiction field. It got numerous very favorable reviews, and my annual income suddenly doubled.

I wasn't doing it all primarily for money, you understand, but my family was growing and I wasn't going to throw money away, either. So there was again that much less urge to return to fiction.

Frederik Pohl, who had succeeded Horace Gold as editor of *Galaxy,* tried to lure a story out of me in March 1965 by sending me a cover painting he intended to run, and asked me to write a story about it. "You have the cover," he said, "so it will be easy."

No, it wasn't. I looked at the cover, which featured a large, sad, space-helmeted face, with several crude crosses in the background, and with a space helmet balanced on each cross. I could make nothing of it. I would have told Fred this, but he was an old friend, and I didn't want to break his heart with the knowledge that there was something I couldn't do. So I made a supreme effort and wrote the following, which appeared in the August 1965 *Galaxy*.

FOUNDING FATHER

The original combination of catastrophes had taken place five years ago—five revolutions of this planet, HC-12549d by the charts, and nameless otherwise. Six-plus revolutions of Earth, but who was counting—anymore?

If the men back home knew, they might say it was a heroic fight, an epic of the Galactic Corps; five men against a hostile world, holding their bitter own for five (or six-plus) years. And now they were dying, the battle lost after all. Three were in final coma, a fourth had his yellow-tinged eyeballs still open, and a fifth was yet on his feet.

But it was no question of heroism at all. It had been five men fighting off boredom and despair and maintaining their metallic bubble of livability only for the most unheroic reason that there was nothing else to do while life remained.

If any of them felt stimulated by the battle, he never mentioned it. After the first year they stopped talking of rescue, and after the second a moratorium descended on the word "Earth."

But one word remained always present. If unspoken it had to be found in their thoughts: "ammonia."

It had come first while the landing was being scratched out, against all odds, on limping motors and in a battered space can.

You allow for bad breaks, of course; you expect a certain number—but one at a time. A stellar flare fries out the hypercircuits—that can be repaired, given time. A meteorite disaligns the feeder valves—they can be straightened, given time. A trajectory is miscalculated under tension and a momentarily unbearable acceleration tears out the Jump-antennae and dulls the senses of every man on board—but antennae can be replaced and senses will recover, given time.

The chances are one in countless many that all three will happen at once; and still less that they will all happen during a particularly tricky landing when the one necessary currency for the correction of all errors, time, is the one thing that is most lacking.

The *Cruiser John* hit that one chance in countless many, and it made a final landing, for it would never lift off a planetary surface again.

That it had landed essentially intact was itself a near-miracle. The five were given life for some years at least. Beyond that, only the blundering arrival of another ship could help, but no one expected that. They had had their life's share of coincidences, they knew, and all had been bad.

That was that.

And the key word was "ammonia." With the surface spiraling upward, and death (mercifully quick) facing them at considerably better than even odds, Chou somehow had time to note the absorption spectrograph, which was registering raggedly.

"Ammonia," he cried out. The others heard but there was no time to pay attention. There was only the wrenching fight against a quick death for the sake of a slow one.

When they landed finally, on sandy ground with sparse bluish (bluish?) vegetation; reedy grass; stunted treelike objects with blue bark and no leaves; no sign of animal life; and with a greenish (greenish?) cloud-streaked sky above—the word came back to haunt them.

"Ammonia?" said Petersen heavily.

Chou said, "Four per cent."

"Impossible," said Petersen.

But it wasn't. The books didn't say impossible. What the Galactic Corps had discovered was that a planet of a certain mass and volume and at a certain temperature was an ocean planet and had one of two atmospheres: nitrogen/oxygen or nitrogen/carbon dioxide. In the former case, life was advanced; in the latter, it was primitive.

No one checked beyond mass, volume, and temperature any longer. One took the atmosphere (one or the other of them) for granted. But the books didn't say it had to be so; just that it always was so. Other atmospheres were thermodynamically possible, but extremely unlikely, so they weren't found in actual practice.

Until now. The men of the *Cruiser John* had found one and were bathed for the rest of such life as they could eke out by a nitrogen/carbon dioxide/ammonia atmosphere.

The men converted their ship into an underground bubble of Earth-type surroundings. They could not lift off the surface, nor could they drive a communicating beam through hyperspace, but all else was salvageable. To make up for inefficiencies in the cycling system, they could even tap the planet's own water and air supply, within limits; provided, of course, they subtracted the ammonia.

They organized exploring parties since their suits were in excellent condition and it passed the time. The planet was harmless; no animal life; sparse plant life everywhere. Blue, always blue; ammoniated chlorophyll; ammoniated protein.

They set up laboratories, analyzed the plant components, studied microscopic sections, compiled vast volumes of findings. They tried growing native plants in ammonia-free atmosphere and failed. They made themselves into geologists and studied the planet's crust; astronomers, and studied the spectrum of the planet's sun.

Barrère would say sometimes, "Eventually, the Corps will reach this planet again and we'll leave a legacy of knowledge for them. It's a unique planet after all. There might not be another Earth-type with ammonia in all the Milky Way."

"Great," said Sandropoulos bitterly. "What luck for us."

Sandropoulos worked out the thermodynamics of the situation. "A metastable system," he said. "The ammonia disappears steadily through geochemical oxidation that forms nitrogen; the plants utilize nitrogen and re-form ammonia, adapting themselves to the presence of ammonia. If the rate of plant formation of ammonia dropped two per cent, a declining spiral would set in. Plant life would wither, reducing the ammonia still further, and so on."

"You mean if we killed enough plant life," said Vlassov, "we could wipe out the ammonia."

"If we had air sleds and wide-angle blasters, and a year to work in, we might," said Sandropoulos, "but we haven't and there's a better way. If we could get our own plants going, the formation of oxygen through photosynthesis would increase the rate of ammonia oxidation. Even a small localized rise would lower the ammonia in the region, stimulate Earth-plant growth further and inhibit the native growth, drop the ammonia further, and so on."

They became gardeners through all the growing season. That was, after all, routine for the Galactic Corps. Life on Earth-type planets was usually of the water/protein type, but variation was infinite and other-world food was rarely nourishing and even more rarely palatable. One had to try Earth plants of different sorts. It often happened (not always, but often) that some types of Earth plants would overrun and drown out the native flora. With the native flora held down, other Earth plants could take root.

Dozens of planets had been converted into new Earths in this fashion. In the process Earthly plants developed hundreds of hardy varieties that flourished under extreme conditions. —All the better with which to seed the next planet.

The ammonia would kill any Earth plant, but the seeds at the disposal of the *Cruiser John* were not true Earth plants but other-world mutations of these plants. They fought hard but not well enough. Some varieties grew in a feeble, sickly manner and then died.

At that they did better than did microscopic life. The planet's bacterioids were far more flourishing than was the planet's straggly blue plant life. The native micro-organisms drowned out any attempt at competition from Earth samples. The attempt to seed the alien soil with Earth-type bacterial flora in order to aid the Earth plants failed.

Vlassov shook his head. "It wouldn't do anyway. If our bacteria survived, it would only be by adapting to the presence of ammonia."

Sandropoulos said, "Bacteria won't help us. We need the plants; they carry the oxygen-manufacturing systems."

"We could make some ourselves," said Petersen. "We could electrolyze water."

"How long will our equipment last? If we could only get our plants going, it would be like electrolyzing water forever, little by little, but year after year, till the planet gave up."

Barrère said, "Let's treat the soil then. It's rotten with ammonium salts. We'll bake the salts out and replace the ammonia-free soil."

"And what about the atmosphere?" asked Chou.

"In ammonia-free soil, they may catch hold despite the atmosphere. They almost make it as is."

They worked like longshoremen, but with no real end in view. None really thought it would work, and there was no future for themselves, personally, even if it did work. But working passed the days.

The next growing season, they had their ammonia-free soil, but Earth plants still grew only feebly. They even placed domes over several shoots and pumped ammonia-free air within. It helped slightly but not enough. They adjusted the chemical composition of the soil in every possible fashion. There was no reward.

The feeble shoots produced their tiny whiffs of oxygen, but not enough to topple the ammonia atmosphere off its narrow base.

"One more push," said Sandropoulos, "one more. We're rocking it; we're rocking it; but we can't knock it over."

Their tools and equipment blunted and wore out with time and the future closed in steadily. Each month there was less room for maneuver.

When the end came at last it was with almost gratifying suddenness. There was no name to place on the weakness and vertigo. No one actually suspected direct ammonia poisoning. Still, they were living off the algal growths of what had once been ship-hydroponics for years, and the growths were themselves aberrant with possible ammonia contamination.

It could have been the workings of some native micro-organism which might finally have learned to feed off them. It might even have been an Earthly micro-organism, mutated under the conditions of a strange world.

So three died at last, and did so, circumstances be praised, painlessly. They were glad to go, and leave the useless fight.

Chou said in a voiceless whisper, "It's foolish to lose so badly."

Petersen, alone of the five to be on his feet (was he immune, whatever it was?) turned a grieving face toward his only living companion. "Don't die," he said, "don't leave me alone."

Chou tried to smile. "I have no choice. —But you can follow us, old friend. Why fight? The tools are gone and there is no way of winning now, if there ever was."

Even now, Petersen fought off final despair by concentrating on the fight against the atmosphere. But his mind was weary, his heart worn-out, and when Chou died the next hour he was left with four corpses to work with.

He stared at the bodies, counting over the memories, stretching them back (now that he was alone and dared wail) to Earth itself, which he had last seen on a visit nearly eleven years before.

He would have to bury the bodies. He would break off the bluish branches of the native leafless trees and build crosses of them. He would hang the space helmet of each man on top and prop the oxygen cylinders below. Empty cylinders to symbolize the lost fight.

A foolish sentiment for men who could no longer care, and for future eyes that might never see.

But he was doing it for himself, to show respect for his friends, and respect for himself, too, for he was not the kind of man to leave his friends untended in death while he himself could stand.

Besides—

Besides? He sat in weary thought for some moments.

While he was still alive he would fight with such tools as were left. He would bury his friends.

He buried each in a spot of ammonia-free soil they had so laboriously built up; buried them without shroud and without clothing; leaving them naked in the hostile ground for the slow decomposition that would come with their own micro-organisms before those, too, died with the inevitable invasion of the native bacterioids.

Petersen placed each cross, with its helmet and oxygen cylinders, propped each with rocks, then turned away, grim and sad-eyed, to return to the buried ship that he now inhabited alone.

He worked each day and eventually the symptoms came for him, too.

He struggled into his spacesuit and came to the surface for what he knew would be one last time.

He fell to his knees on the garden plots. The Earth plants were green. They had lived longer than ever before. They looked healthy, even vigorous.

They had patched the soil, babied the atmosphere, and now Petersen had used the last tool, the only one remaining at his disposal, and he had given them fertilizer as well—

Out of the slowly corrupting flesh of the Earthmen came the nutrients that supplied the final push. Out of the Earth plants came the oxygen that would beat back the ammonia and push the planet out of the unaccountable niche into which it had stuck.

If Earthmen ever came again (when? a million years hence?) they would find a nitrogen/oxygen atmosphere and a limited flora strangely reminiscent of Earth's.

The crosses would rot and decay; the metal, rust and decompose. The bones might fossilize and remain to give a hint as to what happened. Their own records, sealed away, might be found.

But none of that mattered. If nothing at all was ever found, the planet itself, the whole planet, would be their monument.

And Petersen lay down to die amid their victory.

———◆———

Fred Pohl changes titles more frequently than most editors do, and in some cases drove me to distraction by doing so. In this case, though, my own title was *The Last Tool,* and once again the editorial change was for the better, so I kept FOUNDING FATHER. (I hate when Fred changes me for the better, but he won't stop.)

By 1967 it had been ten years since I had switched to nonfiction, and ten years since I had sold anything to John Campbell.

John was just rounding out his third decade as editor of *Astounding.* As the 1960s opened, however, he changed its name to *Analog,* and I had never had any fiction in the magazine in its new incarnation.

So I wrote EXILE TO HELL and sent it in to John. He took it, thank goodness, and it was a great pleasure to appear in the pages of the magazine again, in the May 1968 issue, even if it was just a short-short.

EXILE TO HELL

"The Russians," said Dowling, in his precise voice, "used to send prisoners to Siberia in the days before space travel had become common. The French used Devil's Island for the purpose. The British sailed them off to Australia."

He considered the chessboard carefully and his hand hesitated briefly over the bishop.

Parkinson, at the other side of the chess board, watched the pattern of the pieces absently. Chess was, of course, the professional game of computer programmers, but, under the circumstances, he lacked enthusiasm. By rights, he felt with some annoyance, Dowling should have been even worse off; he was programming the prosecution's case.

There was, of course, a tendency for the programmer to take over some of the imagined characteristics of the computer—the unemotionality, the imperviousness to anything but logic. Dowling reflected that in his precise hair-part and in the restrained elegance of his clothing.

Parkinson, who preferred to program the defense in the law cases in which he was involved, also preferred to be deliberately careless in the minor aspects of his costume.

He said, "You mean exile is a well-established punishment and therefore not particularly cruel."

"No, it *is* particularly cruel, but also it *is* well-established, and nowadays it has become the perfect deterrent."

Dowling moved the bishop and did not look upward. Parkinson, quite involuntarily, did.

Of course, he couldn't see anything. They were indoors, in the comfortable modern world tailored to human needs, carefully protected against the raw environment. Out there, the night would be bright with its illumination.

When had he last seen it? Not for a long time. It occurred to him to wonder what phase it was in right now. Full? Gleaming? Or was it in its crescent phase? Was it a bright fingernail of light low in the sky?

By rights it should be a lovely sight. Once it had been. But that had been centuries ago, before space travel had become common and cheap, and before the surroundings all about them had grown sophisticated and controlled. Now the lovely light in the sky had become a new and more horrible Devil's Island hung in space.

—No one even used its name any longer, out of sheer distaste. It was "It." Or it was less than that, just a silent, upward movement of the head.

Parkinson said, "You might have allowed me to program the case against exile generally."

"Why? It couldn't have affected the result."

"Not this one, Dowling. But it might have affected future cases. Future punishments might be commuted to the death sentence."

"For someone guilty of equipment damage? You're dreaming."

"It was an act of blind anger. There was intent to harm a human being, granted; but there was no intent to harm equipment."

"Nothing; it means nothing. Lack of intent is no excuse in such cases. You know that."

"It *should* be an excuse. That's my point; the one I wanted to make."

Parkinson advanced a pawn now, to cover his knight.

Dowling considered. "You're trying to hang on to the queen's attack, Parkinson, and I'm not going to let you. —Let's see, now." And while he pondered he said, "These are not primitive times, Parkinson. We live in a crowded world with no margin for error. As small a thing as a blown-out consistor could endanger a sizable fraction of our population. When anger endangers and subverts a power line, it's a serious thing."

"I don't question that—"

"You seemed to be doing so, when you were constructing the defense program."

"I was not. Look, when Jenkins' laser beam cut through the Field-warp, I myself was as close to death as anyone. A quarter hour's additional delay would have meant my end, too, and I'm completely aware of that. My point is only that exile is not the proper punishment!"

He tapped his finger on the chessboard for emphasis, and Dowling caught the queen before it went over. "Adjusting, not moving," he mumbled.

Dowling's eyes went from piece to piece and he continued to hesitate. "You're wrong, Parkinson. It *is* the proper punishment, because there's nothing worse and that matches a crime than which there is nothing worse. Look, we all feel our absolute dependence on a complicated and rather fragile technology. A breakdown might kill us all, and it doesn't matter whether the breakdown is deliberate, accidental, or caused by incompetence. Human beings demand the maximum punishment for any such deed as the only way they can feel secure. Mere death is not sufficient deterrent."

"Yes, it is. No one wants to die."

"They want to live in exile up there even less. That's why we've only had one such case in the last ten years, and only one exile. — There, do something about that!" And Dowling nudged his queen's rook one space to the right.

A light flashed. Parkinson was on his feet at once. "The programming is finished. The computer will have its verdict now."

Dowling looked up phlegmatically, "You've no doubt about what that verdict will be, have you? —Keep the board standing. We'll finish afterward."

Parkinson was quite certain he would lack the heart to continue the game. He hurried down the corridor to the courtroom, light and quick on his feet, as always.

Shortly after he and Dowling had entered, the judge took his seat, and then in came Jenkins, flanked by two guards.

Jenkins looked haggard, but stoical. Ever since the blind rage had overcome him and he had accidentally thrown a sector into unpowered darkness while striking out at a fellow worker, he must have known the inevitable consequence of this worst of all crimes. It helps to have no illusions.

Parkinson was not stoical. He dared not look squarely at Jenkins. He could not have done so without wondering, painfully, as to what might be going through Jenkins' mind at that moment. Was he absorbing, through every sense, all the perfections of familiar comfort before being thrust forever into the luminous Hell that rode the night sky?

Was he savoring the clean and pleasant air in his nostrils, the soft lights, the equable temperature, the pure water on call, the secure surroundings designed to cradle humanity in tame comfort?

While up there—

The judge pressed a contact and the computer's decision was converted into the warm, unmannered sound of a standardized human voice.

"A weighing of all pertinent information in the light of the law of the land and of all relevant precedents leads to the conclusion that Anthony Jenkins is guilty on all counts of the crime of equipment damage and is subject to the maximum penalty."

There were only six people in the courtroom itself, but the entire population was listening by television, of course.

The judge spoke in prescribed phraseology. "The defendant will be taken from here to the nearest spaceport and, on the first available transportation, be removed from this world and sent into exile for the term of his natural life."

Jenkins seemed to shrink within himself, but he said no word.

Parkinson shivered. How many, he wondered, would now feel the enormity of such a punishment for *any* crime? How long before there would be enough humanity among men to wipe out forever the punishment of exile?

Could anyone really think of Jenkins up there in space, without flinching? Could they think, and endure the thought, of a fellow man thrown for all his life among the strange, unfriendly, vicious population of a world of unbearable heat by day and frigid cold by night; of a world where the sky was a harsh blue and the ground a harsher, clashing green; where the dusty air moved raucously and the viscous sea heaved eternally?

And the gravity, that heavy—heavy—heavy—eternal—pull!

Who could bear the horror of condemning someone, for whatever reason, to leave the friendly home of the Moon for that Hell in the sky—the Earth?

Considering what John Campbell means to me, I hate to point out any editorial bad points he had—but he was a terrible blurb writer. In those little editorial comments at the beginning of a story, comments that are supposed to lure you into reading it, he all too often gave away the point of the story, when the writer was doing his best to conceal the point till the proper moment.

Here is John's blurb for EXILE TO HELL: "Hell is, of course, the worst imaginable place you least want to be forced to experience.

It's an attitude about a place—Fiji for an Eskimo, Baffin Island for a Polynesian. . . ." If you read the blurb first and *then* read my story, EXILE TO HELL will have the impact of a strand of wet spaghetti.

As the drought of science fiction intensified, it became important to me not to allow any item to go to waste.

A friend of mine, Ed Berkeley, ran a little periodical devoted to computers and automation. (It was even called *COMPUTERS AND AUTOMATION,* as I recall.) In 1959 he asked me to do a little story for him, for friendship's sake, and since I always have trouble fighting off anything put to me in that fashion, I wrote KEY ITEM for him and he paid me a dollar for it. —But then he never printed it.

Eight years passed and I finally said to him, "Hey, Ed, what happened to my story KEY ITEM?" and he told me he had decided not to publish science fiction.

"Give it back, then," I said, and he said, "Oh, can you use it?"

Yes, I could use it. I sent it in to *F & SF* and they took it and ran it in the July 1968 issue of that magazine.

KEY ITEM

Jack Weaver came out of the vitals of Multivac looking utterly worn and disgusted.

From the stool, where the other maintained his own stolid watch, Todd Nemerson said, "Nothing?"

"Nothing," said Weaver. "Nothing, nothing, nothing. No one can find anything wrong with it."

"Except that it won't work, you mean."

"You're no help sitting there!"

"I'm thinking."

"Thinking!" Weaver showed a canine at one side of his mouth.

Nemerson stirred impatiently on his stool. "Why not? There are six teams of computer technologists roaming around in the corridors of Multivac. They haven't come up with anything in three days. Can't you spare one person to think?"

"It's not a matter of thinking. We've got to look. Somewhere a relay is stuck."

"It's not that simple, Jack!"

"Who says it's simple. You know how many million relays we have there?"

"That doesn't matter. If it were just a relay, Multivac would have alternate circuits, devices for locating the flaw, and facilities to repair or replace the ailing part. The trouble is, Multivac won't only not answer the original question, it won't tell us what's wrong with it. —And meanwhile, there'll be panic in every city if we don't do something. The world's economy depends on Multivac, and everyone knows that."

"I know it, too. But what's there to do?"

"I told you, *think*. There must be something we're missing completely. Look, Jack, there isn't a computer bigwig in a hundred years who hasn't devoted himself to making Multivac more complicated. It can do so much now—hell, it can even talk and listen. It's practically as complex as the human brain. We can't understand the human brain, so why should we understand Multivac?"

"Aw, come on. Next you'll be saying Multivac is human."

"Why not?" Nemerson grew absorbed and seemed to sink into himself. "Now that you mention it, why not? Could we tell if Multivac passed the thin dividing line where it stopped being a machine and started being human? *Is* there a dividing line, for that matter? If the brain is just more complex than Multivac, and we keep making Multivac more complex, isn't there a point where . . ." He mumbled down into silence.

Weaver said impatiently, "What are you driving at? Suppose Multivac were human. How would that help us find out why it isn't working?"

"For a human reason, maybe. Suppose *you* were asked the most probable price of wheat next summer and didn't answer. Why wouldn't you answer?"

"Because I wouldn't know. But Multivac would know! We've given it all the factors. It can analyze futures in weather, politics, and economics. We know it can. It's done it before."

"All right. Suppose I asked the question and you knew the answer but didn't tell me. Why not?"

Weaver snarled, "Because I had a brain tumor. Because I had been knocked out. Because I was drunk. Damn it, because my machinery was out of order. That's just what we're trying to find out about Multivac. We're looking for the place where its machinery is out of order, for the key item."

"Only you haven't found it." Nemerson got off his stool. "Listen, ask me the question Multivac stalled on."

"How? Shall I run the tape through you?"

"Come on, Jack. Give me the talk that goes along with it. You do talk to Multivac, don't you?"

"I've got to. Therapy."

Nemerson nodded. "Yes, that's the story. Therapy. That's the official story. We talk to it in order to pretend it's a human being so that we don't get neurotic over having a machine know so much more than we do. We turn a frightening metal monster into a protective father image."

"If you want to put it that way."

Well, it's wrong and you know it. A computer as complex as Multivac *must* talk and listen to be efficient. Just putting in and taking out coded dots isn't sufficient. At a certain level of complexity, Multivac must be made to seem human because, by God, it *is* human. Come on, Jack, ask me the question. I want to see my reaction to it."

Jack Weaver flushed. "This is silly."

"Come on, will you?"

It was a measure of Weaver's depression and desperation that he acceded. Half sullenly, he pretended to be feeding the program into Multivac, speaking as he did so in his usual manner. He commented on the latest information concerning farm unrest, talked about the new equations describing jet-stream contortions, lectured on the solar constant.

He began stiffly enough, but warmed to this task out of long habit, and when the last of the program was slammed home, he almost closed contact with a physical snap at Todd Nemerson's waist.

He ended briskly, "All right, now. Work that out and give us the answer pronto."

For a moment, having done, Jack Weaver stood there, nostrils flaring, as though he was feeling once more the excitement of throwing into action the most gigantic and glorious machine ever put together by the mind and hands of man.

Then he remembered and muttered, "All right. That's it."

Nemerson said, "At least I know now why *I* wouldn't answer, so let's try that on Multivac. Look, clear Multivac; make sure the investigators have their paws off it. Then run the program into it and let me do the talking. Just once."

Weaver shrugged and turned to Multivac's control wall, filled with its somber, unwinking dials and lights. Slowly he cleared it. One by one he ordered the teams away.

Then, with a deep breath, he began once more feeding the program into Multivac. It was the twelfth time all told, the dozenth time. Somewhere a distant news commentator would spread the word that they were trying again. All over the world a Multivac-dependent people would be holding its collective breath.

Nemerson talked as Weaver fed the data silently. He talked diffidently, trying to remember what it was that Weaver had said, but waiting for the moment when the key item might be added.

Weaver was done and now a note of tension was in Nemerson's voice. He said, "All right, now, Multivac. Work that out and give us the answer." He paused and added the key item. He said *"Please!"*

And all over Multivac, the valves and relays went joyously to work. After all, a machine has feelings—when it isn't a machine anymore.

The story didn't stop at *F & SF,* by the way.

The Saturday Evening Post had died in 1966, shortly after serializing my novel FANTASTIC VOYAGE (Houghton Mifflin, 1966), though I don't think there was any connection. It came back to life, however, and its editors were interested in some of my stories. They reprinted A STATUE FOR FATHER, and they also did KEY ITEM, under the title *The Computer That Went On Strike,* in their spring 1972 issue.

The slick magazines were interested in science fiction now. It was not only *The Saturday Evening Post* that was after me for stories. *Boys' Life* was, too. They sent me a painting hoping it would inspire a story, and I tried. I turned out THE PROPER STUDY, which appeared in the September 1968 issue of *Boys' Life.*

THE PROPER STUDY

"The demonstration is ready," said Oscar Harding softly, half to himself, when the phone rang to say that the general was on his way upstairs.

Ben Fife, Harding's young associate, pushed his fists deep into the pockets of his laboratory jacket. "We won't get anywhere," he said. "The general doesn't change his mind." He looked sideways at the older man's sharp profile, his pinched cheeks, his thinning gray hair. Harding might be a wizard with electronic equipment, but he couldn't seem to grasp the kind of man the general was.

And Harding said mildly, "Oh, you can never tell."

The general knocked once on the door, but it was for show only. He walked in quickly, without waiting for a response. Two soldiers took up their position in the corridor, one on each side of the door. They faced outward, rifles ready.

General Gruenwald said crisply, "Professor Harding!" He nodded briefly in Fife's direction and then, for a moment, studied the remaining individual in the room. That was a blank-faced man who sat apart in a straight-backed chair, half-obscured by surrounding equipment.

Everything about the general was crisp; his walk, the way he held his spine, the way he spoke. He was all straight lines and angles, adhering rigidly at all points to the etiquette of the born soldier.

"Won't you sit down, General," murmured Harding. "Thank you. It's good of you to come; I've been trying to see you for some time. I appreciate the fact you're a busy man."

"Since I am busy," said the general, "let us get to the point."

"As near the point as I can, sir. I assume you know about our project here. You know about the Neurophotoscope."

"Your top-secret project? Of course. My scientific aides keep me abreast of it as best they can. I won't object to some further clarification. What is it you want?"

The suddenness of the question made Harding blink. Then he

said, "To be brief—declassification. I want the world to know that—"

"Why do you want them to know anything?"

"Neurophotoscopy is an important problem, sir, and enormously complex. I would like all scientists of all nationalities working on it."

"No, no. That's been gone over many times. The discovery is ours and we keep it."

"It will remain a very small discovery if it remains ours. Let me explain once more."

The general looked at his watch. "It will be quite useless."

"I have a new subject. A new demonstration. As long as you've come here at all, General, won't you listen for just a little while? I'll omit scientific detail as much as possible and say only that the varying electric potentials of brain cells can be recorded as tiny, irregular waves."

"Electroencephalograms. Yes, I know. We've had them for a century. And I know what you do with it."

"Uh—yes." Harding grew more earnest. "The brain waves by themselves carry their information too compactly. They give us the whole complex of changes from a hundred billion brain cells at once. My discovery was of a practical method for converting them to colored patterns."

"With your Neurophotoscope," said the general, pointing. "You see, I recognize the machine." Every campaign ribbon and medal on his chest lay in its proper place to within the millimeter.

"Yes. The 'scope produces color effects, real images that seem to fill the air and change very rapidly. They can be photographed and they're beautiful."

"I have seen photographs," the general said coldly.

"Have you seen the real thing, in action?"

"Once or twice. You were there at the time."

"Oh, yes." The professor was disconcerted. He said, "But you haven't seen this man; our new subject." He pointed briefly to the man in the chair, a man with a sharp chin, a long nose, no sign of hair on his skull, and still that vacant look in his eye.

"Who is he?" asked the general.

"The only name we use for him is Steve. He is mentally retarded but produces the most intense patterns we have yet found. Why this should be we don't know. Whether it has something to do with his mental—"

"Do you intend to show me what he does?" broke in the general.

"If you will watch, General." Harding nodded at Fife, who went into action at once.

The subject, as always, watched Fife with mild interest, doing as he was told and making no resistance. The light plastic helmet fitted snugly over his shaved cranium and each of the complicated electrodes was adjusted properly. Fife tried to work smoothly under the unusual tension of the occasion. He was in agony lest the general look at his watch again, and leave.

He stepped away, panting. "Shall I activate it now, Professor Harding?"

"Yes. Now."

Fife closed a contact gently and at once the air above Steve's head seemed filled with brightening color. Circles appeared and circles within circles, turning, whirling, and splitting apart.

Fife felt a clear sensation of uneasiness but pushed it away impatiently. That was the subject's emotion—Steve's—not his own. The general must have felt it too, for he shifted in his chair and cleared his throat loudly.

Harding said casually, "The patterns contain no more information than the brain waves, really, but are much more easily studied and analyzed. It is like putting germs under a strong microscope. Nothing new is added, but what is there can be seen more easily."

Steve was growing steadily more uneasy. Fife could sense it was the harsh and unsympathetic presence of the general that was the cause. Although Steve did not change his position or give any outward sign of fear, the colors in the patterns his mind created grew harsher, and within the outer circles there were clashing interlocks.

The general raised his hand as though to push the flickering lights away. He said, "What about all this, Professor?"

"With Steve, we can jump ahead even faster than we have been. Already we have learned more in the two years since I devised the first 'scope than in the fifty years before that. With Steve, and with others like him, perhaps, and with the help of the scientists of the world—"

"I have been told you can use this to reach minds," said the general sharply.

"Reach minds?" Harding thought a moment. "You mean telepathy? That's quite exaggerated. Minds are too different for that.

The fine details of your way of thinking are not like mine or like anyone else's, and raw brain patterns won't match. We have to translate thoughts into words, a much cruder form of communication, and even then it is hard enough for human beings to make contact."

"I don't mean telepathy! I mean emotion! If the subject feels anger, the receiver can be made to experience anger. Right?"

"In a manner of speaking."

The general was clearly agitated. "Those things—right there—" His finger jabbed toward the patterns, which were whirling most unpleasantly now. "They can be used for emotion control. With these, broadcast on television, whole populations can be emotionally manipulated. Can we allow such power to fall into the wrong hands?"

"If it were such power," said Harding mildly, "there would be no right hands."

Fife frowned. That was a dangerous remark. Every once in a while Harding seemed to forget that the old days of democracy were gone.

But the general let it go. He said, "I didn't know you had this thing so far advanced. I didn't know you had this—Steve. You get others like that. Meanwhile, the army is taking this over. *Completely!*"

"Wait, General, just ten seconds." Harding turned to Fife. "Give Steve his book, will you, Ben?"

Fife did so with alacrity. The book was one of the new Kaleido-volumes that told their stories by means of colored photographs that slowly twisted and changed once the book was opened. It was a kind of animated cartoon in hard-covers and Steve smiled as he reached out eagerly for it.

Almost at once the colored patterns that clustered above his plastic helmet changed in nature. They slowed their turning and the colors softened. The patterns within the circle grew less discordant.

Fife sighed his relief and let warmth and relaxation sweep over him.

Harding said, "General, don't let the possibility of emotion control alarm you. The 'scope offers less possibility for that than you think. Surely there are men whose emotions can be manipulated, but the 'scope isn't necessary for them. They react mindlessly to catch words, music, uniforms, almost anything. Hitler once con-

trolled Germany without even television, and Napoleon controlled
France without even radio or mass-circulation newspapers. The
'scope offers nothing new."

"I don't believe that," muttered the general, but he had grown
thoughtful again.

Steve stared earnestly at the Kaleido-volume, and the patterns
over his head had almost stilled into warmly colored and intricately
detailed circles that pulsed their pleasure.

Harding's voice was almost coaxing. "There are always the people who resist conformity; who don't go along; and they are the
important ones of society. They won't go along with colored patterns
any more than with any other form of persuasion. So why worry
about the useless bogey of emotion control? Let us instead see the
Neurophotoscope as the first instrument through which mental func-
tion can be truly analyzed. That's what should concern us above all.
The proper study of mankind is man, as Alexander Pope once said,
and what is man but his brain?"

The general remained silent.

"If we can solve the manner of the brain's workings," went on
Harding, "and learn at last what makes a man a man, we are on
our way to understanding ourselves, and nothing more difficult—
or more worthwhile—faces us. And how can this be done by just
one man, by one laboratory? How can it be done in secrecy and
fear? The whole world of science must cooperate. —General, de-
classify the project! Throw it open to all men!"

Slowly the general nodded. "I think you're right after all."

"I have the proper document. If you'll sign it and key it with
your fingerprint; if you use your two guards outside as witnesses;
if you alert the Executive Board by closed video; if you—"

It was all done. Before Fife's astonished eyes it was all done.

When the general was gone, the Neurophotoscope dismantled,
and Steve taken back to his quarters, Fife finally overcame his
amazement long enough to speak.

"How could he have been persuaded so easily, Professor Harding? You've explained your point of view at length in a dozen
reports and it never helped a bit."

"I've never presented it in this room, with the Neurophotoscope
working," said Harding. "I've never had anyone as intensely pro-
jective as Steve before. Many people can withstand emotion con-

trol, as I said, but some people cannot withstand it. Those who have a tendency to conform are easily led to agree with others. I took the gamble that any man who feels comfortable in uniform and who lives by the military book is liable to be swayed, no matter how powerful he imagines himself to be."

"You mean—Steve—"

"Of course, I let the general feel the uneasiness first, then you handed Steve the Kaleido-volume and the air filled with happiness. You felt it, didn't you?"

"Yes. Certainly."

"It was my guess the general couldn't resist that happiness so suddenly following the unease, and he didn't. Anything would have sounded good at that moment."

"But he'll get over it, won't he?"

"Eventually, I suppose, but so what? The key progress reports concerning Neurophotoscopy are being sent out right now to news media all over the world. The general might suppress it here in this country, but surely not elsewhere. —No, he will have to make the best of it. Mankind can begin its proper study in earnest, at last."

———————◆———————

The painting was simply a crudely done head surrounded by a series of aimless psychedelic designs. It meant nothing to me and I had a terrible time thinking up THE PROPER STUDY. Poul Anderson also wrote a story based on the same painting and probably had no trouble at all.

The two stories appeared in the same issue and I suppose it might be interesting to compare the stories and try to get an idea of the different workings of Poul's brain and mine—but, as in the case of BLANK!, I didn't save the other story. Besides, I don't want you to compare brains. Poul is awfully bright and you might come to me with some hard truths I'd rather not face.

In early 1970 *IBM Magazine* came to me with a quote from J. B. Priestley which went as follows: "Between midnight and dawn, when sleep will not come and all the old wounds begin to ache, I often have a nightmare vision of a future world in which there are billions of people, all numbered and registered, with not a gleam of genius anywhere, not an original mind, a rich personality, on the whole packed globe."

The editor of the magazine asked me to write a story based on the quote, and I did the job in late April and mailed it in. The story was 2430 A.D., and in it I took Priestley's quotation seriously and tried to describe the world of his nightmares.

And *IBM Magazine* sent it back. They said they didn't want a story that backed the quotation; they wanted one that refuted the quotation. Well, they had never *said* so.

Under ordinary circumstances I might have been very indignant and might have written a rather scathing letter. However, these were hard times for me and there was another turning point, and a very sad one, coming up in my life.

My marriage had been limping for some years and it finally broke down. On July 3, 1970, with our twenty-eighth anniversary nearly upon us, I moved out and went to New York. I took a two-room hotel suite that I was to use as an office for nearly five years.

You can't make a change like that without all kinds of worries, miseries, and guilts. And among them all, I being what I am, one of my worries, as I sat in the two rooms in a strange environment, with my reference library still undelivered,* was whether I would still be able to write.

I remembered my story 2430 A.D., which ordinarily I might have abandoned in indignation. Now, just to see if I could do it, I began another story, on July 8, 1970, five days after my move, one which would refute Priestley's quotation. I called it THE GREATEST ASSET.

I sent it to *IBM Magazine,* and you'll never believe me but after reading my second story they decided to take my first one after all. It was utterly confusing. Was my second story so bad that it made the first look good? Or had they changed their mind before I had written the second story and had they not gotten round to telling me? I suspect the latter. Anyway, 2430 A.D. was published in the October 1970 issue of *IBM Magazine*.

* As long as I was a fiction writer I needed very little in the way of a library and could write anywhere. One of the less pleasant aspects of my switch to nonfiction was that I gradually built up an enormous reference library which nails me to the ground.

2430 A.D.

Between midnight and dawn, when sleep will not come and all the old wounds begin to ache, I often have a nightmare vision of a future world in which there are billions of people, all numbered and registered, with not a gleam of genius anywhere, not an original mind, a rich personality, on the whole packed globe.

—J. B. Priestley

"He'll talk to us," said Alvarez when the other stepped out the door.

"Good," said Bunting. "Social pressure is bound to get to him eventually. An odd character. How he escaped genetic adjustment I'll never know. —But *you* do the talking. He irritates me past tact."

Together they swung down the corridor along the Executive Trail, which was, as always, sparsely occupied. They might have taken the Moving Strips, but there were only two miles to go and Alvarez enjoyed walking, so Bunting didn't insist.

Alvarez was tall and rather thin, with the kind of athletic figure one would expect of a person who cherished the muscular activities; who routinely used the stairs and rampways, for instance, almost to the edge of being considered an unsettling character himself. Bunting, softer and rounder, avoided even the sunlamps, and was quite pale.

Bunting said dolefully, "I hope the two of us will be enough."

"I should think so. We want to keep it in our sector, if we can."

"Yes! You know, I keep thinking—why does it have to be *our* sector? Fifty million square miles of seven-hundred-level living space, and it has to be in our apartment bloc."

"Rather a distinction, in a grisly kind of way," said Alvarez.

Bunting snorted.

"And a little to our credit," Alvarez added softly, "if we settle the matter. We reach peak. We reach end. We reach goal. All mankind. And *we* do it."

Bunting brightened. He said, "You think they'll look at it that way?"

"Let's see to it that they do."

Their footsteps were muted against the plastic-knit crushed rock underfoot. They passed crosscorridors and saw the endless crowds on the Moving Strips in the middle distance. There was a fugitive whiff of plankton in its varieties. Once, almost by instinct, they could tell that up above, far above, was one of the giant conduits leading in from the sea. And by symmetry they knew there would be another conduit, just as large, far below, leading out to sea.

Their destination was a dwelling room set well back from the corridor, but one that seemed different from the thousands they had passed. There was about it an intangible and disconcerting note of space, for on either side, for hundreds of feet, the wall was blank. And there was something in the air.

"Smell it?" muttered Bunting.

"I've smelled it before," said Alvarez. "Inhuman."

"Literally!" said Bunting. "He won't expect us to look at them, will he?"

"If he does, it's easy enough to refuse."

They signaled, then waited in silence while the hum of infinite life sounded all around them in utterly disregarded manner, for it was always there.

The door opened. Cranwitz was waiting. He looked sullen. He wore the same clothes they all did; light, simple, gray. On him, though, they seemed rumpled. *He* seemed rumpled, his hair too long, his eyes bloodshot and shifting uneasily.

"May we enter?" asked Alvarez with cold courtesy.

Cranwitz stood to one side.

The odor was stronger inside. Cranwitz closed the door behind them and they sat down. Cranwitz remained standing and said nothing.

Alvarez said, "I must ask you, in my capacity as Sector Representative, with Bunting here as Vice-Representative, whether you are now ready to comply with social necessity."

Cranwitz seemed to be thinking. When he finally spoke his deep voice was choked and he had to clear his throat. "I don't want to," he said. "I don't have to. There is a contract with the government of long-standing. My family has always had the right—"

"We know all this and there's no question of force involved," said Bunting irritably. "We're asking you to accede voluntarily."

Alvarez touched the other's knee lightly. "You understand the situation is not what it was in your father's time; or even, really, what it was last year?"

Cranwitz's long jaw quivered slightly. "I don't see that. The birth rate has dropped this year by the amount computerized, and everything else has changed correspondingly. That goes on from year to year. Why should this year be different?"

His voice somehow did not carry conviction. Alvarez was sure he *did* know why this year was different, and he said softly, "This year we've reached the goal. The birth rate now exactly matches the death rate; the population level is now exactly steady; construction is now confined to replacement entirely; and the sea farms are in a steady state. Only you stand between all mankind and perfection."

"Because of a few mice?"

"Because of a few mice. And other creatures. Guinea pigs. Rabbits. Some kinds of birds and lizards. I haven't taken a census—"

"But they're the only ones left in all the world. What harm do they do?"

"What good?" demanded Bunting.

Cranwitz said, "The good of being there to look at. There was once a time when—"

Alvarez had heard that before. He said, with as much sympathy as he could pump into his voice (and, to his surprise, with a certain amount of real sympathy, too), "I know. There was once a time! Centuries ago! There were vast numbers of life forms like those you care for. And millions of years before that there were dinosaurs. But we have microfilms of *everything*. No man need go ignorant of them."

"How can you compare microfilms with the real thing?" asked Cranwitz.

Bunting's lips quirked. "The microfilms don't smell."

"The zoo was much larger once," said Cranwitz. "Year by year we've had to get rid of so many. All the large animals. All the carnivores. The trees. There's nothing left but small plants, tiny creatures. Let them be."

Alvarez said, "What is there to do with them? No one wants to see them. Mankind is against you."

"Social pressure—"

"We couldn't persuade people against real resistance. People don't want to see these life distortions. They're sickening; they really are. What's there to do with them?" Alvarez's voice was insinuating.

Cranwitz sat down now. A certain feverishness heightened the color in his cheeks. "I've been thinking. Someday we'll reach out. Mankind will colonize other worlds. He'll want animals. He'll want other species in these new, empty worlds. He'll start a new ecology of variety. He'll . . ."

His words faded under the hostile stare of the other two.

Bunting said, "What other worlds are we going to colonize?"

"We reached the moon in 1969," said Cranwitz.

"Sure, and we established a colony, and we abandoned it. There's no world in all the solar system capable of supporting human life without prohibitive engineering."

Cranwitz said, "There are worlds circling other stars. Earthlike worlds by the hundred of millions. There must be."

Alvarez shook his head. "Out of reach. We have finally exploited Earth and filled it with the human species. We have made our choice, and it is Earth. There is no margin for the kind of effort needed to build a starship capable of crossing light-years of space. —Have you been immersing yourself in twentieth-century history?"

"It was the last century of the open world," said Cranwitz.

"So it was," said Alvarez dryly. "I hope you haven't over-romanticized it. I've studied its madness, too. The world was empty then, only a few billions, and they thought it was crowded—and with good reason. They spent more than half their substance on war and preparations of war, ran their economy without forethought, wasted and poisoned at will, let pure chance govern the genetic pool, and tolerated the deviants-from-norm of all descriptions. Of course, they dreaded what they called the population explosion, and dreamed of reaching other worlds as a kind of escape. So would we under those conditions.

"I needn't tell you the combination of events and of scientific advances that changed everything, but just let me remind you briefly in case you are trying to forget. There was the establishment of a world government, the development of fusion power, and the growth of the art of genetic engineering. With planetary peace, plentiful energy, and a placid humanity men could multiply peacefully, and science kept up with the multiplication.

"It was known in advance exactly how many men the Earth could support. So many calories of sunlight reached the Earth, and, using that, only so many tons of carbon dioxide could be fixed by green plants each year, and only so many tons of animal life could be supported by those plants. The Earth could support two trillion tons of animal life—"

Cranwitz finally broke in, "And why shouldn't all two trillion tons be human?"

"Exactly."

"Even if it meant killing off all other animal life?"

"That's the way of evolution," said Bunting angrily. "The fit survive."

Alvarez touched the other's knee again. "Bunting is right, Cranwitz," he said gently. "The toleosts replaced the placoderms, who had replaced the trilobites. The reptiles replaced the amphibians and were in turn replaced by the mammals. Now, at last, evolution has reached its peak. Earth bears its mighty population of fifteen trillion human beings—"

"But how?" demanded Cranwitz. "They live in one vast building over all the face of the dry land, with no plants and no animals beside, except what I have right here. And all the uninhabited ocean has become a plankton soup; no life but plankton. We harvest it endlessly to feed our people; and as endlessly we restore organic matter to feed the plankton."

"We live very well," said Alvarez. "There is no war; there is no crime. Our births are regulated; our deaths are peaceful. Our infants are genetically adjusted and on Earth there are now twenty billion tons of normal brain; the largest conceivable quantity of the most complex conceivable matter in the universe."

"And all that weight of brain doing *what?*"

Bunting heaved an audible sigh of exasperation but Alvarez, still calm, said, "My good friend, you confuse the journey with the destination. Perhaps it comes from living with your animals. When the Earth was in process of development, it was necessary for life to experiment and take chances. It was even worthwhile to be wasteful. The Earth was empty then. It had infinite room and evolution had to experiment with ten million species or more—till it found *the* species.

"Even after mankind came, it had to learn the way. While it was learning, it had to take chances, attempt the impossible, be foolish or mad. —But mankind has come home, now. Men have filled the planet and need only to enjoy perfection."

Alvarez paused to let that sink in, then said, "We *want* it, Cranwitz. The whole world wants perfection. It is in our generation that perfection has been reached, and we *want* the distinction of having reached it. Your animals are in the way."

Cranwitz shook his head stubbornly. "They take up so little room; consume so little energy. If all were wiped out, you might have room for what? For twenty-five more human beings? Twenty-five in fifteen trillion?"

Bunting said, "Twenty-five human beings represent another seventy-five pounds of human brain. With what measure can you evaluate seventy-five pounds of human brain?"

"But you already have billions of tons of it."

"I know," said Alvarez, "but the difference between perfection and not-quite-perfection is that between life and not-quite-life. We are so close now. All Earth is prepared to celebrate this year of 2430 A.D. This is the year when the computer tells us that the planet is full at last; the goal is achieved; all the striving of evolution crowned. Shall we fall short by twenty-five—even out of fifteen trillion. It is such a tiny, tiny flaw, but it is a flaw.

"Think, Cranwitz! Earth has been waiting for five billion years to be fulfilled. Must we wait longer? We cannot and will not force you, but if you yield voluntarily you will be a hero to everyone."

Bunting said, "Yes. In all future time men will say that Cranwitz acted and with that one single act perfection was reached."

And Cranwitz said, imitating the other's tone of voice, "And men will say that Alvarez and Bunting persuaded him to do so."

"If we succeed!" said Alvarez with no audible annoyance. "But tell me, Cranwitz, can you hold out against the enlightened will of fifteen trillion people forever? Whatever your motives—and I recognize that in your own way you are an idealist—can you withhold that last bit of perfection from so many?"

Cranwitz looked down in silence and Alvarez's hand waved gently in Bunting's direction and Bunting said not a word. The silence remained unbroken while slow minutes crept by.

Then Cranwitz whispered, "Can I have one more day with my animals?"

"And then?"

"And then—I won't stand between mankind and perfection."

And Alvarez said, "I'll let the world know. You will be honored." And he and Bunting left.

Over the vast continental buildings some five trillion human beings placidly slept; some two trillion human beings placidly ate; half a trillion carefully made love. Other trillions talked without heat, or tended the computers quietly, or ran the vehicles, or studied the machinery, or organized the microfilm libraries, or amused their fellows. Trillions went to sleep; trillions woke up; and the routine never varied.

The machinery worked, tested itself, repaired itself. The plankton soup of the planetary ocean basked under the sun and the cells divided, and divided, and divided, while dredges endlessly scooped them up and dried them and by the millions of tons transferred them to conveyors and conduits that brought them to every corner of the endless buildings.

And in every corner of the buildings human wastes were gathered and irradiated and dried, and human corpses were ground and treated and dried and endlessly the residue was brought back to the ocean. And for hours, while all this was going on, as it had gone on for decades, and might be doomed to go on for millennia, Cranwitz fed his little creatures a last time, stroked his guinea pig, lifted a tortoise to gaze into its uncomprehending eye, felt a blade of living grass between his fingers.

He counted them over, all of them—the last living things on Earth that were neither humans nor food for humans—and then he seared the soil in which the plants grew and killed them. He flooded the cages and rooms in which the animals moved with appropriate vapors, and they moved no more and soon they lived no more.

The last of them was gone and now between mankind and perfection there was only Cranwitz, whose thoughts still rebelliously departed from the norm. But for Cranwitz there were also the vapors, and he didn't want to live.

And, after that, there was really perfection, for over all the Earth, through all its fifteen trillion inhabitants and over all its twenty billion tons of human brain, there was (with Cranwitz gone) not one unsettling thought, not one unusual idea, to disturb the universal placidity that meant that the exquisite nothingness of uniformity had at last been achieved.

———————◀◆▶———————

Even though 2430 A.D. was published, and had been paid for very generously indeed, it left my neurotic fears unallayed. That story, which had been accepted, was written while I still lived in Newton. The one which had not been taken was written in New York.

So I took THE GREATEST ASSET to John Campbell (we were now in the same city again for the first time in twenty-one years) and told him the story of *IBM Magazine*. I said I was handing him the one that they had rejected, but I wouldn't if he would scorn to look at a story under those conditions.

Good old John shrugged and said, "One editor doesn't necessarily agree with another."

He read the story and bought it. I hadn't told him about my crazy worry about being unable to write in New York, because I was ashamed of it and John was still the great man before whom I feared to show myself in my role as jackass. Still, by taking that story he had added one more favor to the many, many he had done for me.

(And in case you're worried, I might as well tell you that my years in New York have so far been even more prolific than the Newton years were. I stayed 57 months in my two-room office and in that period of time published 57 books.)

NOTE: The population of Earth in 1970 is estimated to be 3.68 billion. The present rate of increase doubles that population every 35 years. If this present rate of increase can be maintained for 460 years then in the year 2430 A.D. the weight of human flesh and blood will be equal to the total weight of animal life now present on Earth. To that extent, the story above is not fiction.

THE GREATEST ASSET

The Earth was one large park. It had been tamed utterly.

Lou Tansonia saw it expand under his eyes as he watched somberly from the Lunar Shuttle. His prominent nose split his lean face into inconsiderable halves and each looked sad always—but this time in accurate reflection of his mood.

He had never been away so long—almost a month—and he anticipated a none-too-pleasant acclimation period once Earth's large gravity made its grip fiercely evident.

But that was for later. That was not the sadness of now as he watched Earth grow larger.

As long as the planet was far enough to be a circle of white spirals, glistening in the sun that shone over the ship's shoulders, it had its primeval beauty. When the occasional patches of pastel browns and greens peeped through the clouds, it might still have been the planet it was at any time since three hundred million years before, when life had first stretched out of the sea and moved over the dry land to fill the valleys with green.

It was lower, lower—when the ship sank down—that the tameness began to show.

There was no wilderness anywhere. Lou had never seen Earthly wilderness; he had only read of it, or seen it in old films.

The forests stood in rank and file, with each tree carefully ticketed by species and position. The crops grew in their fields in orderly rotation, with intermittent and automated fertilization and weeding. The few domestic animals that still existed were numbered and Lou wryly suspected that the blades of grass were as well.

Animals were so rarely seen as to be a sensation when glimpsed. Even the insects had faded, and none of the large animals existed anywhere outside the slowly dwindling number of zoos.

The very cats had become few in number, for it was much more patriotic to keep a hamster, if one had to have a pet at all.

Correction! Only Earth's nonhuman animal population had diminished. Its mass of animal life was as great as ever, but most of it, about three fourths of its total, was one species only—*Homo sapiens.*

And, despite everything the Terrestrial Bureau of Ecology could do (or said it could do), that fraction very slowly increased from year to year.

Lou thought of that, as he always did, with a towering sense of loss. The human presence was unobtrusive, to be sure. There was no sign of it from where the shuttle made its final orbits about the planet; and, Lou knew, there would be no sign of it even when they sank much lower.

The sprawling cities of the chaotic pre-Planetary days were gone. The old highways could be traced from the air by the imprint they still left on the vegetation, but they were invisible from close quarters. Individual men themselves rarely troubled the surface, but they were there, underground. All mankind was, in all its billions, with the factories, the food-processing plants, the energics, the vacu-tunnels.

The tame world lived on solar energy and was free of strife, and to Lou it was hateful in consequence.

Yet at the moment he could almost forget, for, after months of failure, he was going to see Adrastus, himself. It had meant the pulling of every available string.

Ino Adrastus was the Secretary General of Ecology. It was not an elective office; it was little-known. It was simply the most important post on Earth, for it controlled everything.

Jan Marley said exactly that, as he sat there, with a sleepy look of absent-minded dishevelment that made one think he would have been fat if the human diet were so uncontrolled as to allow of fatness.

He said, "For my money this is the most important post on Earth, and no one seems to know it. I want to write it up."

Adrastus shrugged. His stocky figure, with its shock of hair, once a light brown and now a brown-flecked gray, his faded blue eyes nested in darkened surrounding tissues, finely wrinkled, had been an unobtrusive part of the administrative scene for a generation. He had been Secretary-General of Ecology ever since the regional ecological councils had been combined into the Terrestrial Bureau. Those who knew of him at all found it impossible to think of ecology without him.

He said, "The truth is I hardly ever make a decision truly my own. The directives I sign aren't mine, really. I sign them because it would be psychologically uncomfortable to have computers sign them. But, you know, it's only the computers that can do the work.

"The Bureau ingests an incredible quantity of data each day; data forwarded to it from every part of the globe and dealing not only with human births, deaths, population shifts, production, and consumption, but with all the tangible changes in the plant and animal population as well, to say nothing of the measured state of the major segments of the environment—air, sea, and soil. The information is taken apart, absorbed, and assimilated into crossfiled memory indices of staggering complexity, and from that memory comes answers to the questions we ask."

Marley said, with a shrewd, sidelong glance, "Answers to *all* questions?"

Adrastus smiled. "We learn not to bother to ask questions that have no answer."

"And the result," said Marley, "is ecological balance."

"Right, but a *special* ecological balance. All through the planet's history, the balance has been maintained, but always at the cost of catastrophe. After temporary imbalance, the balance is restored by famine, epidemic, drastic climatic change. We maintain it now without catastrophe by daily shifts and changes, by never allowing imbalance to accumulate dangerously."

Marley said, "There's what you once said—'Man's greatest asset is a balanced ecology.'"

"So they tell me I said."

"It's there on the wall behind you."

"Only the first three words," said Adrastus dryly. There it was on a long Shimmer-plast, the words winking and alive: MAN'S GREATEST ASSET . . .

"You don't have to complete the statement."

"What else can I tell you?"

"Can I spend some time with you and watch you at your work?"

"You'll watch a glorified clerk."

"I don't think so. Do you have appointments at which I may be present?"

"One appointment today; a young fellow named Tansonia; one of our Moon-men. You can sit in."

"Moon-men? You mean—"

"Yes, from the lunar laboratories. Thank heaven for the moon. Otherwise all their experimentation would take place on Earth, and we have enough trouble containing the ecology as it is."

"You mean like nuclear experiments and radiational pollution?"

"I mean many things."

Lou Tansonia's expression was a mixture of barely suppressed excitement and barely suppressed apprehension. "I'm glad to have this chance to see you, Mr. Secretary," he said breathlessly, puffing against Earth's gravity.

"I'm sorry we couldn't make it sooner," said Adrastus smoothly. "I have excellent reports concerning your work. The other gentleman present is Jan Marley, a science writer, and he need not concern us."

Lou glanced at the writer briefly and nodded, then turned eagerly to Adrastus. "Mr. Secretary—"

"Sit down," said Adrastus.

Lou did so, with the trace of clumsiness to be expected of one acclimating himself to Earth, and with an air, somehow, that to pause long enough to sit was a waste of time. He said, "Mr. Secretary, I am appealing to you personally concerning my Project Application Num—"

"I know it."

"You've read it, sir?"

"No, I haven't, but the computers have. It's been rejected."

"Yes! But I appeal from the computers to you."

Adrastus smiled and shook his head. "That's a difficult appeal for me. I don't know from where I could gather the courage to override the computer."

"But you *must*," said the young man earnestly. "My field is genetic engineering."

"Yes, I know."

"And genetic engineering," said Lou, running over the interruption, "is the handmaiden of medicine and it shouldn't be so. Not entirely, anyway."

"Odd that you think so. You have your medical degree, and you have done impressive work in medical genetics. I have been told that in two years time your work may lead to the full suppression of diabetes mellitus for good."

"Yes, but I don't care. I don't want to carry that through. Let someone else do it. Curing diabetes is just a detail and it will merely mean that the death rate will go down slightly and produce just a bit more pressure in the direction of population increase. I'm not interested in achieving that."

"You don't value human life?"

"Not infinitely. There are too many people on Earth."

"I know that some think so."

"You're one of them, Mr. Secretary. You have written articles saying so. And it's obvious to any thinking man—to you more than anyone—what it's doing. Overpopulation means discomfort, and to reduce the discomfort private choice must disappear. Crowd enough people into a field and the only way they can all sit down is for all to sit down at the same time. Make a mob dense enough and they can move from one point to another quickly only by marching in formation. That is what men are becoming; a blindly marching mob knowing nothing about where it is going or why."

"How long have you rehearsed this speech, Mr. Tansonia?"

Lou flushed slightly. "And the other life forms are decreasing in numbers of species and individuals, except for the plants we eat. The ecology gets simpler every year."

"It stays balanced."

"But it loses color and variety and we don't even know how good the balance is. We accept the balance only because it's all we have."

"What would you do?"

"Ask the computer that rejected my proposal. I want to initiate a program for genetic engineering on a wide variety of species from worms to mammals. I want to create new variety out of the dwindling material at hand before it dwindles out altogether."

"For what purpose?"

"To set up artificial ecologies. To set up ecologies based on plants and animals not like anything on Earth."

"What would you gain?"

"I don't know. If I knew exactly what I would gain there would be no need to do the research. But I know what we ought to gain. We ought to learn more about what makes an ecology tick. So far, we've only taken what nature has handed us and then ruined it and broken it down and made do with the gutted remains. Why not build something up and study that?"

"You mean build it blindly? At random?"

"We don't know enough to do it any other way. Genetic engineering has the random mutation as its basic driving force. Applied to medicine, this randomness must be minimized at all costs, since a specific effect is sought. I want to take the random component of genetic engineering and make use of it."

Adrastus frowned for a moment. "And how are you going to set up an ecology that's meaningful? Won't it interact with the ecology that already exists, and possibly unbalance it? That is something we can't afford."

"I don't mean to carry out the experiments on Earth," said Lou. "Of course not."

"On the moon?"

"Not on the moon, either. —On the asteroids. I've thought of that since my proposal was fed to the computer which spit it out. Maybe this will make a difference. How about small asteroids, hollowed-out; one per ecology? Assign a certain number of asteroids for the purpose. Have them properly engineered; outfit them with energy sources and transducers; seed them with collections of life forms which might form a closed ecology. See what happens. If it doesn't work, try to figure out why and subtract an item, or, more likely, add an item, or change the proportions. We'll develop a science of applied ecology, or, if you prefer, a science of ecological engineering; a science one step up in complexity and significance beyond genetic engineering."

"But the good of it, you can't say."

"The specific good, of course not. But how can it avoid some good? It will increase knowledge in the very field we need it most." He pointed to the shimmering lettering behind Adrastus. "You said it yourself, 'Man's greatest asset is a balanced ecology.' I'm offering you a way of doing basic research in experimental ecology; something that has never been done before."

"How many asteroids will you want?"

Lou hesitated. "Ten?" he said with rising inflection. "As a beginning."

"Take five," said Adrastus, drawing the report toward himself and scribbling quickly on its face, cancelling out the computer's decision.

Afterward, Marley said, "Can you sit there and tell me that you're a glorified clerk now? You cancel the computer and hand out five asteroids. Like that."

"The Congress will have to give its approval. I'm sure it will."

"Then you think this young man's suggestion is really a good one."

"No, I don't. It won't work. Despite his enthusiasm, the matter is so complicated that it will surely take far more men than can possibly be made available for far more years than that young man will live to carry it through to any worthwhile point."

"Are you sure?"

"The computer says so. It's why his project was rejected."

"Then why did you cancel the computer's decision?"

"Because I, and the government in general, are here in order to preserve something far more important than the ecology."

Marley leaned forward. "I don't get it."

"Because you misquoted what I said so long ago. Because everyone misquotes it. Because I spoke two sentences and they were telescoped into one and I have never been able to force them apart again. Presumably, the human race is unwilling to accept my remarks as I made them."

"You mean you didn't say 'Man's greatest asset is a balanced ecology'?"

"Of course not. I said, 'Man's greatest *need* is a balanced ecology.'"

"But on your Shimmer-plast you say, 'Man's greatest asset—'"

"That begins the second sentence, which men refuse to quote, but which I never forget—'Man's greatest asset is the unsettled mind.' I haven't overruled the computer for the sake of our ecology. We only need that to live. I overruled it to save a valuable mind and keep it at work, an unsettled mind. We need that for man to be man— which is more important than merely to live."

Marley rose. "I suspect, Mr. Secretary, you wanted me here for this interview. It's this thesis you want me to publicize, isn't it?"

"Let's say," said Adrastus, "that I'm seizing the chance to get my remarks correctly quoted."

Alas, that was my last sale to John. The check arrived on August 18, 1970, and less than a year later he was dead.

When the story appeared in the January 1972 issue of *Analog* my good and gentle friend, Ben Bova, was editor of the magazine. It isn't possible to fill John Campbell's shoes, but Ben is filling his own very successfully.

The next story was written as the result of a comedy of errors. In January 1971, as a result of a complicated set of circumstances,

I promised Bob Silverberg that I would write a short story for an anthology of originals he was preparing.*

I wrote the short story but it turned out not to be a short story. To my enormous surprise, I wrote a novel, THE GODS THEMSELVES (Doubleday, 1972), my first science fiction novel in fifteen years (if you don't count FANTASTIC VOYAGE, which wasn't entirely mine).

It wasn't a bad novel at all, since it won the Hugo and the Nebula, and showed the science fiction world that the old man still had it. Nevertheless, it put me in a hole since there was the short story I had promised Bob. I wrote another, therefore, TAKE A MATCH, and it appeared in Bob's anthology *New Dimensions II* (Doubleday, 1972).

* You may be surprised that I don't explain the complicated set of circumstances, since I am such a blabbermouth, but Bob finds my version a little on the offensive side, so we'll let it go.

TAKE A MATCH

Space was black; black all around in every direction. There was nothing to be seen; not a star.

It was not because there were no stars—

Actually the thought that there might be no stars, literally no stars, had chilled Per Hanson's vitals. It was the old nightmare that rested just barely subliminally beneath the skin of every deep-spacer's brain.

When you took the Jump through the tachyon-universe, how sure were you *where* you would emerge? The timing and quantity of the energy input might be as tightly controlled as you liked, and your Fusionist might be the best in space, but the uncertainty principle reigned supreme and there was always the chance, even the inevitability of a random miss.

And by way of tachyons, a paper-thin miss might be a thousand light-years.

What, then, if you landed nowhere; or at least so distant from anywhere that nothing could possibly ever guide you to knowledge of your own position and nothing, therefore, could guide you back to anywhere?

Impossible, said the pundits. There was no place in the universe from which the quasars could not be seen, and from those alone you could position yourself. Besides, the chance that in the course of ordinary Jumps mere chance would take you outside the galaxy was only one in about ten million, and to the distance of, say, the Andromeda galaxy or Maffei 1, perhaps one in a quadrillion.

Forget it, said the pundits.

So when a ship comes out of its Jump, and returns from the weird paradoxes of the faster-than-light tachyons to the healthy we-know-it-all of all the tardyons from protons down to protons up, there *must* be stars to be seen. If they are not seen nevertheless, you are in a dust cloud; it is the only explanation. There are smoggy areas in the galaxy, or in any spiral galaxy, as once there were on Earth, when it was the sole home of humanity, rather than the carefully preserved, weather-controlled, life-preserve museum-piece it now was.

Hanson was tall and gloomy; his skin was leathery; and what he didn't know about the hyperships that ploughed the length and breadth of the galaxy and immediately neighboring regions—always barring the Fusionists' mysteries—was yet to be worked out. He was alone, now, in the Captain's Corner, as he liked to be. He had at hand all that was needed to be connected with any man or woman on board, and with the results of any device and instrument, and it pleased him to be the unseen presence.

—Though now nothing pleased him. He closed contact and said, "What else, Strauss?"

"We're in an open cluster," said Strauss's voice. (Hanson did not turn on the visual attachment; it would have meant revealing his own face and he preferred his look of sick worry to be held private.)

"At least," Strauss continued, "it seems to be an open cluster, from the level of radiation we can get in the far infrared and micro-wave regions. The trouble is we just can't pinpoint the positions well enough to locate ourselves. Not a hope."

"Nothing in visible light?"

"Nothing at all; or in the near-infrared, either. The dust cloud is as thick as soup."

"How big is it?"

"No way of telling."

"Can you estimate the distance to the nearest edge?"

"Not even to an order of magnitude. It might be a light-week. It might be ten light-years. Absolutely no way of telling."

"Have you talked to Viluekis?"

Strauss said briefly, "Yes!"

"What does he say?"

"Not much. He's sulking. He's taking it as a personal insult, of course."

"Of course." Hanson sighed noiselessly. Fusionists were as child-ish as children and because theirs was the romantic role in deep space, they were indulged. He said, "I suppose you told him that this sort of thing is unpredictable and could happen at any time."

"I did. And he said, as you can guess—'Not to Viluekis.'"

"Except that it did, of course. Well, I can't speak to him. Noth-ing I say will mean anything at all except that I'm trying to pull rank and then we'll get nothing further out of him. —He won't start the scoop?"

"He says he can't. He says it will be damaged."

"How can you damage a magnetic field!"

Strauss grunted. "Don't say that to him. He'll tell you there's more to a fusion tube than a magnetic field and then say you're trying to downgrade him."

"Yes, I know. —Well, look, put everyone and everything on the cloud. There must be some way to make some sort of guess as to the direction and distance of the nearest edge." He broke connection.

Hanson frowned into the middle distance, then.

Nearest edge! It was doubtful if at the ship's speed (relative to the surrounding matter) they dared expend the energy required for radical alteration of course.

They had moved into the Jump at half-light speed relative to the galactic nucleus in the tardyon-universe, and they emerged from the Jump at (of course) the same speed. There always seemed an element of risk in that. After all, suppose you found yourself, on the return, in the near neighborhood of a star and heading toward it at half-light speed.

The theoreticians denied the possibility. To get dangerously close to a massive body by way of a Jump was not reasonably to be expected. So said the pundits. Gravitational forces were involved in the Jump and for the transition from tardyon to tachyon and back to tardyon those forces were repulsive in nature. In fact, it was the random effect of a net gravitational force that could never be worked out in complete detail that accounted for a good deal of the uncertainty in the Jump.

Besides, they would say, trust to the Fusionist's instinct. A good Fusionist never goes wrong.

Except that this Fusionist had Jumped them into a cloud.

—Oh, that! It happens all the time. It doesn't matter. Do you know how *thin* most clouds are. You won't even know you're in one.

(Not this cloud, O Pundit.)

—In fact, clouds are good for you. The scoops don't have to work so long or so hard to keep fusion going and energy storing.

(Not this cloud, O Pundit.)

—Well, then, rely on the Fusionist to think of a way out.

(But if there was no way out?)

Hanson shied away from that last thought. He tried hard not to think it. —But how do you not think a thought that is the loudest thing in your head?

Henry Strauss, ship's astronomer, was himself in a mood of deep depression. If what had taken place were undiluted catastrophe, it might be accepted. No one on the hyperships could entirely close his eyes to the possibility of catastrophe. You were prepared for that, or you tried to be. —Though it was worse for the passengers, of course.

But when the catastrophe involved something that you would give your eye-teeth to observe and study, and when you find that the professional find of a lifetime was precisely what was killing you—

He sighed heavily.

He was a stout man, with tinted contact lenses that gave a spurious brightness and color to eyes that would otherwise have precisely matched a colorless personality.

There was nothing the captain could do. He knew that. The captain might be autocrat of all the rest of the ship, but a Fusionist was a law to himself, and always had been. Even to the passengers (he thought with some disgust) the Fusionist is the emperor of the spaceways and everyone beside dwindles to impotence.

It was a matter of supply and demand. The computers might calculate the exact quantity and timing of the energy input and the exact place and direction (if "direction" had any meaning in the transition from tardyon to tachyon), but the margin of error was huge and only a talented Fusionist could lower it. What it was that gave a Fusionist his talent, no one knew—they were born, not made. But Fusionists knew they had the talent and there was never one that didn't trade on that.

Viluekis wasn't bad as Fusionists went—though they never went far. He and Strauss were at least on speaking terms, even though Viluekis had effortlessly collected the prettiest passenger on board after Strauss had seen her first. (That was somehow part of the Imperial rights of the Fusionists en route.)

Strauss contacted Anton Viluekis. It took time for it to go through and when it did, Viluekis looked irritated in a rumpled, sad-eyed way.

"How's the tube?" asked Strauss gently.

"I think I shut it down in time. I've gone over it and I don't see any damage. Now," he looked down at himself, "I've got to clean up."

"At least it isn't harmed."

"But we can't use it."

"We *might* use it, Vil," said Strauss in an insinuating voice. "We can't say what will happen out there. If the tube were damaged, it wouldn't matter what happened out there, but, as it is, if the cloud cleans up—"

"If—if—if— I'll tell you an 'if.' If you stupid astronomers had known this cloud was here, I might have avoided it."

That was flatly irrelevant, and Strauss did not rise to the bait. He said, "It might clear up."

"What's the analysis?"

"Not good, Vil. It's the thickest hydroxyl cloud that's ever been observed. There is nowhere in the galaxy, as far as I know, a place where hydroxyl has been concentrated so densely."

"And no hydrogen?"

"Some hydrogen, of course. About five per cent."

"Not enough," said Viluekis curtly. "There's something else there besides hydroxyl. There's something that gave me more trouble than hydroxyl could. Did you locate it?"

"Oh, yes. Formaldehyde. There's more formaldehyde than hydrogen. Do you realize what it means, Vil? Some process has concentrated oxygen and carbon in space in unheard-of amounts; enough to use up the hydrogen over a volume of cubic light-years, perhaps. There isn't anything I know or can imagine which would account for such a thing."

"What are you trying to say, Strauss? Are you telling me that this is the only cloud of this type in space and I am stupid enough to land in it?"

"I'm not saying that, Vil. I only say what you hear me say and you haven't heard me say that. But, Vil, to get out we're depending on you. I can't call for help because I can't aim a hyperbeam without knowing where we are: I can't find out where we are because I can't pinpoint any stars—"

"And I can't use the fusion tube, so why am I the villain? You can't do your job, either, so why is the Fusionist always the villain." Viluekis was simmering. "It's up to you, Strauss, up to you. Tell me where to cruise the ship to find hydrogen. Tell me where the edge of the cloud is. —Or to hell with the edge of the cloud; find me the edge of the hydroxyl-formaldehyde business."

"I wish I could," said Strauss, "but so far I can't detect anything but hydroxyl and formaldehyde as far as I can probe."

"We can't fuse that stuff."

"I know."

"Well," said Viluekis violently, "this is an example of why it's wrong for the government to try to legislate supersafety instead of leaving it to the judgment of the Fusionist on the spot. If we had the capacity for the Double-Jump, there'd be no trouble."

Strauss knew perfectly well what Viluekis meant. There was always the tendency to save time by making two Jumps in rapid succession, but if one Jump involved certain unavoidable uncertainties, two in succession greatly multiplied those uncertainties, and even the best Fusionist couldn't do much. The multiplied error almost invariably greatly lengthened the total time of the trip.

It was a strict rule of hypernavigation that one full day of cruising between Jumps was necessary—three full days was preferable. That gave time enough to prepare the next Jump with all due caution. To avoid breaking that rule, each Jump was made under conditions that left insufficient energy supply for a second. For at least some time, the scoops had to gather and compress hydrogen, fuse it, and store the energy, building up to Jump-ignition. And it usually took at least a day to store enough to allow a Jump.

Strauss said, "How far short in energy are you, Vil?"

"Not much. This much." Viluekis held his thumb and forefinger apart by a quarter of an inch. "It's enough, though."

"Too bad," said Strauss flatly. The energy supply was recorded and could be inspected, but even so, Fusionists had been known to organize the records in such a way as to leave themselves some leeway for that second Jump.

"Are you sure?" he said. "Suppose you throw in the emergency generators, turn off all the lights—"

"And the air circulation and the appliances and the hydroponics apparatus. I know. I know. I figured that all in and we don't quite make it. —There's your stupid Double-Jump safety regulation."

Strauss still managed to keep his temper. He knew—everyone knew—that it had been the Fusionist Brotherhood that had been the driving force behind that regulation. A Double-Jump, sometimes insisted on by the captain, much more often than not made the

Fusionist look bad. —But then, there was at least one advantage. With an obligatory cruise between every Jump, there ought to be at least a week before the passengers grew restless and suspicious, and in that week something might happen. So far, it was not quite a day.

He said, "Are you sure you can't do something with your system; filter out some of the impurities?"

"Filter them out! They're not impurities; they're the whole thing. Hydrogen is the impurity here. Listen, I'll need half a billion degrees to fuse carbon and oxygen atoms; probably a full billion. It can't be done and I'm not going to try. If I try something and it doesn't work, it's my fault, and I won't stand for that. It's up to you to get me to the hydrogen and you do it. You just cruise this ship to the hydrogen. I don't care how long it takes."

Strauss said, "We can't go faster than we're going now, considering the density of the medium, Vil. And at half-light speed we might have to cruise for two years—maybe twenty years—"

"Well, *you* think of a way out. Or the captain."

Strauss broke contact in despair. There was just no way of carrying on a rational conversation with a Fusionist. He'd heard the theory advanced (and perfectly seriously) that repeated Jumps affected the brain. In the Jump, every tardyon in ordinary matter had to be turned into an equivalent tachyon and then back again to the original tardyon. If the double conversion was imperfect in even the tiniest way, surely the effect would show up first in the brain, which was by far the most complex piece of matter ever to make the transition. Of course, no ill effects had ever been demonstrated experimentally, and no class of hypership officers seemed to deteriorate with time past what could be attributed to simple aging. But perhaps whatever it was in the Fusionists' brains that made them Fusionists and allowed them to go, by sheer intuition, beyond the best of computers might be particularly complex and therefore particularly vulnerable.

Nuts! There was nothing to it! Fusionists were merely spoiled!

He hesitated. Ought he to try to reach Cheryl? She could smooth matters if anyone could, and once old Vil-baby was properly dandled, he might think of a way to put the fusion tubes into operation —hydroxyl or not.

Did he really believe Viluekis could, under any circumstances? Or was he trying to avoid the thought of cruising for years? To be sure, hyperships were prepared for such an eventuality, in principle, but the eventuality had never come to pass and the crews—and still less the passengers—were surely *not* prepared for it.

But if he did talk to Cheryl, what could he say that wouldn't sound like an order for seduction? It was only one day so far and he was not yet ready to pimp for a Fusionist.

Wait! Awhile, anyway!

Viluekis frowned. He felt a little better having bathed and he was pleased that he had been firm with Strauss. Not a bad fellow, Strauss, but like all of them ("them," the captain, the crew, the passengers, all the stupid non-Fusionists in the universe) he wanted to shed responsibility. Put it all on the Fusionist. It was an old, old song, and he was one Fusionist who wouldn't take it.

That talk about cruising for years was just a way of trying to frighten him. If they really put their minds to it, they could work out the limits of the cloud and somewhere there had to be a nearer edge. It was too much to ask that they had landed in the precise center. Of course, if they had landed near one edge and were heading for the other—

Viluekis rose and stretched. He was tall and his eyebrows hung over his eyes like canopies.

Suppose it did take years. No hypership had ever cruised for years. The longest cruise had been eighty-eight days and thirteen hours, when one of them had managed to find itself in an unfavorable position with respect to a diffuse star and had to recede at speeds that built up to over 0.9 light before it was reasonably able to Jump.

They had survived and that was a quarter-year cruise. Of course, *twenty* years—

But that was impossible.

The signal light flashed three times before he was fully aware of it. If that was the captain coming to see him personally, he would leave at a rather more rapid rate than he had come.

"Anton!"

The voice was soft, urgent, and part of his annoyance seeped away. He allowed the door to recede into its socket and Cheryl came in. The door closed again behind her.

She was about twenty-five, with green eyes, a firm chin, dull red hair, and a magnificent figure that did not hide its light under a bushel.

She said, "Anton. Is there something wrong?"

Viluekis was not caught so entirely by surprise as to admit any such thing. Even a Fusionist knew better than to reveal anything prematurely to a passenger. "Not at all. What makes you think so?"

"One of the other passengers says so. A man named Martand."

"Martand? What does he know about it?" Then, suspiciously, "And what are you doing listening to some fool passenger? What does he look like?"

Cheryl smiled wanly. "Just someone who struck up a conversation in the lounge. He must be nearly sixty years old, and quite harmless, though I imagine he would like not to be. But that's not the point. There are no stars in view. Anyone can see that, and Martand said it was significant."

"Did he? We're just passing through a cloud. There are lots of clouds in the galaxy and hyperships pass through them all the time."

"Yes, but Martand says you can usually see some stars even in a cloud."

"What does he know about it?" Viluekis repeated. "Is he an old hand at deep space?"

"No-o," admitted Cheryl. "Actually, it's his first trip, I think. But he seems to know a lot."

"I'll bet. Listen, you go to him and tell him to shut up. He can be put in solitary for this. And don't you repeat stories like that, either."

Cheryl put her head to one side. "Frankly, Anton, you sound as though there *were* trouble. This Martand—Louis Martand is his name—is an interesting fellow. He's a schoolteacher—eighth grade general science."

"A grade-school teacher! Good Lord, Cheryl—"

"But you ought to listen to him. He says that teaching children is one of the few professions where you have to know a little bit about everything because kids ask questions and can spot phonies."

"Well, then, maybe your specialty should be spotting phonies, too. Now, Cheryl, you go and tell him to shut up, or I will."

"All right. But first—is it true that we're going through a hydroxyl cloud and the fusion tube is shut down?"

Viluekis's mouth opened, then shut again. It was quite a while before he said, "Who told you that?"

"Martand. I'll go now."

"No," said Viluekis sharply. "Wait awhile. How many others has Martand been telling all this?"

"Nobody. He said he doesn't want to spread panic. I was there when he was thinking about it, I suppose, and I guess he couldn't resist saying something."

"Does he know you know me?"

Cheryl's forehead furrowed slightly. "I think I mentioned something about it."

Viluekis snorted, "Don't you suppose that this crazy old man you've picked up is bound to try to show you how great he is. It's me he's trying to impress through you."

"Nothing of the sort," said Cheryl. "In fact, he specifically said I wasn't to tell you anything."

"Knowing, of course, that you'd come to me at once."

"Why should he want me to do that?"

"To show me up. Do you know what it's like being a Fusionist? To have everyone resenting you, against you, because you're so *needed,* because you—"

Cheryl said, "But what's any of that got to do with it? If Martand's all wrong, how would that show you up? And if he's right— Is he right, Anton?"

"Well, exactly what did he say?"

"I'm not sure I can remember it all, of course," Cheryl said thoughtfully. "It was after we came out of the Jump, actually quite a few hours after. By that time all anyone was talking about was that there were no stars in view. In the lounge everyone was saying there ought to be another Jump soon because what was the good of deep-space travel without a view. Of course, we knew we had to cruise at least a day. Then Martand came in, saw me, and came over to speak to me. —I think he rather likes me."

"I think I rather don't like him," said Viluekis grimly. "Go on."

"I said to him that it was pretty dreary without a view and he said it would stay that way for a while, and he sounded worried. Naturally I asked why he said such a thing and he said it was because the fusion tube had been turned off."

"Who told him that?" demanded Viluekis.

"He said there was a low hum that you could hear in one of the men's rooms that you couldn't hear anymore. And he said there was a place in the closet of the game room where the chess sets were kept where the wall felt warm because of the fusion tube and that place was not warm now."

"Is that all the evidence he has?"

Cheryl ignored that and went on, "He said there were no stars visible because we were in a dust cloud and the fusion tubes must have stopped because there was no hydrogen to speak of in it. He said there probably wouldn't be enough energy to spark another Jump and that if we looked for hydrogen we might have to cruise years to get out of the cloud."

Viluekis's frown became ferocious. "He's panic-mongering. Do you know what that—"

"He's *not*. He told me not to tell anyone because he said it would create panic and that besides it wouldn't happen. He only told me because he had just figured it out and was all excited about it and had to talk to someone, but he said there was an easy way out and that the Fusionist would know what to do so that there was no need to worry at all. —But you're the Fusionist, so it seemed to me I had to ask whether he was really right about the cloud and whether you had really taken care of it."

Viluekis said, "This grade-school teacher of yours knows nothing about anything. Just stay away from him. —Uh, did he *say* what his so-called easy way out was?"

"No. Should I have asked him?"

"No! Why should you have asked him? What would he know about it? But then again— All right, ask him. I'm curious what the idiot has in mind. Ask him."

Cheryl nodded. "I can do that. But are we in trouble?"

Viluekis said shortly. "Suppose you leave that to me. We're not in trouble till I say we're in trouble."

He looked for a long time at the closed door after she had left, both angry and uneasy. What was this Louis Martand—this grade-school teacher—doing with his lucky guesses?

If it finally came about that an extended cruise was necessary, the passengers would have to have it broken to them carefully, or none of them would survive. With Martand shouting it to all who would listen—

Almost savagely Viluekis clicked shut the combination that would bring him the captain.

Martand was slim and of neat appearance. His lips seemed forever on the verge of a smile, though his face and bearing were marked by a polite gravity; an almost expectant gravity, as though he was forever waiting for the person with him to say something truly important.

Cheryl said to him, "I spoke to Mr. Viluekis. —He's the Fusionist, you know. I told him what you said."

Martand looked shocked and shook his head. "I'm afraid you shouldn't have done that!"

"He did seem displeased."

"Of course. Fusionists are very special people and they don't like to have outsiders—"

"I could see that. But he insisted there was nothing to worry about."

"Of course not," said Martand, taking her hand and patting it in a consoling gesture, but then continuing to hold it. "I told you there was an easy way out. He's probably setting it up now. Still, I suppose it could be a while before he thinks of it."

"Thinks of what?" Then, warmly, "Why shouldn't he think of it, if *you* have?"

"But he's a specialist, you see, my dear young lady. Specialists think in their specialty and have a hard time getting out of it. As for myself, I don't dare fall into ruts. When I set up a class demonstration I've got to improvise most of the time. I have never yet been at a school where proton micropiles have been available, and I've had to work up a kerosene thermoelectric generator when we're off on field trips."

"What's kerosene?" asked Cheryl.

Martand laughed. He seemed delighted. "You see? People forget. Kerosene is a kind of flammable liquid. A still-more-primitive source of energy that I have many times had to use was a wood fire which you start by friction. Did you ever come across one of those? You take a match—"

Cheryl was looking blank and Martand went on indulgently, "Well, it doesn't matter. I'm just trying to get across the notion that your Fusionist will have to think of something more primitive than fusion and that will take him a while. As for me, I'm used to working with primitive methods. —For instance, do you know what's out there?"

He gestured at the viewing port, which was utterly featureless; so featureless that the lounge was virtually depopulated for lack of a view.

"A cloud; a dust cloud."

"Ah, but what kind? The one thing that's always to be found everywhere is hydrogen. It's the original stuff of the universe and hyperships depend on it. No ship can carry enough fuel to make repeated Jumps or to accelerate to near-light-speed and back repeatedly. We have to scoop the fuel out of space."

"You know, I've always wondered about that. I thought outer space was empty!"

"*Nearly* empty, my dear, and 'nearly' is as good as a feast. When you travel at a hundred thousand miles a second, you can scoop up and compress quite a bit of hydrogen, even when there's only a few atoms per cubic centimeter. And small amounts of hydrogen, fusing steadily, provide all the energy we need. In clouds the hydrogen is usually even thicker, but impurities may cause trouble, as in this one."

"How can you tell this one has impurities?"

"Why else would Mr. Viluekis have shut down the fusion tube. Next to hydrogen, the most common elements in the universe are helium, oxygen, and carbon. If the fusion pumps have stopped, that means there's a shortage of fuel, which is hydrogen, and a presence of something that will damage the complex fusion system. This can't be helium, which is harmless. It is possibly hydroxyl groups, an oxygen-hydrogen combination. Do you understand?"

"I think so," said Cheryl. "I had general science in college, and some of it is coming back. The dust is really hydroxyl groups attached to solid dust grains."

"Or actually free in the gaseous state, too. Even hydroxyl is not too dangerous to the fusion system, in moderation, but carbon compounds are. Formaldehyde is most likely and I should imagine with a ratio of about one of those to four hydroxyls. Do you see now?"

"No, I don't," said Cheryl flatly.

"Such compounds won't fuse. If you heat them to a few hundred million degrees, they break down into single atoms and the concentration of oxygen and carbon will simply damage the system. But why not take them in at ordinary temperatures. Hydroxyl will combine with formaldehyde, after compression, in a chemical reaction that will cause no harm to the system. At least, I'm sure a good Fusionist could modify the system to handle a chemical reaction at room temperature. The energy of the reaction can be stored and, after a while, there will be enough to make a Jump possible."

Cheryl said, "I don't see that at all. Chemical reactions produce hardly any energy, compared to fusion."

"You're quite right, dear. But we don't need much. The previous Jump has left us with insufficient energy for an immediate second Jump—that's regulations. But I'll bet your friend, the Fusionist, saw to it that as little energy as possible was lacking. Fusionists usually do that. The little extra required to reach ignition can be collected from ordinary chemical reactions. Then, once a Jump takes us out of the cloud, cruising for a week or so will refill our energy tanks and we can continue without harm. Of course—" Martand raised his eyebrows and shrugged.

"Yes?"

"Of course," said Martand, "if for any reason Mr. Viluekis should delay, there may be trouble. Every day we spend before Jumping uses up energy in the ordinary life of the ship, and after a while chemical reactions won't supply the energy required to reach Jump-ignition. I hope he doesn't wait long."

"Well, why don't you tell him? Now."

Martand shook his head. "Tell a Fusionist? I couldn't do that, dear."

"Then I will."

"Oh, no. He's *sure* to think of it himself. In fact, I'll make a bet with you, my dear. You tell him exactly what I said and say that I told you he had already thought of it himself and that the fusion tube was in operation. And, of course, if I win—"

Martand smiled.

Cheryl smiled, too. "I'll see," she said.

Martand looked after her thoughtfully as she hastened away, his thoughts not entirely on Viluekis's possible reaction.

He was not surprised when a ship's guard appeared from almost nowhere and said, "Please come with me, Mr. Martand."

Martand said quietly. "Thank you for letting me finish. I was afraid you wouldn't."

Something more than six hours passed before Martand was allowed to see the captain. His imprisonment (which was what he considered it) was one of isolation, but was not onerous; and the captain, when he did see him, looked tired and not particularly hostile.

Hanson said, "It was reported to me that you were spreading rumors designed to create panic among the passengers. That is a serious charge."

"I spoke to one passenger only, sir; and for a purpose."

"So we realize. We put you under surveillance at once and I have a report, a rather full one, of the conversation you had with Miss Cheryl Winter. It was the second conversation on the subject."

"Yes, sir."

"Apparently you intended the meat of the conversation to be passed on to Mr. Viluekis."

"Yes, sir."

"You did not consider going to Mr. Viluekis personally?"

"I doubt that he would have listened, sir."

"Or to me."

"You might have listened, but how would you pass on the information to Mr. Viluekis? You might then have had to use Miss Winter yourself. Fusionists have their peculiarities."

The captain nodded abstractedly. "What was it you expected to happen when Miss Winter passed on the information to Mr. Viluekis?"

"My hope, sir," said Martand, "was that he would be less defensive with Miss Winter than with anyone else; that he would feel less threatened. I was hoping that he would laugh and say the idea was a simple one that had occurred to him long before, and that, indeed, the scoops were already working, with the intent of promoting the chemical reaction. Then, when he got rid of Miss Winter, and I imagine he would do that quickly, he would start the scoops and report his action to you, sir, omitting any reference to myself or Miss Winter."

"You did not think he might dismiss the whole notion as unworkable?"

"There was that chance, but it didn't happen."

"How do you know?"

"Because half an hour after I was placed in detention, sir, the lights in the room in which I was kept dimmed perceptibly and did not brighten again. I assumed that energy expenditure in the ship was being cut to the bone, and assumed further that Viluekis was throwing everything into the pot so that the chemical reaction would supply enough for ignition."

The captain frowned. "What made you so sure you could manipulate Mr. Viluekis? Surely you have never dealt with Fusionists, have you?"

"Ah, but I teach the eighth-grade, captain. I have dealt with other children."

For a moment the captain's expression remained wooden. And then slowly it relaxed into a smile. "I like you, Mr. Martand," he said, "but it won't help you. Your expectations *did* come to pass; as nearly as I can tell, exactly as you had hoped. But do you understand what followed?"

"I will, if you tell me."

"Mr. Viluekis had to evaluate your suggestion and decide, at once, whether it was practical. He had to make a number of careful adjustments to the system to allow chemical reactions without knocking out the possibility of future fusion. He had to determine the maximum safe rate of reaction; the amount of stored energy to save; the point at which ignition might safely be attempted; the kind and nature of the Jump. It all had to be done quickly and no one else but a Fusionist could have done it. In fact, not every Fusionist could have done it; Mr. Viluekis is exceptional even for a Fusionist. Do you see?"

"Quite well."

The captain looked at the timepiece on the wall and activated his viewport. It was black, as it had been now for the better part of two days. "Mr. Viluekis has informed me of the time at which he will attempt Jump-ignition. He thinks it will work and I am confident in his judgment."

"If he misses," said Martand somberly, "we may find ourselves in the same position as before, but stripped of energy."

"I realize that," said Hanson, "and since you might feel a certain responsibility over having placed the idea in the Fusionist's mind, I thought you might want to wait through the few moments of suspense ahead of us."

Both men were silent now, watching the screen, while first seconds, then minutes, moved past. Hanson had not mentioned the exact deadline and Martand had no way of telling how imminent it was or whether it had passed. He could only shift his glance, occasionally and momentarily, to the captain's face, which maintained a studied expressionlessness.

And then came that queer internal wrench that disappeared almost at once, like a tic in the abdominal wall. They had Jumped.

"Stars!" said Hanson in a whisper of deep satisfaction. The viewport had burst into a riot of them, and at that moment Martand could recall no sweeter sight in all his life.

"And on the second," said Hanson. "A beautiful job. We're energy-stripped now, but we'll be full again in anywhere from one to three weeks, and during that time the passengers will have their view."

Martand felt too weak with relief to speak.

The captain turned to him. "Now, Mr. Martand. Your idea had merit. One could argue that it saved the ship and everyone on it. One could also argue that Mr. Viluekis was sure to think of it himself soon enough. But there will be no argument about it at all, for under no conditions can your part in this be known. Mr. Viluekis did the job and it was a great one of pure virtuosity even after we take into account the fact that you may have sparked it. He will be commended for it and receive great honors. *You* will receive nothing."

Martand was silent for a moment. Then he said, "I understand. A Fusionist is indispensable and I am of no account. If Mr. Viluekis's pride is hurt in the slightest, he may become useless to you, and you can't afford to lose him. For myself—well, be it as you wish. Good day, Captain."

"Not quite," said the captain. "We can't trust you."

"I won't say anything."

"You may not intend to, but things happen. We can't take the chance. For the remainder of the flight you will be under house arrest."

Martand frowned. "For *what?* I saved you and your damned ship —*and* your Fusionist."

"For exactly that. For saving it. That's the way it works out."

"Where's the justice?"

Slowly the captain shook his head. "It's a rare commodity, I admit, and sometimes too expensive to afford. You can't even go back to your room. You will be seeing no one in what remains of the trip."

Martand rubbed the side of his chin with one finger. "Surely you don't mean that literally, Captain."

"I'm afraid I do."

"But there is another who might talk—accidentally and without meaning to. You had better place Miss Winter under house arrest, too."

"And double the injustice?"

"Misery loves company," said Martand.

And the captain smiled. "Perhaps you're right," he said.

Writer-friends come and go, too, alas. After I moved to New York, I frequently saw a number of writers whom, while I was in Boston, I had seen only occasionally. Lester del Rey and Robert Silverberg are examples. But then in 1972 Bob moved to California and I lost him again.

I had a chance to do one last thing for John Campbell, by the way. It occurred to Harry Harrison to do an anthology of stories of the kind that John Campbell had made famous by the authors he had made famous. Naturally, I was one of the authors, and in March 1972 I offered to do another "thiotimoline" article.

I had done three in my time and they had made a considerable stir. The first was *The Endochronic Properties of Resublimated Thiotimoline* and it had appeared in the March 1948, *Astounding* under circumstances described in THE EARLY ASIMOV (where the article was reprinted).

The second was *The Micropsychiatric Applications of Thiotimoline,* which appeared in the December 1953 *Astounding*. It, along with the first, was included in my collection ONLY A TRILLION (Abelard-Schuman, 1957).

The third was *Thiotimoline and the Space Age,* which appeared in the September 1960 *Analog* and was included in my book OPUS 100 (Houghton Mifflin, 1969).

Now I wrote a fourth, a quarter century after the first, and it was THIOTIMOLINE TO THE STARS.

THIOTIMOLINE
TO THE STARS

"Same speech, I suppose," said Ensign Peet wearily.

"Why not?" said Lieutenant Prohorov, closing his eyes and care-fully sitting down on the small of his back. "He's given it for fifteen years, once to each graduating class of the Astronautic Academy."

"Word for word, I'll bet," said Peet, who had heard it the year before for the first time.

"As far as I can tell. —What a pompous bore! Oh, for a pin that would puncture pretension."

But the class was filing in now, uniformed and expectant, march-ing forward, breaking into rows with precision, each man and woman moving to his or her assigned seat to the rhythm of a subdued drum-beat, and then all sitting down to one loud boom.

At that moment Admiral Vernon entered and walked stiffly to the podium.

"Graduating class of '22, welcome! Your school days are over. Your education will now begin.

"You have learned all there is to know about the classic theory of space flight. You have been filled to overflowing with astrophysics and celestial relativistic mechanics. But you have not been told about thiotimoline.

"That's for a very good reason. Telling you about it in class will do you no good. You will have to learn to *fly* with thiotimoline. It is thiotimoline and that alone that will take you to the stars. With all your book learning, you may still never learn to handle thiotimo-line. If so, there will yet be many posts you can fill in the astronautic way of life. Being a pilot will not, however, be one of them.

"I will start you off on this, your graduation day, with the only lec-ture you will get on the subject. After this, your dealings will thio-timoline will be in flight and we will find out quickly whether you have any talent for it at all."

The admiral paused, and seemed to be looking from face to face as though he was trying to assay each man's talent to begin with. Then he barked:

"Thiotimoline! First mentioned in 1948, according to legend, by Azimuth or, possibly, Asymptote, who may, very likely, never have existed. There is no record of the original article supposed to have been written by him; merely vague references to it, none earlier than the twenty-first century.

"Serious study began with Almirante, who either discovered thiotimoline, or rediscovered it, if the Azimuth/Asymptote tale is accepted. Almirante worked out the theory of hypersteric hindrance and showed that the molecule of thiotimoline is so distorted that one bond is forced into extension through the temporal dimension into the past; and another into the future.

"Because of the future-extension, thiotimoline can interact with an event that has not yet taken place. It can, for instance, to use the classic example, dissolve in water approximately one second before the water is added.

"Thiotimoline is, of course, a very simple compound, comparatively. It has, indeed, the simplest molecule capable of displaying endochronic properties—that is, the past-future extension. While this makes possible certain unique devices, the true applications of endochronicity had to await the development of more complicated molecules; polymers that combined endochronicity with firm structure.

"Pellagrini was the first to form endochronic resins and plastics, and, twenty years later, Cudahy demonstrated the technique for binding endochronic plastics to metal. It became possible to make large objects endochronic—entire spaceships, for instance.

"Now let us consider what happens when a large structure is endochronic. I will describe it qualitatively only; it is all that is necessary. The theoreticians have it all worked out mathematically, but I have never known a physics-johnny yet who could pilot a starship. Let them handle the theory, then, and you handle the ship.

"The small thiotimoline molecule is extraordinarily sensitive to the probabilistic states of the future. If you are certain you are going to add the water, it will dissolve before the water is added. If there is even the slightest doubt in your mind as to whether you will add the water, the thiotimoline will not dissolve until you actually add it.

"The larger the molecule possessing endochronicity, the less sensitive it is to the presence of doubt. It will dissolve, swell, change its electrical properties, or in some way interact with water, even if you are almost certain you may not add the water. But then what if you don't, in actual fact, add the water? The answer is simple. The endochronic structure will move into the future in search of water; not finding it, it will continue to move into the future.

"The effect is very much that of the donkey following the carrot fixed to a stick and held two feet in front of the donkey's nose; except that the endochronic structure is not as smart as the donkey, and never gets tired.

"If an entire ship is endochronic—that is, if endochronic groupings are fixed to the hull at frequent intervals—it is easy to set up a device that will deliver water to key spots in the structure, and yet so arrange that device that although it is always apparently on the point of delivering the water, it never actually does.

"In that case, the endochronic groupings move forward in time, carrying all the ship with it and all the objects on board the ship, including its personnel.

"Of course, there are no absolutes. The ship is moving forward in time relative to the universe; and this is precisely the same as saying that the universe is moving backward in time relative to the ship. The rate at which the ship is moving forward, or the universe is moving backward, in time, can be adjusted with great delicacy by the necessary modification of the device for adding water. The proper way of doing this can be taught, after a fashion; but it can be applied perfectly only by inborn talent. That is what we will find out about you all; whether you have that talent."

Again he paused and appraised them. Then he went on, amid perfect silence:

"But what good is it all? Let's consider starflights and review some of the things you have learned in school.

"Stars are incredibly far apart and to travel from one to another, considering the light-speed limit on velocity, takes years; centuries; millennia. One way of doing it is to set up a huge ship with a closed ecology; a tiny, self-contained universe. A group of people will set out and the tenth generation thereafter reaches a distant star. No one man makes the journey, and even if the ship eventually returns home, many centuries may have passed.

"To take the original crew to the stars in their own lifetime, freezing techniques may keep them in suspended animation for virtually all the trip. But freezing is a very uncertain procedure, and even if the crew survives and returns home, they will find that many centuries have passed on Earth.

"To take the original crew to the stars in their own lifetime, without freezing them, it is only necessary to accelerate to near-light velocities. Subjective time slows, and it will seem to the crew that it will have taken them only months to make the trip. But time travels at the normal rate for the rest of the universe, and when the crew returns they will find that although they, themselves, have aged and experienced no more than two months of time, perhaps, the Earth itself will have experienced many centuries.

"In every case, star travel involves enormous duration of time on Earth, even if not to the crew. One must return to Earth, if one returns at all, far into the Earth's future, and this means interstellar travel is not psychologically practical.

"But— *But,* graduates—"

He peered piercingly at them and said in a low, tense voice, *"If* we use an endochronic ship, we can match the time-dilatation effect exactly with the endochronic effect. While the ship travels through space at enormous velocity, and experiences a large slowdown in rate of experienced time, the endochronic effect is moving the universe back in time with respect to the ship. Properly handled, when the ship returns to Earth, with the crew having experienced, say, only two months of duration, the entire universe will have likewise experienced only two months' duration. At last, interstellar travel became practical.

"But only if very delicately handled.

"If the endochronic effect lags a little behind the time-dilatation effect, the ship will return after two months to find an Earth four months older. This is not much, perhaps; it can be lived with, you might think; but not so. The crew members are out of phase. They feel everything about them to have aged two months with respect to themselves. Worse yet, the general population feels that the crew members are two months younger than they ought to be. It creates hard feelings and discomforts.

"Similarly, if the endochronic effect races a little ahead of the time-dilatation effect, the ship may return after two months to find an Earth that has not experienced any time duration at all. The ship returns, just as it is rising into the sky. The hard feelings and discomforts will still exist.

"No, graduates, no interstellar flight will be considered successful in this star fleet unless the duration to the crew and the duration to Earth match minute for minute. A sixty-second deviation is a sloppy job that will gain you no merit. A hundred-twenty-second deviation will not be tolerated.

"I know, graduates, very well what questions are going through your minds. They went through mine when I graduated. Do we not in the endochronic ship have the equivalent of a time machine? Can we not, by proper adjustment of our endochronic device, deliberately travel a century into the future, make our observations, then travel a century into the past to return to our starting point? Or vice versa, can we not travel a century into the past and then back into the future to the starting point? Or a thousand years, or a billion? Could we not witness the Earth being born, life evolving, the sun dying?

"Graduates, the mathematical-johnnies tell us that this sort of thing creates paradoxes and requires too much energy to be practical. But *I* tell you the hell with paradoxes. We can't do it for a very simple reason. The endochronic properties are unstable. Molecules that are puckered into the time dimension are sensitive indeed. Relatively small effects will cause them to undergo chemical changes that will allow unpuckering. Even if there are no effects at all, random vibrations will produce the changes that will unpucker them.

"In short, an endochronic ship will slowly go isochronic and become ordinary matter without temporal extension. Modern technology has reduced the rate of unpuckering enormously and may reduce it further still, but nothing we do, theory tells us, will ever create a truly stable endochronic molecule.

"This means that your starship has only a limited life as a starship. It must get back to Earth while its endochronicity still holds, and that endochronicity must be restored before the next trip.

"Now, then, what happens if you return out-of-time? If you are not very nearly in your own time, you will have no assurance that the state of the technology will be such as to enable you to re-endochronicize your ship. You may be lucky if you are in the future; you will certainly be unlucky in the past. If, through carelessness on your part, or simply through lack of talent, you come back a substantial distance into the past, you will be certain to be stuck there because there will be no way of treating your ship in such a fashion as to bring it back into what will then be your future.

"And I want you to understand, graduates," here he slapped one hand against the other, as though to emphasize his words, "there is no time in the past where a civilized astronautic officer would care to spend his life. You might, for instance, be stranded in sixth-century France or, worse still, twentieth-century America.

"Refrain, then, from any temptation to experiment with time.

"Let us now pass on to one more point which may not have been more than hinted at in your formal school days, but which is something you will be experiencing.

"You may wonder how it is that a relatively few endochronic atomic bonds placed here and there among matter which is overwhelmingly isochronic can drag all with it. Why should one endochronic bond, racing toward water, drag with it a quadrillion atoms with isochronic bonds? We feel this should not happen, because of our lifelong experience with inertia.

"There is, however, no inertia in the movement toward past or future. If one part of an object moves toward the past or future, the rest of the object does so as well, and at precisely the same speed. There is no mass-factor at all. That is why it is as easy for the entire universe to move backward in time as for this single ship to move forward—and at the same rate.

"But there is even more to it than that. The time-dilatation effect is the result of your acceleration with respect to the universe generally. You learned that in grade school, when you took up elementary relativistic physics. It is part of the inertial effect of acceleration.

"But by using the endochronic effect, we wipe out the time-dilatation effect. If we wipe out the time-dilatation effect, then we are, so to speak, wiping out that which produces it. In short, when the endochronic effect exactly balances the time-dilatation effect, the inertial effect of acceleration is canceled out.

"You cannot cancel out one inertial effect without canceling them all. Inertia is therefore wiped out altogether and you can accelerate at any rate without feeling it. Once the endochronic effect is well-adjusted, you can accelerate from rest relative to Earth, to 186,000 miles per second relative to Earth in anywhere from a few hours to a few minutes. The more talented and skillful you are at handling the endochronic effect, the more rapidly you can accelerate.

"You are experiencing that now, gentlemen. It seems to you that you are sitting in an auditorium on the surface of the planet Earth, and I'm sure that none of you has had any reason or occasion to doubt the truth of that impression. But it's wrong just the same.

"You are in an auditorium, I admit, but it is not on the surface of the planet, Earth; not anymore. You—I—all of us—are in a large starship, which took off the moment I began this speech and which accelerated at an enormous rate. We reached the outskirts of the solar system while I've been talking, and we are now returning.

"At no time have any of you felt any acceleration, either through change in speed, change in direction of travel, or both, and therefore you have all assumed that you have remained at rest with respect to the surface of the Earth.

"Not at all, graduates. You have been out in space all the time I was talking, and have passed, according to calculations, within two million miles of the planet Saturn."

He seemed grimly pleased at the distinct stir in the audience.

"You needn't worry, graduates. Since we experience no inertial effects, we experience no gravitational effects either (the two are essentially the same), so that our course has not been affected by Saturn. We will be back on Earth's surface any moment now. As a special treat we will be coming down in the United Nations Port in Lincoln, Nebraska, and you will all be free to enjoy the pleasures of the metropolis for the weekend.

"Incidentally, the mere fact that we have experienced no inertial effects at all shows how well the endochronic effect matched the time-dilatation. Had there been any mismatch, even a small one, you would have felt the effects of acceleration—another reason for making no effort to experiment with time.

"Remember, graduates, a sixty-second mismatch is sloppy and a hundred-twenty-second mismatch is intolerable. We are about to land now; Lieutenant Prohorov, will you take over in the conning tower and oversee the actual landing?"

Prohorov said briskly, "Yes, sir," and went up the ladder in the rear of the assembly hall, where he had been sitting.

Admiral Vernon smiled. "You will all keep your seats. We are exactly on course. My ships are always exactly on course."

But then Prohorov descended again and came running up the aisle to the admiral. He reached him and spoke in a whisper. "Admiral, if this is Lincoln, Nebraska, something is wrong. All I can see are Indians; hordes of Indians. Indians in Nebraska, *now*, Admiral?"

Admiral Vernon turned pale and made a rattling sound in his throat. He crumpled and collapsed, while the graduating class rose to its feet uncertainly. Ensign Peet had followed Prohorov onto the platform and had caught his words and now stood there thunder-struck.

Prohorov raised his arms. "All's well, ladies and gentlemen. Take it easy. The admiral has just had a momentary attack of vertigo. It happens on landing, sometimes, to older men."

Peet whispered harshly, "But we're stuck in the past, Prohorov."

Prohorov raised his eyebrows. "Of course not. You didn't feel any inertial effects, did you? We can't even be an hour off. If the admiral had any brains to go with his uniform, he would have realized it, too. He had just *said* it, for God's sake."

"Then why did you say there was something wrong? Why did you say there are Indians out there?"

"Because there was and there are. When Admiral Sap comes to, he won't be able to do a thing to me. We didn't land in Lincoln, Nebraska, so there was something wrong all right. And as for the Indians—well, if I read the traffic signs correctly, we've come down on the outskirts of Calcutta."

Harry Harrison's anthology, in which THIOTIMOLINE TO THE STARS appeared, was called simply *Astounding*. It had been Harry's aim to make it one last issue of that magazine. Not *Analog* now, but *Astounding*.

There is nothing wrong with *Analog,* but to us old-timers no name change can possibly replace *Astounding* in our hearts.

In the spring of 1973 *The Saturday Evening Post,* having reprinted a couple of my short pieces, asked me to write an original piece for them. On May 3, 1973, caught in the grip of inspiration, I wrote LIGHT VERSE in one quick session at the typewriter and scarcely had to change a word in preparing final copy. It appeared in the September-October 1973 issue of *The Saturday Evening Post.*

LIGHT VERSE

The very last person anyone would expect to be a murderer was Mrs. Avis Lardner. Widow of the great astronaut-martyr, she was a philanthropist, an art collector, a hostess extraordinary, and, everyone agreed, an artistic genius. But above all, she was the gentlest and kindest human being one could imagine.

Her husband, William J. Lardner, died, as we all know, of the effects of radiation from a solar flare, after he had deliberately remained in space so that a passenger vessel might make it safely to Space Station 5.

Mrs. Lardner had received a generous pension for that, and she had then invested wisely and well. By late middle age she was very wealthy.

Her house was a showplace, a veritable museum, containing a small but extremely select collection of extraordinarily beautiful jeweled objects. From a dozen different cultures she had obtained relics of almost every conceivable artifact that could be embedded with jewels and made to serve the aristocracy of that culture. She had one of the first jeweled wristwatches manufactured in America, a jeweled dagger from Cambodia, a jeweled pair of spectacles from Italy, and so on almost endlessly.

All was open for inspection. The artifacts were not insured, and there were no ordinary security provisions. There was no need for anything conventional, for Mrs. Lardner maintained a large staff of robot servants, all of whom could be relied on to guard every item with imperturbable concentration, irreproachable honesty, and irrevocable efficiency.

Everyone knew the existence of those robots and there is no record of any attempt at theft, ever.

And then, of course, there was her light-sculpture. How Mrs. Lardner discovered her own genius at the art, no guest at her many lavish entertainments could guess. On each occasion, however, when her house was thrown open to guests, a new symphony of light shone throughout the rooms; three-dimensional curves and solids in melting color, some pure and some fusing in startling, crystalline effects that bathed every guest in wonder and somehow always adjusted itself so as to make Mrs. Lardner's blue-white hair and soft, unlined face gently beautiful.

It was for the light-sculpture more than anything else that the guests came. It was never the same twice, and never failed to explore new experimental avenues of art. Many people who could afford light-consoles prepared light-sculptures for amusement, but no one could approach Mrs. Lardner's expertise. Not even those who considered themselves professional artists.

She herself was charmingly modest about it. "No, no," she would protest when someone waxed lyrical. "I wouldn't call it 'poetry in light.' That's far too kind. At most, I would say it was mere 'light verse.'" And everyone smiled at her gentle wit.

Though she was often asked, she would never create light-sculpture for any occasion but her own parties. "That would be commercialization," she said.

She had no objection, however, to the preparation of elaborate holograms of her sculptures so that they might be made permanent and reproduced in museums of art all over the world. Nor was there ever a charge for any use that might be made of her light-sculptures.

"I couldn't ask a penny," she said, spreading her arms wide. "It's free to all. After all, I have no further use for it myself." It was true! She never used the same light-sculpture twice.

When the holograms were taken, she was cooperation itself. Watching benignly at every step, she was always ready to order her robot servants to help. "Please, Courtney," she would say, "would you be so kind as to adjust the step ladder?"

It was her fashion. She always addressed her robots with the most formal courtesy.

Once, years before, she had been almost scolded by a government functionary from the Bureau of Robots and Mechanical Men. "You can't do that," he said severely. "It interferes with their efficiency. They are constructed to follow orders, and the more clearly you give those orders, the more efficiently they follow them. When you ask with elaborate politeness, it is difficult for them to understand that an order is being given. They react more slowly."

Mrs. Lardner lifted her aristocratic head. "I do not ask for speed and efficiency," she said. "I ask goodwill. My robots love me."

The government functionary might have explained that robots cannot love, but he withered under her hurt but gentle glance.

It was notorious that Mrs. Lardner never even returned a robot to the factory for adjustment. Their positronic brains are enormously complex, and once in ten times or so the adjustment is not perfect as it leaves the factory. Sometimes the error does not show up for a period of time, but whenever it does, U. S. Robots and Mechanical Men, Inc., always makes the adjustment free of charge.

Mrs. Lardner shook her head. "Once a robot is in my house," she said, "and has performed his duties, any minor eccentricities must be borne with. I will not have him manhandled."

It was the worse thing possible to try to explain that a robot was but a machine. She would say very stiffly, "Nothing that is as intelligent as a robot can ever be *but* a machine. I treat them as people."

And that was that!

She kept even Max, although he was almost helpless. He could scarcely understand what was expected of him. Mrs. Lardner denied that strenuously, however. "Not at all," she would say firmly. "He can take hats and coats and store them very well, indeed. He can hold objects for me. He can do many things."

"But why not have him adjusted?" asked a friend, once.

"Oh, I couldn't. He's himself. He's very lovable, you know. After all, a positronic brain is so complex that no one can ever tell in just what way it's off. If he were made perfectly normal there would be no way to adjust him back to the lovability he now has. I won't give that up."

"But if he's maladjusted," said the friend, looking at Max nervously, "might he not be dangerous?"

"Never," laughed Mrs. Lardner. "I've had him for years. He's completely harmless and quite a dear."

Actually he looked like all the other robots, smooth, metallic, vaguely human but expressionless.

To the gentle Mrs. Lardner, however, they were all individual, all sweet, all lovable. It was the kind of woman she was.

How could she commit murder?

The very last person anyone would expect to be murdered would be John Semper Travis. Introverted and gentle, he was in the world but not of it. He had that peculiar mathematical turn of mind that made it possible for him to work out in his mind the complicated tapestry of the myriad positronic brain-paths in a robot's mind.

He was chief engineer of U. S. Robots and Mechanical Men, Inc.

But he was also an enthusiastic amateur in light-sculpture. He had written a book on the subject, trying to show that the type of mathematics he used in working out positronic brain-paths might be modified into a guide to the production of aesthetic light-sculpture.

His attempt at putting theory into practice was a dismal failure, however. The sculptures he himself produced, following his mathematical principles, were stodgy, mechanical, and uninteresting.

It was the only reason for unhappiness in his quiet, introverted, and secure life, and yet it was reason enough for him to be very unhappy indeed. He *knew* his theories were right, yet he could not make them work. If he could but produce *one* great piece of light-sculpture—

Naturally, he knew of Mrs. Lardner's light-sculpture. She was universally hailed as a genius, yet Travis knew she could not understand even the simplest aspect of robotic mathematics. He had corresponded with her but she consistently refused to explain her methods, and he wondered if she had any at all. Might it not be mere intuition? —but even intuition might be reduced to mathematics. Finally he managed to receive an invitation to one of her parties. He simply had to see her.

Mr. Travis arrived rather late. He had made one last attempt at a piece of light-sculpture and had failed dismally.

He greeted Mrs. Lardner with a kind of puzzled respect and said, "That was a peculiar robot who took my hat and coat."

"That is Max," said Mrs. Lardner.

"He is quite maladjusted, and he's a fairly old model. How is it you did not return it to the factory?"

"Oh, no," said Mrs. Lardner. "It would be too much trouble."

"None at all, Mrs. Lardner," said Travis. "You would be surprised how simple a task it was. Since I am with U. S. Robots, I took the liberty of adjusting him myself. It took no time and you'll find he is now in perfect working order."

A queer change came over Mrs. Lardner's face. Fury found a place on it for the first time in her gentle life, and it was as though the lines did not know how to form.

"You adjusted him?" she shrieked. "But it was *he* who created my light-sculptures. It was the maladjustment, the *maladjustment,* which you can never restore, that—that—"

It was really unfortunate that she had been showing her collection at the time and that the jeweled dagger from Cambodia was on the marble tabletop before her.

Travis's face was also distorted. "You mean if I had studied his uniquely maladjusted positronic brain-paths I might have learned—"

She lunged with the knife too quickly for anyone to stop her and he did not try to dodge. Some said he came to meet it—as though he *wanted* to die.

In sending the story to *The Saturday Evening Post* I was anxious to make it clear that I had not sent them an old story. I explained rather emphatically that "I have written it *today.*"

In doing this I had forgotten the prejudice many people have against any story that is written quickly. There is the legend that a good story must be written and rewritten and must take days and days of agony for each pain-wracked paragraph. I think writers spread that piece of embroidery to collect public sympathy for themselves.

Anyway, I *don't* write slowly, but editors who don't have much experience with me don't realize it. I got a letter from the *Post* people raving about the story and expressing the utmost astonishment that I had managed to write it in *one day.* I kept quiet and said nothing.

However, I can tell you because you're my friends. From the moment of sitting down at the typewriter to the moment of placing the envelope in the mailbox, it did *not* take me one day. It took me two and a half hours. But don't tell the *Post.*

What, then, is left to tell you to bring you up to date?

Well, on November 30, 1973, I married a second time. My wife is Janet Jeppson. She is a psychiatrist, a writer, and a wonderful woman, in order of increasing importance. She has published a science fiction novel of her own, THE SECOND EXPERIMENT

(Houghton Mifflin, 1974) and received final word of the acceptance of that novel on November 30, 1973, half an hour after we had been married. It was a big day.

I, for one, wish that her professional career left her a little more time for writing. Then we could perhaps work up a man-and-wife collection someday.